BUT ERIC VON EMMELMAN DID NOT DIE! THERE IN THAT POLISH SWAMP A MIRACLE TOOK PLACE! THE VINES AND CREEPERS COVERED HIS BODY, MERGED WITH IT AND BECAME *THE HEAP*....

desert sands, Sturgeon's idea of a regenerated creature composed of, or caked with, the material of its surroundings abounds in books, magazines, film, and comics.

Especially in comics.

One of the two characters I mentioned above is the DC Comics villain Solomon Grundy, created by Alfred Bester in 1944 for *All-American Comics* #61. (There's an even chance Bester—at the time, a pulp science fiction writer—had read Sturgeon's story in *Unknown* four years earlier.) As the story goes, Grundy had previously been a wealthy merchant, who was murdered and then dumped in the swamp, where his decaying corpse is eventually reanimated into a rampaging, chalk-faced hulk with no memory of its previous life.

The other character, a bit closer to Sturgeon's original, is the Heap—appearing two years after *It* and two years before Solomon Grundy.

The Heap made his first appearance in the Hillman Periodicals' comic *Air Fighters* #3 (Dec. 1942), and eventually became a recurring character in the retitled *Airboy Comics* until that magazine's final issue in 1953. This muck monster, the first "swamp thing" in comics, had its genesis after a World War One German fighter pilot crashes his plane into a Polish swamp. The pilot's burned and battered body is slowly transformed by the mold and rotting vegetation of the swamp.

The Heap, and hence (indirectly) Sturgeon's *It*, would soon inspire other swamp creatures, all of them similar or similarly created: a dead or dying human regenerated and transformed in the swamp—or the sewer or ... whatever. Toward the end of the Heap's run in *Airboy*, *Mad Magazine* published a satire in its fifth issue (June-July 1953) that strangely anticipated the arrival of generations of muck monsters made of mud and decaying vegetation; and characterized, one might imagine, by occasional and somewhat rude and embarrassing emissions of swamp

Top: The origin of the Heap; and (from Airboy #100) the Heap fights a similarly regenerated creature. Left: Grundy emerges from the swamp, on the cover of *All American Comics* #61. (DC Comics)

...SPILLED OUT THE WINDOW WHERE IT LAY...COMBINING WITH THE SWAMP WATERS IN A FESTERING MISH-MOSH!

NIGHT FELL!...NIGHT ON THE OKEEFENO-KEEKEE SWAMP! SOUNDS OF *THINGS*... MOVING THROUGH THE BACKWATERS!

...HIDDEN THINGS WITH STRANGE CRIES SHATTERING THE SLEEPING CALM OF OLD OKEEFENOKEEKENOFEE!

...AND... BENEATH THE PROFESSOR'S WINDOW... THE MIXTURE CONTINUED TO PULSATE AND QUIVER WHERE IT HAD LAIN... *PULSATED...QUIVERED...AND GREW!*

GREW! STOOD UP! ERECT! A HORRIBLE STANDING GLOB OF SWAMP THING! THERE WAS NOTHING TO CALL IT BUT... HEAP!

gas. (Never accompany a swamp thing for a ride in an elevator.)

In their *Mad* satire "Outer Sanctum," Harvey Kurtzman and Bill Elder depict a swamp-dwelling mad scientist who dumps a failed experiment to create life into the murky water surrounding his shack. Overnight a heap-like creature is born, which according to the comic, "Grew! Stood up! Erect! A horrible standing GLOB of SWAMP THING! There was nothing to call it but ... HEAP!" And apparently someone at *Mad* wanted to give credit where credit was due, for when the scientist "woke up, he found *IT!* ... 'HEAP,' standing outside the door!"

Prophetic? It might seem so. Marvel Comics unleashed the GLOB! on its reading audience in 1961, in *Journey into Mystery* #72; and, ten years after that, DC Comics published a primitive, early version of its

popular character the SWAMP THING.

In between, Marvel, DC, and other comics companies published a variety of muck monsters that oozed and slimed their way into the hearts and nightmares of kids of all ages. But let's jump ahead to the early '70s, and the debut of dueling swamp creatures.

In 1971, within two months of one another, DC and Marvel each concocted a feared but misunderstood creature spawned in the swamp—*half* man, *half* monster, but *totally* similar in concept. Which was first?

Marvel's Man-Thing premiered in May 1971, in the first issue of the black-and-white magazine *Savage Tales*. Two months later, DC's the Swamp Thing debuted in *House of Secrets* #92 (July '71). Both characters were scientists working on a drug for the government; both suffer a mishap and end up being fused with swamp muck.

NIGHTMARE ABBEY

WINTER SOLSTICE 2022

COVER AND INTERIOR ILLUSTRATIONS: ALLEN KOSZOWSKI
PHOTO ART BY NATU SHABBEY
EDITOR AND PUBLISHER: TOM ENGLISH

WELCOME TO THE ABBEY

DO COME IN and make yourself at home. Do you prefer the rack or the iron maiden? On second thought, take *my* chair. Please, I insist. What's that? A motorized recliner? No, I'm afraid it's *not* motorized. But it *is* electric.

Comfortable, dear friend? Excellent. Tea and cakes? Oh, you'd like something a bit stronger. Pardon me for a moment while I step out to throw the switch.

Shocking, isn't it, the degree of hospitality at Nightmare Abbey?

We're extremely pleased to once again host David Surface, Helen Grant, Steve Duffy, Gregory L. Norris, James Dorr and Matt Cowan. And, lest we forget our manners, we welcome our new guests Gary Fry and John Llewellyn Probert, who've already made themselves *quite* at home —Boys! Take your feet off the coffin table! *Ahem.*

These fine souls have no misgivings about spending a stormy night here at the Abbey, and neither should you. After all, we pride ourselves in providing elegantly uncomfortable accomodations for an uneasy rest. We've even instructed the bedbugs to take their meals across the street at the neighbors' house. So, do come in!

In addition to our fine lineup of great contemporary writers, we've managed to dig up three chilling, time-honored classics, including our cover-featured story, Theodore Sturgeon's iconic weird tale *It*—with art by Allen Koszowski.

It was first published over eighty years ago, in the August 1940 issue of *Unknown*, and since then, has inspired numerous imitations. The story's titular monster is created when mud and rotting forest vegetation, clinging to a human skeleton, takes on a strange life of its own. In the story's opening paragraphs, Sturgeon describes the creature in masterful, poetic prose:

It walked in the woods.

It was never born. It existed. Under the pine needles the fires burn, deep and smokeless in the mold. In heat and in darkness and decay there is growth. There is life and there is growth. It grew, but it was not alive. It walked unbreaking through the woods, and thought and saw and was hideous and strong, and it was not born and it did not live. It grew and moved about without living.... It crawled out of its mound in the wood and lay pulsing in the sunlight....

The unlikely creature in Sturgeon's tale is now considered one of the great archetypes in weird literature, and it served as the template for at least two other pop-culture fantasy characters, as well as a host of others indirectly. (One needn't be familiar with the original to create a copy of a copy.) Whether transplanted from the forest-setting of *It* to the swamp, or a sewer, or even to the

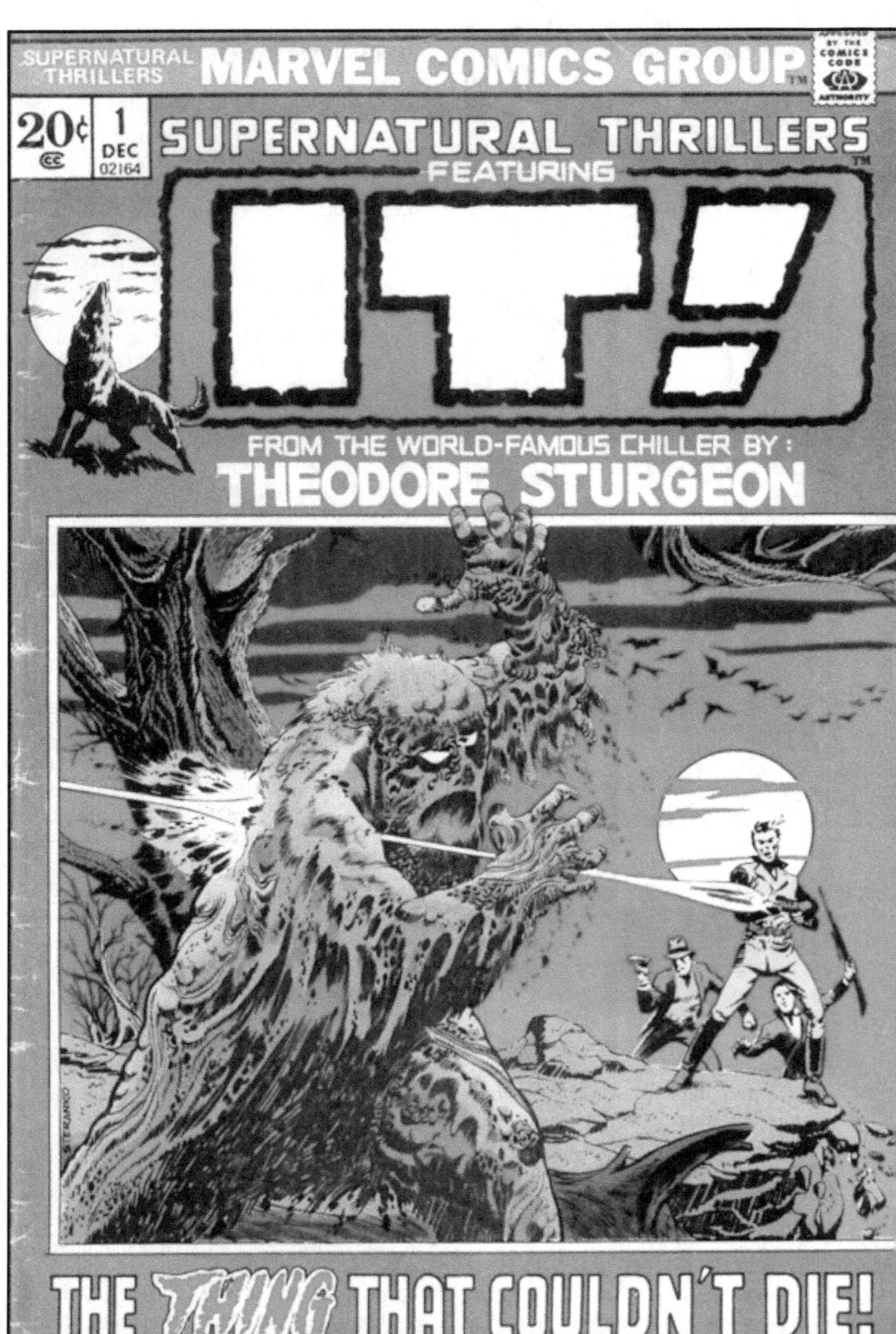

Had the creators of DC's *Swamp* Thing ripped off Marvel's *Man*-Thing? Probably not. And yet, how could two rival comics companies separately concoct two muck monsters so similar? The answer is simple.

Stan Lee, who'd recently been promoted to publisher at Marvel, phoned his chief competitor and good friend Carmine Infantino, who'd recently been promoted to publisher at DC (not sure who was copying who with these career moves) and threatened to *sue* him! Infantino simply laughed and reminded his pal Stan that the origins of both their muck monsters were deeply rooted in a character called the Heap, published in 1942. And, as we all know, the Heap was directly inspired by the character *IT*.

Marvel's Man-Thing and DC's Swamp Thing may have been birthed by different creative teams, but they had the same daddy, and his name was Theodore Sturgeon!

By the way, legend has it that after their phone call, Stan Lee and Carmine Infantino, two highly competitive comic book pioneers, met for a friendly lunch. (Definitely a lesson there, if one would only apply it.)

One last thing: the long, evolving comics journey of Sturgeon's *It* came full circle in late 1972 when Marvel finally went straight to the source material and published an adaptation of the original story in the first issue of *Supernatural Thrillers*. It must have dawned on the publisher, quite suddenly, that if copies of the character were making money, then the original ought to be good for a few bucks, too.

Well, included in this volume of *Nightmare Abbey* is the original—often reprinted, but perhaps not so much as of late. And yet, *It* remains a literary gem, untarnished by time and imitation.

So, my dear friends, let's stop mucking about and get on with IT!

Tom English
New Kent, VA

Previous page: Bernie Wrightson's gothic cover art for *Swamp Thing* #4. Below: The Living Dead rise from the swamp in art by Allen Koszowski.

The Man-Thing, Glob, Journey into Mystery, Strange Tales, Supernatural Thrillers, and all associated images copyright © Marvel Comics.

Swamp Thing and all associated images copyright © DC Comics.

IT

By Theodore Sturgeon

IT WALKED IN THE WOODS.

It was never born. It existed. Under the pine needles the fires burn, deep and smokeless in the mold. In heat and in darkness and decay there is growth. There is life and there is growth. It grew, but it was not alive. It walked unbreathing through the woods, and thought and saw and was hideous and strong, and it was not born and it did not live. It grew and moved about without living.

It crawled out of the darkness and hot, damp mold into the cool of a morning. It was huge. It was lumped and crusted with its own hateful substances, and pieces of it dropped off as it went its way, dropped off and lay writhing, and stilled, and sank putrescent into the forest loam.

It had no mercy, no laughter, no beauty. It had strength and great intelligence. And—perhaps it could not be destroyed. It crawled out of its mound in the wood and lay pulsing in the sunlight for a long moment. Patches of it shone wetly in the golden glow, parts of it were nubbled and flaked. And whose dead bones had given it the form of a man?

It scrabbled painfully with its half-formed hands, beating the ground and the bole of a tree. It rolled and lifted itself up on its crumbling elbows, and it tore up a great handful of herbs and shredded them against its chest, and it paused and gazed at the gray-green juices with intelligent calm. It wavered to its feet, and seized a young sapling and destroyed it, folding the slender trunk back on itself again and again, watching attentively the useless, fibered splinters. And it snatched up a fear-frozen field creature, crushing it slowly, letting blood and pulpy flesh and fur ooze from between its fingers, run down and rot on the forearms.

It began searching.

KIMBO DRIFTED THROUGH the tall grasses like a puff of dust, his bushy tail curled tightly over his back and his long jaws agape. He ran with an easy lope, loving his freedom and the power of his flanks and furry shoulders. His tongue lolled listlessly over his lips. His lips were black and serrated, and each tiny pointed liplet swayed with his doggy gallop. Kimbo was all dog, all healthy animal.

He leaped high over a boulder and landed with a startled yelp as a long-eared coney shot from its hiding place under the rock. Kimbo hurtled after it, grunting with each great thrust of his legs. The rabbit bounced just ahead of him, keeping its distance, its ears flattened on its curving back and its little legs nibbling away at distance hungrily. It stopped, and Kimbo pounced, and the rabbit shot away at a tangent and

popped into a hollow log. Kimbo yelped again and rushed snuffling at the log, and knowing his failure, curvetted but once around the stump and ran on into the forest. The thing that watched from the wood raised its crusted arms and waited for Kimbo.

Kimbo sensed it there, standing dead-still by the path. To him it was a bulk that smelled of carrion not fit to roll in, and he snuffled distastefully and ran to pass it.

The thing let him come abreast and dropped a heavy twisted fist on him. Kimbo saw it coming and curled up tight as he ran, and the hand clipped stunningly on his rump, sending him rolling and yipping down the slope. Kimbo straddled to his feet, shook his head, shook his body with a deep growl, came back to the silent thing with green murder in his eyes. He walked stiffly, straight-legged, his tail as low as his lowered head and a ruff of fury around his neck. The thing raised its arms again, waited.

Kimbo slowed, then flipped himself through the air at the monster's throat. His jaws closed on it; his teeth clicked together through a mass of filth, and he fell choking and snarling at its feet. The thing leaned down and struck twice, and after the dog's back was broken, it sat beside him and began to tear him apart.

"BE BACK IN AN hour or so," said Alton Drew, picking up his rifle from the corner behind the woodbox. His brother laughed.

"Old Kimbo 'bout runs your life, Alton," he said.

"Ah, I know the ol' devil," said Alton. "When I whistle for him for half an hour and he don't show up, he's in a jam or he's treed something wuth shootin' at. The ol' son of a gun calls me by not answerin'."

Cory Drew shoved a full glass of milk over to his nine-year-old daughter and smiled. "You think as much o' that houn' dog o' yours as I do of Babe here."

Babe slid off her chair and ran to her uncle. "Gonna catch me the bad fella, Uncle Alton?" she shrilled. The "bad fella" was Cory's invention—the one who lurked in corners ready to pounce on little girls who chased the chickens and played around mowing machines and hurled green apples with a powerful young arm at the sides of the hogs, to hear the synchronized thud and grunt; little girls who swore with an Austrian accent like an ex-hired man they had had; who dug caves in haystacks till they tipped over, and kept pet crawfish in tomorrow's milk cans, and rode work horses to a lather in the night pasture.

"Get back here and keep away from Uncle Alton's gun!" said Cory. "If you see the bad fella, Alton, chase him back here. He has a date with Babe here for that stunt of hers last night." The preceding evening, Babe had kindheartedly poured pepper on the cows' salt block.

"Don't worry, kiddo," grinned her uncle, "I'll bring you the bad fella's hide if he don't get me first."

ALTON DREW WALKED up the path toward the wood, thinking about Babe. She was a phenomenon—a pampered farm child. Ah, well—she had to be. They'd both loved Clissa Drew, and she'd married Cory, and they had to love Clissa's child. Funny thing, love. Alton was a man's man, and thought things out that way; and his reaction to love was a strong and frightened one. He knew what love was because he felt it still for his brother's wife and would feel it as long as he lived for Babe. It led him through his life, and yet he embarrassed himself by thinking of it. Loving a dog was an easy thing, because you and the old devil could love one another completely without talking about it. The smell of gun smoke and wet fur in the rain were perfume enough for Alton Drew, a grunt of satisfaction and the scream of something hunted and hit were poetry enough. They weren't like love for a human that choked his throat so he could not say words he could not have thought of anyway. So Alton loved his dog Kimbo and his Winchester for all to see, and let his love for his brother's women, Clissa and Babe, eat at him quietly and unmentioned.

His quick eyes saw the fresh indentations in the soft earth behind the boulder, which showed where Kimbo had turned and leaped with a single surge, chasing the rabbit. Ignoring the tracks, he looked for the nearest place where a rabbit might hide, and strolled over to the stump. Kimbo had been there, he saw, and had been there too late. "You're an ol' fool," muttered Alton, "Y' can't catch a coney by chasin' it. You want to cross him up someway." He gave a peculiar trilling whistle, sure that Kimbo was digging frantically under some nearby stump for a rabbit that was three counties away by now. No answer. A little puzzled, Alton went back to the path. "He never done this before," he said softly.

He cocked his .32-40 and cradled it. At the county fair someone had once said of Alton Drew that he could shoot at a handful of corn and peas thrown in the air and hit only the corn. Once he split a bullet on the blade of a knife and put two candles out. He had no need to fear anything that could be shot at. That's what he believed.

THE THING IN THE woods looked curiously down at what it had done to Kimbo, and tried to moan the way Kimbo had before he died. It stood a minute storing away facts in its foul, unemotional mind. Blood was warm. The sunlight was warm. Things that moved and bore fur had a muscle to force the thick liquid through tiny tubes in their bodies. The liquid coagulated after a time. The liquid on rooted green things was thinner and the loss of a limb did not mean loss of life. It was very interesting, but the thing, the mold with a mind, was not pleased. Neither was it displeased. Its accidental urge was a thirst for knowledge, and it was only—interested.

It was growing late, and the sun reddened and rested awhile on the hilly horizon, teaching the clouds to be inverted flames. The thing threw up its head suddenly, noticing the dusk. Night was ever a strange thing, even for those of us who have known it in life. It would have been frightening for the monster had it been capable of fright, but it could only be curious; it could only reason from what it had observed.

What was happening? It was getting harder to see. Why? It threw its shapeless head from side to side. It was true—things were dim, and growing dimmer. Things were changing shape, taking on a new and darker color. What did the creatures it had crushed and torn apart see? How did they see? The larger one, the one that had attacked, had used two organs in its head. That must have been it, because after the thing had torn off two of the dog's legs it had struck at the hairy muzzle; and the dog, seeing the blow coming, had dropped folds of skin over the organs—closed its eyes. Ergo, the dog saw with its eyes. But then after the dog was dead, and its body still, repeated blows had had no effect on the eyes. They remained open and staring. The logical conclusion was, then, that a being that had ceased to live and breathe and move about lost the use of its eyes. It must be that to lose sight was, conversely, to die. Dead things did not walk about. They lay down and did not move. Therefore the thing in the wood concluded that it must be dead, and so it lay down by the path, not far away from Kimbo's scattered body, lay down and believed itself dead.

ALTON DREW CAME UP through the dusk to the wood. He was frankly worried. He whistled again, and then called, and there was still no response, and he said again, "The ol' flea-bus never done this before," and shook his heavy head. It was past milking time, and Cory would need him. "Kimbo!" he roared. The cry echoed through the shadows, and Alton flipped on the safety catch of his rifle and put the butt on the ground beside the path. Leaning on it, he took off his cap and scratched the back of his head, wondering. The rifle butt sank into what he thought was soft earth; he staggered and stepped into the chest of the thing that lay beside the path. His foot went up to the ankle in its yielding rottenness, and he swore and jumped back.

"*Whew!* Somp'n sure dead as hell there! Ugh!" He swabbed at his boot with a handful of leaves while the monster lay in the growing blackness with the edges of the deep footprint in its chest sliding into it, filling it up. It lay there regarding him dimly out of its muddy eyes, thinking it was dead because of the darkness, watching the articulation of Alton Drew's joints,

wondering at this new uncautious creature.

Alton cleaned the butt of his gun with more leaves and went on up the path, whistling anxiously for Kimbo.

CLISSA DREW STOOD in the door of the milk shed, very lovely in red-checked gingham and a blue apron. Her hair was clean yellow, parted in the middle and stretched tautly back to a heavy braided knot. "Cory! Alton!" she called a little sharply.

"Well?" Cory responded gruffly from the barn, where he was stripping off the Ayrshire. The dwindling streams of milk plopped pleasantly into the froth of a full pail.

"I've called and called," said Clissa. "Supper's cold, and Babe won't eat until you come. Why—where's Alton?"

Cory grunted, heaved the stool out of the way, threw over the stanchion lock and slapped the Ayrshire on the rump. The cow backed and filled like a towboat, clattered down the line and out into the barnyard. "Ain't back yet."

"Not back?" Clissa came in and stood beside him as he sat by the next cow, put his forehead against the warm flank. "But, Cory, he said he'd—"

"Yeh, yeh, I know. He said he'd be back fer the milkin'. I heard him. Well, he ain't."

"And you have to—oh, Cory, I'll help you finish up. Alton would be back if he could. Maybe he's—"

"Maybe he's treed a bluejay," snapped her husband. "Him an' that damn dog." He gestured hugely with one hand while the other went on milking. "I got twenty-six head o' cows to milk. I got pigs to feed an' chickens to put to bed. I got to toss hay for the mare and turn the team out. I got harness to mend and a wire down in the night pasture. I got wood to split an' carry." He milked for a moment in silence, chewing on his lip. Clissa stood twisting her hands together, trying to think of something to stem the tide. It wasn't the first time Alton's hunting had interfered with the chores. "So I got to go ahead with it. I can't interfere with Alton's spoorin'. Every damn time that hound o' his smells out a squirrel I go without my supper. I'm gettin' sick and—"

"Oh, I'll help you!" said Clissa. She was thinking of the spring, when Kimbo had held four hundred pounds of raging black bear at bay until Alton could put a bullet in its brain, the time Babe had found a bear cub and started to carry it home, and had fallen into a freshet, cutting her head. You can't hate a dog that has saved your child for you, she thought.

"You'll do nothin' of the kind!" Cory growled. "Get back to the house. You'll find work enough there. I'll be along when I can. Dammit, Clissa, don't cry! I didn't mean to— Oh, shucks!" He got up and put his arms around her. "I'm wrought up," he said. "Go on now. I'd no call to speak that way to you. I'm sorry. Go back to Babe. I'll put a stop to this for good tonight. I've had enough. There's work here for four farmers, an' all we've got is me an' that ... that huntsman.

"Go on now, Clissa."

"All right," she said into his shoulder. "But, Cory, hear him out first when he comes back. He might be unable to come back. He might be unable to come back this time. Maybe he ... he—"

"Ain't nothin' kin hurt my brother that a bullet will hit. He can take care of himself. He's got no excuse good enough this time. Go on, now. Make the kid eat." Clissa went back to the house, her young face furrowed. If Cory quarreled with Alton now and drove him away, what with the drought and the creamery about to close and all, they just couldn't manage. Hiring a man was out of the question. Cory'd have to work himself to death, and he just wouldn't be able to make it. No one man could. She sighed and went into the house. It was seven o'clock, and the milking not done yet. Oh, why did Alton have to—

Babe was in bed at nine when Clissa heard Cory in the shed, slinging the wire cutters into a corner. "Alton back yet?" they both said at once as Cory stepped into the kitchen; and as she shook her head he clumped over to the stove, and lifting a lid, spat into the coals. "Come to bed," he said.

She laid down her stitching and looked at his broad back. He was twenty-eight, and he walked and acted like a man ten years older, and looked like a man five years younger. "I'll be up in a while," Clissa said.

Cory glanced at the corner behind the woodbox where Alton's rifle usually stood, then made an unspellable, disgusted sound and sat down to take off his heavy muddy shoes.

"It's after nine," Clissa volunteered timidly. Cory said nothing, reaching for his house slippers. "Cory, you're not going to—"

"Not going to what?"

"Oh, nothing. I just thought that maybe Alton—"

"Alton," Cory flared. "The dog goes hunting field mice. Alton goes hunting the dog. Now you want me to go hunting Alton. That's what you want?"

"I just— He was never this late before."

"I won't do it! Go out lookin' for him at nine o'clock in the night? I'll be damned! He has no call to use us so, Clissa."

Clissa said nothing. She went to the stove, peered into the wash boiler, set aside at the back of the range. When she turned around, Cory had his shoes and coat on again.

"I knew you'd go," she said. Her voice smiled though she did not.

"I'll be back durned soon," said Cory. "I don't reckon he's strayed far. It *is* late. I ain't feared for him, but—" He broke his 12-gauge shotgun, looked through the barrels, slipped two shells in the breech and a box of them into his pocket. "Don't wait up," he said over his shoulder as he went out.

"I won't," Clissa replied to the closed door, and went back to her stitching by the lamp.

THE PATH UP THE slope to the wood was very dark when Cory went up it, peering and calling. The air was chill and quiet, and a fetid odor of mold hung in it. Cory blew the taste of it out through impatient nostrils, drew it in again with the next breath, and swore. "Nonsense," he muttered. "Houn' dawg. Huntin', at ten in th' night, too. Alton!" he bellowed. "Alton Drew!" Echoes answered him, and he entered the wood. The huddled thing he passed in the dark heard him and felt the vibrations of his footsteps and did not move because it thought it was dead.

Cory strode on, looking around and ahead and not down since his feet knew the path.

"Alton!"

"That you, Cory?"

Cory Drew froze. That corner of the wood was thickly set and as dark as a burial vault. The voice he heard was choked, quiet, penetrating. "Alton?"

"I found Kimbo, Cory."

"Where the hell have you been?" shouted Cory furiously. He disliked this pitch-darkness; he was afraid at the tense hopelessness of Alton's voice, and he mistrusted his ability to stay angry at his brother.

"I called him, Cory. I whistled at him, an' the ol' devil didn't answer."

"I can say the same for you, you ... you louse. Why weren't you to milkin'? Where are you? You caught in a trap?"

"The houn' never missed answerin' me before, you know," said the tight, monotonous voice from the darkness.

"Alton! What the devil's the matter with you? What do I care if your mutt didn't answer? Where—"

"I guess because he ain't never died before," said Alton, refusing to be interrupted.

"You *what?*" Cory clicked his lips together twice and then said, "Alton, you turned crazy? What's that you say?"

"Kimbo's dead."

"Kim ... oh! Oh!" Cory was seeing that picture again in his mind—Babe sprawled unconscious in the freshet, and Kimbo raging and snapping against a monster bear, holding her back until Alton could get there. "What happened, Alton?" he asked more quietly.

"I aim to find out. Someone tore him up."

"Tore him up?"

"There ain't a bit of him left tacked together, Cory. Every damn joint in his body tore apart. Guts out of him."

"Good God! Bear, you reckon?"

"No bear, nor nothin' on four legs. He's all here. None of him's been et. Whoever done it just killed him an'—tore him up.

"Good God!" Cory said again. "Who could've—" There was a long silence, then, "Come 'long home," he said almost gently.

"There's no call for you to set up by him all night."

"I'll set. I aim to be here at sunup, an' I'm going to start trackin', an' I'm goin' to keep trackin' till I find the one done this job on Kimbo."

"You're drunk or crazy, Alton."

"I ain't drunk. You can think what you like about the rest of it. I'm stickin' here."

"We got a farm back yonder. Remember? I ain't going to milk twenty-six head o' cows again in the mornin' like I did jest now, Alton."

"Somebody's got to. I can't be there. I guess you'll just have to, Cory."

"You dirty scum!" Cory screamed. "You'll come back with me now or I'll know why!"

Alton's voice was still tight, half sleepy. "Don't you come no nearer, bud."

Cory kept moving toward Alton's voice.

"I said"—the voice was very quiet now—*"stop where you are."* Cory kept coming. A sharp click told of the release of the .32-40's safety. Cory stopped.

"You got your gun on me, Alton?" Cory whispered.

"Thass right, bud. You ain't a-trompin' up these tracks for me. I need 'em at sunup."

A full minute passed, and the only sound in the blackness was that of Cory's pained breathing. Finally:

"I got my gun, too, Alton. Come home."

"You can't see to shoot me."

"We're even on that."

"We ain't. I know just where you stand, Cory. I been here four hours."

"My gun scatters."

"My gun kills."

Without another word, Cory Drew turned on his heel and stamped back to the farm.

BLACK AND LIQUIDESCENT it lay in the blackness, not alive, not understanding death, believing itself dead. Things that were alive saw and moved about. Things that were not alive could do neither. It rested its muddy gaze on the line of trees at the crest of the rise, and deep within it thoughts trickled wetly. It lay huddled, dividing its new-found facts, dissecting them as it had dissected live things when there was light, comparing, concluding, pigeonholing.

The trees at the top of the slope could just be seen, as their trunks were a fraction of a shade lighter than the dark sky behind them. At length they, too, disappeared, and for a moment sky and trees were a monotone. The thing knew it was dead now, and like many a being before it, it wondered how long it must stay like this. And then the sky beyond the trees grew a little lighter. That was a manifestly impossible occurrence, thought the thing, but it could see it and it must be so. Did dead things live again? That was curious. What about dismembered dead things? It would wait and see.

The sun came hand over hand up a beam of light. A bird somewhere made a high yawning peep, and as an owl killed a shrew, a skunk pounced on another, so that the night-shift deaths and those of the day could go on without cessation. Two flowers nodded archly to each other, comparing their pretty clothes. A dragonfly nymph decided it was tired of looking serious and cracked its back open, to crawl out and dry gauzily. The first golden ray sheared down between the trees, through the grasses, passed over the mass in the shadowed bushes. "I am alive again," thought the thing that could not possibly live. "I am alive, for I see clearly." It stood up on its thick legs, up into the golden glow. In a little while the wet flakes that had grown during the night dried in the sun, and when it took its first steps, they cracked off and a small shower of them fell away. It walked up the slope to find Kimbo, to see if he, too, was alive again.

BABE LET THE SUN come into her room by opening her eyes. Uncle Alton was gone—that was the first thing that ran through her head. Dad had come home last night and had shouted at mother for an hour. Alton was plumb crazy. He'd turned a gun on his own brother. If Alton ever came ten feet into Cory's land, Cory would fill him so full of holes, he'd look like a tumbleweed. Alton was lazy, shiftless, selfish, and one or two other things of questionable taste but undoubted vividness. Babe knew her father. Uncle Alton would never be safe in this county.

She bounced out of bed in the enviable way of the very young, and ran to the window. Cory was trudging down to the night pasture with two bridles over his arm, to get the team. There were kitchen noises from downstairs.

Babe ducked her head in the washbowl and shook off the water like a terrier before she toweled. Trailing clean shirt and dungarees, she went to the head of the stairs, slid into the shirt, and began her morning ritual with the trousers. One step down was a step through the right leg. One more, and she was into the left. Then, bouncing step by step on both feet, buttoning one button per step, she reached the bottom fully dressed and ran into the kitchen.

"Didn't Uncle Alton come back a-tall, Mum?"

"Morning, Babe. No, dear." Clissa was too quiet, smiling too much, Babe thought shrewdly. Wasn't happy.

"Where'd he go, Mum?"

"We don't know, Babe. Sit down and eat your breakfast."

"What's a misbegotten, Mum?" Babe asked suddenly.

Her mother nearly dropped the dish she was drying. "Babe! You must never say that again!"

"Oh. Well, why is Uncle Alton, then?"

"Why is he what?"

Babe's mouth muscled around an outsize spoonful of oatmeal. "A misbe—"

"Babe!"

"All right, Mum," said Babe with her mouth full. "Well, why?"

"I *told* Cory not to shout last night," Clissa said half to herself.

"Well, whatever it means, he isn't," said Babe with finality. "Did he go hunting again?"

"He went to look for Kimbo, darling."

"Kimbo? Oh Mummy, is Kimbo gone, too? Didn't he come back either?"

"No, dear. Oh, please, Babe, stop asking questions!"

"All right. Where do you think they went?"

"Into the north woods. Be quiet."

Babe gulped away at her breakfast. An idea struck her; and as she thought of it she ate slower and slower and cast more and more glances at her mother from under the lashes of her tilted eyes. It would be awful if Daddy did anything to Uncle Alton. Someone ought to warn him.

Babe was halfway to the woods when Alton's .32-40 sent echoes giggling up and down the valley.

CORY WAS IN THE south thirty, riding a cultivator and cussing at the team of grays when he heard the gun. "Hoa," he called to the horses, and sat a moment to listen to the sound. "One-two-three. Four," he counted. "Saw someone, blasted away at him. Had a chance to take aim and give him another, careful. My God!" He threw up the cultivator points and steered the team into the shade of three oaks. He hobbled the gelding with swift tosses of a spare strap and headed for the woods. "Alton a killer," he murmured, and doubled back to the house for his gun. Clissa was standing just outside the door.

"Get shells!" he snapped and flung into the house. Clissa followed him. He was strapping his hunting knife on before she could get a box off the shelf. "Cory—"

"Hear that gun, did you? Alton's off his nut. He don't waste lead. He shot at someone just then, and he wasn't fixin' to shoot pa'tridges when I saw him last. He was out to get a man. Gimme my gun."

"Cory, Babe—"

"You keep her here. Oh, God, this is a helluva mess. I can't stand much more." Cory ran out the door.

Clissa caught his arm: "Cory, I'm trying to tell you. Babe isn't here. I've called, and she isn't here." Cory's heavy, young-old face tautened. "Babe— Where did you last see her?"

"Breakfast." Clissa was crying now.

"She say where she was going?"

"No. She asked a lot of questions about Alton and where he'd gone."

"Did you say?"

Clissa's eyes widened, and she nodded, biting the back of her hand.

"You shouldn't ha' done that, Clissa," he gritted, and ran toward the woods, Clissa looking after him, and in that moment she could have killed herself.

Cory ran with his head up, straining with his legs and lungs and eyes at the long path. He puffed up the slope to the woods, agonized for breath after the forty-five minutes' heavy going. He couldn't even notice the damp smell of mold in the air.

He caught a movement in a thicket to his right, and dropped. Struggling to keep his breath, he crept forward until he could see clearly. There was something in there, all right. Something black, keeping still. Cory relaxed his legs and torso completely to make it easier for his heart to pump some strength back into them, and slowly raised the 12-gauge until it bore on the thing hidden in the thicket.

"Come out!" Cory said when he could speak.

Nothing happened.

"Come out or by God I'll shoot!" rasped Cory.

There was a long moment of silence, and his finger tightened on the trigger.

"You asked for it," he said, and as he fired, the thing leaped sideways into the open, screaming.

It was a thin little man dressed in sepulchral black and bearing the rosiest baby face Cory had ever seen. The face was twisted with fright and pain. The man scrambled to his feet and hopped up and down saying over and over, "Oh, my hand. Don't shoot again! Oh, my hand. Don't shoot again!" He stopped after a bit, when Cory had climbed to his feet, and he regarded the farmer out of sad china-blue eyes. "You shot me," he said reproachfully, holding up a little bloody hand. "Oh, my goodness."

Cory said, "Now, who the hell are you?"

The man immediately became hysterical, mouthing such a flood of broken sentences that Cory stepped back a pace and half-raised his gun in self-defense. It seemed to consist mostly of "I lost my papers," and "I didn't do it," and "It was horrible, horrible, horrible," and "The dead man," and "Oh, don't shoot again."

Cory tried twice to ask him a question, and then he stepped over and knocked the man down. He lay on the ground writhing and moaning and blubbering and putting his bloody hand to his mouth where Cory had hit him.

"Now what's going on around here?"

The man rolled over and sat up. "I didn't do it!" he sobbed. "I didn't. I was walking along and I heard the gun and I heard some swearing and an awful scream and I went over there and peeped and I saw the dead man and I ran away and you came and I hid and you shot me and—"

"*Shut up!*" The man did, as if a switch had been thrown. "Now," said Cory, pointing along the path, "you say there's a dead man up there?"

The man nodded and began crying in earnest. Cory helped him up. "Follow this path back to my farmhouse," he said. "Tell my wife to fix up your hand. *Don't* tell her anything else. And wait there until I come. Hear?"

"Yes. Thank you. Oh, thank you. *Snff.*"

"Go on now." Cory gave him a gentle shove in the right direction and went alone, in cold fear, up the path to the spot where he had found Alton the night before.

He found him here now, too, and Kimbo. Kimbo and Alton had spent several years together in the deepest friendship; they had hunted and fought and slept together, and the lives they owed each other were finished now. They were dead together.

It was terrible that they died the same way. Cory Drew was a strong man, but he gasped and fainted dead away when he saw what the thing of the mold had done to his brother and his brother's dog.

The little man in black hurried down the path, whimpering and holding his injured hand as if he rather wished he could limp with it. After a while the whimper faded away, and the hurried stride changed to a walk as the gibbering terror of the last hour receded. He drew two deep breaths, said: "My goodness!" and felt almost normal. He bound a linen handkerchief around his wrist, but the hand kept bleeding. He tried the elbow, and that made it hurt. So he stuffed the handkerchief back in his pocket and simply waved the hand stupidly in the air until the blood clotted. He did not see the great moist horror that clumped along

behind him, although his nostrils crinkled with its foulness.

The monster had three holes close together on its chest, and one hole in the middle of its slimy forehead. It had three close-set pits in its back and one on the back of its head. These marks were where Alton Drew's bullets had struck and passed through. Half of the monster's shapeless face was sloughed away, and there was a deep indentation on its shoulder. This was what Alton Drew's gun butt had done after he clubbed it and struck at the thing that would not lie down after he put his four bullets through it. When these things happened the monster was not hurt or angry. It only wondered why Alton Drew acted that way. Now it followed the little man without hurrying at all, matching his stride step by step and dropping little particles of muck behind it.

The little man went on out of the wood and stood with his back against a big tree at the forest's edge, and he thought. Enough had happened to him here. What good would it do to stay and face a horrible murder inquest, just to continue this silly, vague search? There was supposed to be the ruin of an old, old hunting lodge deep in this wood somewhere, and perhaps it would hold the evidence he wanted. But it was a vague report—vague enough to be forgotten without regret. It would be the height of foolishness to stay for all the hick-town red tape that would follow that ghastly affair back in the woods. Ergo, it would be ridiculous to follow that farmer's advice, to go to his house and wait for him. He would go back to town.

The monster was leaning against the other side of the big tree.

The little man snuffled disgustedly at a sudden overpowering odor of rot. He reached for his handkerchief, fumbled and dropped it. As he bent to pick it up, the monster's arm *whuffed* heavily in the air where his head had been—a blow that would certainly have removed that baby-faced protuberance. The man stood up and would have put the handkerchief to his nose had it not been so bloody. The creature behind the tree lifted its arm again just as the little man tossed the handkerchief away and stepped out into the field, heading across country to the distant highway that would take him back to town. The monster pounced on the handkerchief, picked it up, studied it, tore it across several times and inspected the tattered edges. Then it gazed vacantly at the disappearing figure of the little man, and finding him no longer interesting, turned back into the woods.

BABE BROKE INTO a trot at the sound of the shots. It was important to warn Uncle Alton about what her father had said, but it was more interesting to find out what he had bagged. Oh, he'd bagged it, all right. Uncle Alton never fired without killing. This was about the first time she had ever heard him

blast away like that. Must be a bear, she thought excitedly, tripping over a root, sprawling, rolling to her feet again, without noticing the tumble. She'd love to have another bearskin in her room. Where would she put it? Maybe they could line it and she could have it for a blanket. Uncle Alton could sit on it and read to her in the evening— Oh, no. No. Not with this trouble between him and dad. Oh, if she could only do something! She tried to run faster, worried and anticipating, but she was out of breath and went more slowly instead.

At the top of the rise by the edge of the woods she stopped and looked back. Far down in the valley lay the south thirty. She scanned it carefully, looking for her father. The new furrows and the old were sharply

defined, and her keen eyes saw immediately that Cory had left the line with the cultivator and had angled the team over to the shade trees without finishing his row. That wasn't like him. She could see the team now, and Cory's pale-blue denim was nowhere in sight.

A little nearer was the house, and as her gaze fell on it she moved out of the cleared pathway. Her father was coming; she had seen his shotgun and he was running. He could really cover ground when he wanted to. He must be chasing her, she thought immediately. He guessed that she would run toward the sound of the shots, and he was going to follow her tracks to Uncle Alton and shoot him. She knew that he was as good a woodsman as Alton; he would most certainly see her tracks. Well, she'd fixed him.

She ran along the edge of the wood, being careful to dig her heels deeply into the loam. A hundred yards of this, and she angled into the forest and ran until she reached a particularly thick grove of trees. Shinnying up like a squirrel, she squirmed from one close-set tree to another until she could go no farther back toward the path, then dropped lightly to the ground and crept on her way, now stepping very gently. It would take him an hour to beat around for her trail, she thought proudly, and by that time she could easily get to Uncle Alton. She giggled to herself as she thought of the way she had fooled her father. And the little sound of laughter drowned out, for her, the sound of Alton's hoarse dying scream.

She reached and crossed the path and slid through the brush beside it. The shots came from up around here somewhere. She stopped and listened several times, and then suddenly heard something coming toward her, fast. She ducked under cover, terrified, and a little baby-faced man in black, his blue eyes wide with horror, crashed blindly past her, the leather case he carried catching on the branches. It spun a moment and then fell right in front of her. The man never missed it.

Babe lay there for a long moment and then picked up the case and faded into the woods. Things were happening too fast for her. She wanted Uncle Alton, but she dared not call. She stopped again and strained her ears. Back toward the edge of the woods she heard her father's voice, and another's—probably the man who had dropped the briefcase. She dared not go over there. Filled with enjoyable terror, she thought hard, then snapped her fingers in triumph. She and Alton had played Injun many times up here; they had a whole repertoire of secret signals. She had practiced birdcalls until she knew them better than the birds themselves. What would it be? Ah—bluejay. She threw back her head and by some youthful alchemy produced a nerve-shattering screech that would have done justice to any jay that ever flew. She repeated it, and then twice more.

The response was immediate—the call of a bluejay, four times, spaced two and two. Babe nodded to herself happily. That was the signal that they were to meet immediately at The Place. The Place was a hideout that he had discovered and shared with her, and not another soul knew of it; an angle of rock beside a stream not far away. It wasn't exactly a cave, but almost. Enough so to be entrancing. Babe trotted happily away toward the brook. She had just known that Uncle Alton would remember the call of the bluejay, and what it meant.

In the tree that arched over Alton's scattered body perched a large jaybird, preening itself and shining in the sun. Quite unconscious of the presence of death, hardly noticing Babe's realistic cry, it screamed again four times, two and two.

It took Cory more than a moment to recover himself from what he had seen. He turned away from it and leaned weakly against a pine, panting. Alton. That was Alton lying there, in—parts.

"God! God, God, God—"

Gradually his strength returned, and he forced himself to turn again. Stepping carefully, he bent and picked up the .32-40. Its barrel was bright and clean, but the butt and stock were smeared with some kind of stinking rottenness. Where had he seen the stuff before? Somewhere—no matter. He cleaned it off absently, throwing the befouled bandanna away afterward. Through his mind ran Alton's words—was that only last night?—*"I'm goin' to start trackin', an' I'm goin' to keep trackin' till I find the one done this job on Kimbo."*

Cory searched shrinkingly until he found Alton's box of shells. The box was wet and sticky. That made it—better, somehow. A bullet wet with Alton's blood was the right thing to use. He went away a short distance, circled around till he found heavy footprints, then came back.

"I'm a-trackin' for you, bud," he whispered thickly, and began. Through the brush he followed its wavering spoor, amazed at the amount of filthy mold about, gradually associating it with the thing that had killed his brother. There was nothing in the world for him anymore but hate and doggedness. Cursing himself for not getting Alton home last night, he followed the tracks to the edge of the woods. They led him to a big tree there, and there he saw something else—the footprints of the little city man. Nearby lay some tattered scraps of linen, and—what was that?

Another set of prints—small ones. Small, stub-toed ones. "Babe!"

No answer. The wind sighed. Somewhere a bluejay called.

BABE STOPPED AND TURNED when she heard her father's voice, faint with distance, piercing.

"Listen at him holler," she crooned delightedly. "Gee, he sounds mad." She sent a jaybird's call disrespectfully back to him and hurried to The Place.

It consisted of a mammoth boulder beside the brook. Some upheaval in the glacial age had cleft it, cutting out a huge V-shaped chunk. The widest part of the cleft was at the water's edge, and the narrowest was hidden by bushes. It made a little ceilingless room, rough and uneven and full of potholes and cavelets inside, and yet with quite a level floor. The open end was at the water's edge.

Babe parted the bushes and peered down the cleft.

"Uncle Alton!" she called softly. There was no answer. Oh, well, he'd be along. She scrambled in and slid down to the floor.

She loved it here. It was shaded and cool, and the chattering stream filled it with shifting golden lights and laughing gurgles. She called again, on principle, and then perched on an outcropping to wait. It was only then she realized that she still carried the little man's briefcase.

She turned it over a couple of times and then opened it. It was divided in the middle by a leather wall. On one side were a few papers in a large yellow envelope, and on the other some sandwiches, a candy bar, and an apple. With a youngster's complacent acceptance of manna from heaven, Babe fell to. She saved one sandwich for Alton, mainly because she didn't like its highly spiced bologna. The rest made quite a feast.

She was a little worried when Alton hadn't arrived, even after she had consumed the apple core. She got up and tried to skim some flat pebbles across the roiling brook, and she stood on her hands, and she tried to think of a story to tell herself, and she tried just waiting. Finally, in desperation, she turned again to the briefcase, took out the papers, curled up by the rocky wall and began to read them. It was something to do, anyway.

There was an old newspaper clipping that told about strange wills that people had left. An old lady had once left a lot of money to whoever would make the trip from the Earth to the Moon and back. Another had financed a home for cats whose masters and mistresses had died. A man left thousands of dollars to the first person who could solve a certain mathematical problem and prove his solution. But one item was blue-penciled. It was:

One of the strangest of wills still in force is that of Thaddeus M. Kirk, who died in 1926. It appears that he built an elaborate mausoleum with burial vaults for all the remains of his family. He collected and removed caskets from all over the country to fill the designated niches. Kirk was the last of his line; there were no relatives when he died. His will stated that the mausoleum was to be kept in repair permanently, and that a certain sum was to be set aside as a reward for whoever could produce the body of his grandfather, Roger Kirk, whose niche is still empty. Anyone finding this body is eligible to receive a substantial fortune.

Babe yawned vaguely over this, but kept on reading because there was nothing else to do. Next was a thick sheet of business correspondence, bearing the letterhead of a firm of lawyers. The body of it ran:

In regard to your query regarding the will of Thaddeus Kirk, we are authorized to state that his grandfather was a man about five feet, five inches, whose left arm had been broken and who had a triangular silver plate set into his skull. There is no information as to the whereabouts of his death. He disappeared and was declared legally dead after the lapse of fourteen years.

The amount of the reward as stated in the will, plus accrued interest, now amounts to a fraction over sixty-two thousand dollars. This will be paid to anyone who produces the remains, providing that said remains answer descriptions kept in our private files.

There was more, but Babe was bored. She went on to the little black notebook. There was nothing in it but penciled and highly abbreviated records of visits to libraries; quotations from books with titles like "History of Angelina and Tyler Counties" and "Kirk Family History." Babe threw that aside, too. Where could Uncle Alton be?

She began to sing tunelessly, "Tumalumalum tum, ta ta ta," pretending to dance a minuet with flowering skirts like a girl she had seen in the movies. A rustle of the bushes at the entrance to The Place stopped her. She peeped upward, saw them being thrust aside. Quickly she ran to a tiny cul-de-sac in the rock wall, just big enough for her to hide in. She giggled at the thought of how surprised Uncle Alton would be when she jumped out at him.

She heard the newcomer, shuffling down the steep slope of the crevice and land heavily on the floor. There was something about the sound—What was it? It occurred to her that though it was a hard job for a big man like Uncle Alton to get through the little opening in the bushes, she could hear no heavy breathing. She heard no breathing at all!

Babe peered out into the main cave and squealed in utmost horror. Standing there was, not Uncle Alton, but a massive caricature of a man: a huge thing like an irregular mud doll, clumsily made. It quivered and parts of it glistened and parts of it were dried and crumbly. Half of the lower left part of its face was gone, giving it a lopsided look. It had no perceptible mouth or nose, and its eyes were crooked, one higher than the other, both a dingy brown with no whites at all. It stood quite still looking at her, its only movement a steady unalive quivering.

It wondered about the queer little noise Babe had made.

Babe crept far back against a little pocket of stone, her brain running around and around in tiny circles of agony. She opened her mouth to cry out, and could not. Her eyes bulged and her face flamed with the strangling effort, and the two golden ropes of her braided hair twitched and twitched as she hunted hopelessly for a way out. If only she were out in the open—or in the wedge-shaped half-cave where the thing was—or home in bed!

The thing clumped toward her, expressionless, moving with a slow inevitability that was the sheer crux of horror. Babe lay wide-eyed and frozen, mounting pressure of terror stilling her lungs, making her heart shake the whole world. The monster came to the mouth of the little pocket, tried to walk to her and was stopped by the sides. It was such a narrow little fissure, and it was all Babe could do to get in. The thing from the woods stood straining against the rock at its shoulders, pressing harder and harder to get to Babe. She sat up slowly, so near to the thing that its odor was almost thick enough to see, and a wild hope burst through her voiceless fear. It couldn't get in! It couldn't get in because it was too big!

The substance of its feet spread slowly under the tremendous strain, and at its shoulder appeared a slight crack. It widened as the monster unfeelingly crushed itself against the rock, and suddenly a large piece of the shoulder came away and the being twisted slushily three feet farther in. It lay quietly with its muddy eyes fixed on her, and then brought one thick arm up over its head and reached.

Babe scrambled in the inch farther she had believed impossible, and the filthy clubbed hand stroked down her back, leaving a trail of muck on the blue denim of the shirt she wore. The monster surged suddenly and, lying full length now, gained that last precious inch. A black hand seized one of her braids, and for Babe the lights went out.

When she came to, she was dangling by her hair from that same crusted paw. The thing held her high, so that her face and its featureless head were not more than a foot apart. It gazed at her with a mild curiosity in its eyes, and it swung her slowly back and forth. The agony of her pulled hair did what fear could not do—gave her a voice. She screamed. She opened her mouth and puffed up her powerful young lungs, and she sounded off. She held her throat in the position of the first scream, and her chest labored and pumped more air through the frozen throat. Shrill and monotonous and infinitely piercing, her screams.

The thing did not mind. It held her as she was, and watched. When it had learned all it could from this phenomenon, it dropped her jarringly, and looked around the half-cave, ignoring the stunned and huddled Babe. It reached over and picked up the leather briefcase and tore it twice across as if it were tissue. It saw the sandwich Babe had left, picked it up, crushed it, dropped it.

Babe opened her eyes, saw that she was free, and just as the thing turned back to her she dived between its legs and out in the shallow pool in front of the rock, paddled across and hit the other bank screaming. A vicious little light of fury burned in her; she picked up a grapefruit-sized stone and hurled it with all her frenzied might. It flew low and fast, and struck squashily on the monster's ankle. The thing was just taking a step toward the water; the stone caught it off balance, and its unpracticed equilibrium could not save it. It tottered for a long, silent moment at the edge and then splashed into the stream. Without a second look Babe ran shrieking away.

CORY DREW WAS following the little gobs of mold that somehow indicated the path of the murderer, and he was nearby when he first heard her scream. He broke into a run, dropping his shotgun and holding the .32-40 ready to fire. He ran with such deadly panic in his heart that he ran right past the huge cleft rock and was a hundred yards past it before she burst out through the pool and ran up the bank. He had to run hard and fast to catch her, because anything behind her was that faceless horror in the cave, and she was living for the one idea of getting away from there. He caught her in his arms and swung her to him, and she screamed on and on and on.

Babe didn't see Cory at all, even when he held her and quieted her.

THE MONSTER LAY in the water. It neither liked nor disliked this new element. It rested on the bottom, its massive head a foot beneath the surface, and it curiously considered the facts that it had garnered. There was the little humming noise of Babe's voice that sent the monster questing into the cave. There was the black material of the briefcase that resisted so much more than green things when he tore it. There was the little two-legged one who sang and brought him near, and who screamed when he came. There was this new cold moving thing that he had fallen into. It was washing his body away. That had never happened before. That was interesting. The monster decided to stay and observe the new thing. It felt no urge to save itself; it could only be curious.

The brook came laughing down out of its spring, ran down from its source beckoning to the sunbeams and embracing freshets and helpful brooklets. It shouted and played with steaming little roots and nudged the minnows and pollywogs about in its tiny backwaters. It was a happy brook. When it came to the pool by the cloven rock it found the monster there, and plucked at it. It soaked the foul substances and smoothed and melted the molds, and the waters below the thing eddied darkly with its diluted matter. It was a thorough brook. It washed all it touched, persistently. Where it found filth, it removed filth; and if there were layer on layer of foulness, then layer by foul layer it was removed. It was a good brook. It did not mind the poison of the monster, but took it up and thinned it and spread it in little rings and around rocks downstream, and let it drift to the rootlets of water plants, that they might grow greener and lovelier. And the monster melted.

"I am smaller," the thing thought. "That is interesting. I could not move now. And now this part of me which thinks is going, too. It will stop in just a moment, and drift away with the rest of the body. It will stop thinking and I will stop being, and that, too, is a very interesting thing."

So the monster melted and dirtied the water, and the water was clean again, washing and washing the skeleton that the monster had left. It was not very big, and there was a badly healed knot on the left arm. The sunlight flickered on the triangular silver plate set into the pale skull, and the skeleton was very clean now. The brook laughed about it for an age.

THEY FOUND THE SKELETON, six grim-lipped men who came to find a killer. No one had believed Babe, when she told her story days later. It had to be days later because Babe had screamed for seven hours without stopping, and had lain like a dead child for a day. No one believed her at all, because her story was all about the bad fella, and they knew that the bad fella was simply a thing that her father had made up to frighten her with. But it was through her that the skeleton was found, and so the men at the bank sent a check to the Drews for more money than they had ever dreamed about. It was old Roger Kirk, sure enough, that skeleton, though it was found five miles from where he had died and sank into the forest floor where the hot molds built around his skeleton and emerged—a monster.

So the Drews had a new barn and fine new livestock and they hired four men. But they didn't have Alton. And they didn't have Kimbo. And Babe screams at night and has grown very thin.

"IT" first appeared in the August 1940 issue of Unknown, *copyright © 1940 in U.S.A. and Great Britain by Street & Smith Publications, Inc., and reprinted here by permission of The Theodore Sturgeon Literary Trust c/o The Lotts Agency, Ltd. Special thanks to Noël Sturgeon.*

Before turning to full-time writing, American author, critic, and screenwriter Theodore Sturgeon (1918–1985) sailed as a merchant marine, worked at a drydock for the U.S. Army, operated a bulldozer in Puerto Rico, managed a hotel in Jamaica, sold refrigerators door to door, ran a gas station, and even opened his own literary agency. Having penned 11 novels, 120 short stories, 400 reviews, and several television scripts, Sturgeon is perhaps best known today for two wildly popular episodes of the original Star Trek series, "Shore Leave" (1966) and "Amok Time" (1967), which introduced the Vulcan mating ritual pon farr. He also introduced the Prime Directive in a third Trek script that was never produced.

Sturgeon's fiction inspired numerous writers and creative works, in film, television and comics. "It" spawned a host of muck monsters, including Marvel Comics' Man-Thing *and DC Comics'* Swamp Thing. *"Killdozer!" —his 1944 novella about an alien intelligence possessing a piece of hardware, an idea frequently revisited in SF—was adapted as a made-for-TV movie (a 1974 cult classic with a script by Sturgeon) and as a comics story published in Marvel's* Worlds Unknown #6 *(1974). Another, unauthorized, comics adaptation, "The Steel Monster," had previously appeared in the second issue of* Amazing Adventures *(May 1951)*

In 1954, Sturgeon won the International Fantasy Award for his SF novel More Than Human *('53), In 2000, he was posthumously inducted into the Science Fiction and Fantasy Hall of Fame.*

Sturgeon once stated that "Ninety percent of everything is crap." (Sturgeon's Law) If true, we can be thankful for his outstanding "tithe."

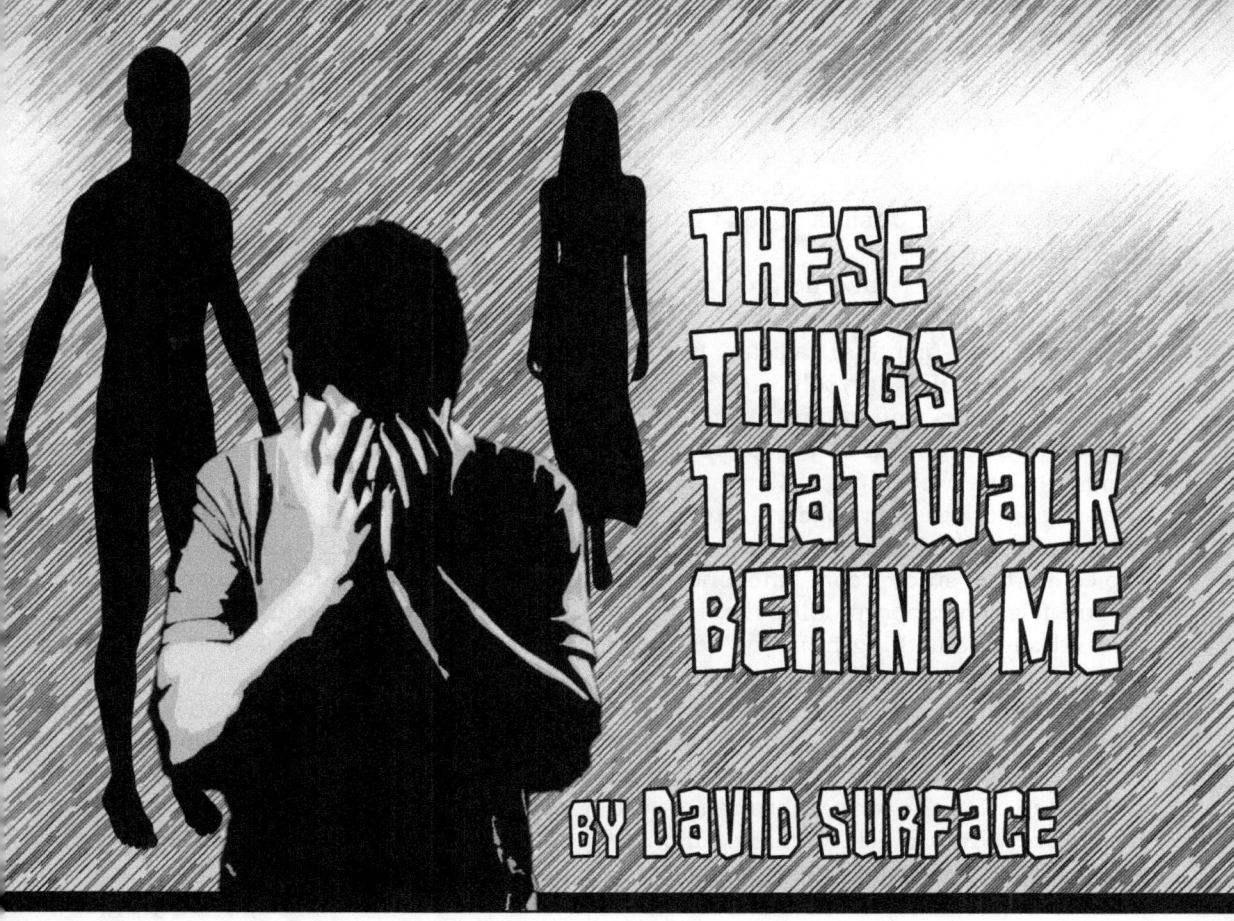

THESE THINGS THAT WALK BEHIND ME

BY DAVID SURFACE

"YOU KNOW A GROWN MAN ISN'T SUPPOSED TO SLEEP WITH A LIGHT ON."

That's what Robert used to say every night when we went to bed, back when it was one of those little lover's idiosyncrasies that we could still joke about. I told him that I couldn't see well in the dark, that I was afraid of tripping and falling if I had to get up in the middle of the night. That seemed to satisfy him. But it wasn't true.

I've always been afraid of going to sleep. Even when I was very young, I was terrified by the idea of unconsciousness, that there was a precise moment when my awareness was going to be extinguished like a light being turned out. I lay in my bed and waited for that moment, horribly frightened of it, then I'd wake up, surprised to see the sunlight coming through my window. I'd missed the moment I was so afraid of, but the morning light felt tainted by the realization that I was going to have to live through that moment again and again and again.

I make the mistake of telling this to Robert one night as we lay side by side on our backs, our voices floating up to the ceiling in the dark.

"What were you afraid of?" he asks. I listen for some note of tenderness or concern, but all I hear is curiosity. I don't think Robert has ever been afraid of anything in his life, so for him, the question is a purely academic one.

"I don't know," I say. "I guess it was just the idea of losing consciousness. Being completely defenseless…"

Robert is silent for a moment. I can feel the gears in his brain working, coming up with something practical and intelligent to say.

"Defenseless? Against what? I mean, if you were afraid of losing consciousness, of nothingness, then that's just ridiculous. Nothingness means there's nothing there. You can't be afraid of *nothing*."

Robert is right. It wasn't really the idea

of nothingness that I was afraid of. It was the idea that there might be something behind it. Something alive and aware that might show its face at any moment. But I can't tell him that. Just like I can't tell him about the grey people.

The first time I saw the grey people, I was in college. It was finals week and I'd been pulling all-nighters, basically living in the library, fueling myself with vending machine snacks and coffee. On my third day without any real sleep, there was a constant, low-level ringing in my ears, and my arms and legs felt rubbery and numb.

I was hunched over one of the long wood tables in the study room late one night when I felt someone watching me. I looked up and saw something from the corner of my eye, standing about twenty feet away next to a pillar. I had the impression of something thin and grey. When I looked directly at it, it slipped out of sight behind the pillar. Not the way a human would move, but with a quick, slithering motion, like some kind of dark fluid slipping down a drain.

I sat there for a moment, trying to understand what I'd just seen. I decided that I must have fallen asleep and dreamed it, so I sat up straight and tried to focus on my book. But the words drifted and pulsed on the page under the ugly florescent light, so I closed my eyes for a moment. Again, I felt like I was being watched. I opened my eyes, and the thin grey thing was there again, closer than before. It quickly slipped behind another pillar with that same liquid motion, but I thought I could make out a long, loose robe, and a face that was somehow not a face.

I looked around at the other bleary-eyed students, lost in their books and papers. None of them seemed to notice. For a moment, I tried to make myself get up and look behind that pillar, but I was afraid of what I might find. I decided to keep my head down and not look up.

A moment later, I could feel it watching me again. This time I knew it was standing right over me. I could no longer read the words on the page, but I forced my eyes to stay on the book in front of me. I knew that if I looked up again, the thing standing over me would show me its face and then take me with it.

When the sun finally came up, I left the library and walked across the campus toward my dorm, and they were everywhere. Behind every building, behind every tree. Watching me. I slept for twelve hours, and when I opened my eyes, they were gone. But there was no comfort in that word. *Gone* meant that they'd once been there. That they were real. And that they could come back at any time.

SITTING AT THE KITCHEN table the next morning trying to drink my coffee, I can feel Robert looking at me, inspecting me for flaws. I sit straighter and try to look alert. Robert has been patient with my occasional sleepless nights, my insecurities, anxieties, and quiet spells. But even with the most supportive and understanding lover, there's a point you can't afford to fall below.

"You're not having trouble sleeping again, are you?"

"No," I say. I feel him studying me—Robert can always tell when I'm lying.

"Maybe it's hormonal," he says. "You should try to get more exercise."

More than anyone I know, Robert likes to explain things. Robert is older than me by one year, handsomer by far, and taller by three inches. Five foot eleven, to be exact. Most men would just say they're six feet, but Robert likes to be precise about things. Facts have a sort of moral weight for him, and he chides me when he thinks I'm ignoring them. Working as communications director of a government healthcare agency satisfies his desire for precision and orderliness, as well as his sense of importance. As he likes to say, he's helping people in ways that matter.

You help people too, he says whenever he senses that I'm feeling low about the differences between us. *You're a teacher. Teachers help people.* Sometimes I believe him. At other times, his earnest and well-meaning attempts to make me feel like his equal only show me how much less he thinks I'm worth.

"You should go to the gym after school

today," he says on his way out the door. Robert's always trying to get me to improve myself. He says he's worried about me. Worrying about me is a distraction, an annoyance he wishes he didn't have to put up with.

Don't worry about me, I want to say. But he's already gone.

TODAY A NEW STUDENT appears in my classroom, a quiet boy with a pale, somber face who keeps his eyes cast downward. There is a young woman with him whom I've never seen before; his case worker, obviously. She sits behind him, hands folded in her lap, occasionally leaning forward to whisper something to him, although I never see him respond. At one point, I look up and see his lips moving as if he's talking to someone. The other students don't seem to notice until they're working silently on something. The new boy's voice stands out in the silence, muttering softly, his eyes shut tight. I see one or two students nervously glance at him.

At one point, the new boy shouts out a single word that sounds like *No.* One of the girls sitting close to him screams, then the whole class explodes into whispers and nervous laughter. The young woman sitting with the new boy blushes and leans close to say something to him. The boy keeps on muttering, eyes shut tight, but I know he's not talking to her.

"SOUNDS LIKE SCHIZOPHRENIA," Robert says. "Ten's a little young for that." He says it with the kind of confidence that I used to find reassuring, but now I just feel a spark of annoyance.

"I don't know," I say. "I never really like to know what kind of diagnosis those students have. I don't like to label them like that."

Robert gives me the kind of patient smile that a parent gives a child who's prattling on about something they've heard a hundred times before. "Well," he says, moving to the refrigerator and digging around inside for a bottle of wine, "They probably don't even bother to tell you that stuff anyway, do they?"

Robert pours us each a big glass of Merlot, and we sit down. The wine tastes bitter for some reason, but I take deep swallows, trying to melt the knot of anxiety deep in my chest. I catch Robert staring at me intently. "Are you still not sleeping?" he asks, a concerned scowl creeping across his handsome face.

"I'm sleeping enough."

"What's *enough*? Six hours? Four?"

I don't answer because I don't like lying to him.

"Dean, you're not, like … *afraid* to go to sleep or something, are you?"

"No," I say a little too loudly. "Why should I be?"

"I don't know. Just … you know … that thing you told me about when you were a kid…."

"Jesus, Robert, I'm sorry I even told you now. God, why do I tell you anything?"

"Okay, I'm sorry, I'm sorry," Robert says, raising both hands, palms-out. "It's just … you know. I want you to be alright."

You think I don't want the same thing? That's what I want to say, but I don't. I've said enough already. Probably too much.

In bed later, I try to make my breathing as slow and regular as I can to make myself relax. I'm also doing it so Robert will think I'm asleep. Pretty soon, I hear his slow, ragged breathing. I lay there listening and try to take some comfort in that sound.

Three hours later, I'm still awake, staring into the dark. Robert has stopped snoring, so I'm unprotected from all the sounds around me. The long sigh of a car passing by and fading. The staccato pop of wood swelling in the heat. And a new sound from down the hall, in the kitchen. A ceramic clink and scrape that sounds like a coffee cup being clumsily placed in a saucer and picked up again. I wait, certain that it won't happen again, afraid that it will. When it does, the sound is unmistakable.

The third time it happens, I can't stop myself. I get up and walk down the hall toward that noise. I pause outside of the kitchen door and look in. Light from the streetlight outside pours in through the windows, illuminating everything.

There's a man standing by the kitchen

counter. He's heavy-set, and wears some kind of baggy gray suit that's too big for him. There's plenty of light, but I can't seem to see his face. He picks up a coffee cup, appears to study it, then puts it back down again, making that small rattling sound, over and over. At first, he doesn't seem to notice me. Then he turns his face toward me and slowly smiles, double rows of sharp teeth, long as butcher knives, gleaming in the kitchen light. At the same time, I see the baggy gray suit that sags in folds around him is skin.

This can't be happening. I say those words to myself, closing my eyes and repeating them to push out everything else. *This can't be happening.* I open my eyes again and the thing in the kitchen is still there, grinning at me.

"No." I say out loud, then, louder. *"No."* The thing smiles even wider. A long string of saliva stretches slowly from its lips all the way to the floor.

I turn and walk quickly back to the bedroom. I don't run—I know that running will only make this worse. I get into bed next to Robert, but I don't try to wake him or even touch him. Instead, I lay there and listen for that rattling sound, for *any* sound, but it's quiet now.

I watch the door all night, but nothing happens.

"WHAT THE HELL were you doing in here last night?"

Robert is standing near the kitchen sink, a confused scowl on his face. I'm bleary-eyed and light-headed from lack of sleep, and my heart is beating too fast. I lean against the door frame and try to focus on what Robert is holding in his hand and peering at. It's the white cup and saucer from last night.

"You spill a cup of coffee on the floor and don't clean it up?" I watch Robert scowl harder and bend down to touch a wet spot on the floor. He pulls his fingers away, something sticky and viscous trailing from them. "Jesus, Dean! what the hell…"

"Don't!" I shout. I push him out of the way, and he staggers back against the counter, the white cup and saucer fall to the floor and break.

"What the hell is wrong with you?" he yells. In his eyes I see anger and something I've never seen in them before. Fear. He's afraid of me.

Now we're both afraid.

I WANT YOU TO see somebody. Those are the words Robert uses, the ones I knew were coming. *I want you to see somebody.* I know what that means. I don't argue. I agree, just to keep the peace. Maybe it will help. But something tells me it won't. I don't want anyone else to explain what's happening to me. Not some doctor. Not Dean. Not anyone.

I stay up late, doing my research. I'm learning about the limits of human visual perception. I read about the whole spectrum of invisible light that humans can't see, about infrared light that shines from our bodies, x-ray light that penetrates flesh and bone, gamma light and radio light.

I bring these things up before dinner, trying to sound casual.

"Stop it, Dean," Robert sighs. "Just stop, okay?"

"Stop what?" I know he's on to me, but the reflex to deflect and deny is too strong.

"I mean … you go on Google, you write down a bunch of big scientific-sounding words, then you throw them at me like you know what you're talking about, but you don't. You don't even understand half the stuff you're saying."

Normally, I'd get up and walk away, but tonight my anger flies out at him. "Why do you always have to call me stupid?"

"I'm not calling you stupid…"

"That's what you meant."

"You're not stupid, Dean," Robert says, trying to make his voice go softer. "You're just…" He trails off and looks down, his lips tight. I try to imagine the word he doesn't want to say. *Gullible? Weak?*

Later, I start to wonder if he's right. I don't want him to put a label on what's happening to me and stick me in some kind of box. But isn't that what I'm doing with my invisible spectrum and gamma rays and radio light—trying to put what I've seen into some other kind of box?

BACK IN THE CLASSROOM, I try to lose myself

in my job, in all the young faces around me, but it's hard. The new boy seems to be getting worse. He shouts out loud at least once every day, flailing his hands like he's trying to push something away. The other kids almost seem used to it by now. They've stopped reacting with startled squeals and nervous laughter. Instead, they stop in the middle of whatever they're saying and wait patiently until the boy's case worker has calmed him down. Their kindness almost makes me weep, then I wonder if it's really kindness that I'm witnessing, or something else.

Today I approach the case worker after class. She's standing by the boy's desk, picking up her things, and looks a little startled to see me walk over to her. We've never talked.

"Hi," I say, glancing down at the boy. "I was just wondering ... is there anything I can do? You know, to help?"

"No," she says. "Thank you." Behind her polite smile and strained eyes, I can see the part of her that's given up. I glance down at the boy sitting alone at his desk and feel sorrier for him than before.

It must be terrible to have people give up on you.

THERE ARE NO SEATS on the bus today, so I stand, hanging onto the metal bar as best I can. No sleep now for four days. One moment, my body feels heavy as lead, the next moment, it's so light, I imagine that people can see right through me.

I'm gazing at the window, at the ghostly reflection of the other passengers packed in around me. Then I see the reflection of a face over my shoulder, looking right at me. I freeze, unable to understand what I'm seeing. Two dead eyes like black marbles. A lipless, snake-like mouth that stretches all the way from ear to ear.

I close my eyes as tight as I can and try to concentrate on the rumble and roar of the bus, the voices of people talking around me. Familiar sounds. I open my eyes, and the face behind me is closer than before, just a few feet away, staring at me. He's taller than the other passengers, but they don't seem to notice him. I can't turn around and look.

I'm afraid that if I do, he might really be there. When the urge to turn around becomes too much, I shut my eyes again as tightly as I can, and squeeze the metal bar over my head so hard that my hand becomes numb. *No.* Am I saying it out loud? *No!* I hear people around me start to whisper and mutter. I know they're talking about me. When I can't bear it anymore, I open my eyes and the thing is standing right behind me. A long, thin tongue flickers out of its mouth and slides across the back of my neck.

WHEN I WAKE UP, there are strangers hovering over me and asking me questions, and a terrible hospital smell all around. My throat feels raw from screaming, but as soon as I can speak, I say, *"Robert ... Robert Denning."* I can't give them his number—the only two phone numbers I've ever memorized in my life are my mother's, and my childhood best friend, and they're both dead now. So I keep telling them, *"Robert. Robert Denning,"* over and over, until the words are just meaningless sounds

When Robert finally arrives, his face is flushed red, and his blue eyes are hard. "Christ, Dean! I begged you to see somebody!" Those are his first words to me. I don't know what else I expected of him, but there they are, so I say what I know he wants from me.

"I'm sorry..."

I watch him looking around at the cold, stark hallways, a nervous expression on his face. "Jesus," he says. "You don't belong in this god damn place..." But when he looks back at me, I see a glimpse of the same fearful anger I saw in his eyes the morning I pushed him, and I understand what he really means. *I don't belong with someone who belongs in this god damn place.*

Two men in white walk up to Dean. One of them touches Dean on the shoulder and says something I can't hear. Dean walks away with him and they disappear around a corner. The other man stays and watches me, an unreadable look on his face. *Don't worry about me,* I want to say. *He's going to get me out of here.* But when the doctor comes back, Dean isn't with him. I understand what's happened before he says anything.

"Your friend believes it's in your best interest for you to stay here with us for a while."

All the breath leaves my body, and for a moment I feel my heart actually stop. *I'm going to die now,* I think. But I don't. Somehow, I don't.

THE TV BLARING—that's the one thing you can't get away from in this place. The doctors and nurses come and go, and you can close your eyes if you don't want to see all the other men and women with their vacant, frightened stares. But there's no escaping the sound of the TV. They turn it up all the way, so it keeps battering away at your ears and nerves until you learn to tune it out.

There's a man here who yells at the other patients. An older man, maybe in his sixties, very thin with hard muscles like knots. His head is shaved and his eyes are bright and wild. I watch him walk over to a middle-aged woman huddled in a chair, shouting angrily and flailing his arms until a couple of orderlies come and take him away. An hour later he's back again, sitting alone in the corner, his bright, angry eyes darting all over the room as if he's looking for someone.

All night long, I can hear someone crying in the room next to mine. I wish I could cry. I wish I could scream or shout, anything to get rid of this tight, terrified feeling trapped in my chest. It hits me that nothing in my entire life has prepared me for this. Nothing I've ever done, nothing I've learned can help me now.

In the morning, I look across the community room and see a frightened-looking man in striped pajamas huddled in one of the ugly green Naugahyde chairs. His eyes are shut, his lips are moving rapidly. His head jerks and twists as if he's trying to get away from something.

"Ugly mother..."

I turn and see the angry man from yesterday sitting right next to me, glaring at the man across the room. Before I can react, he gets up and strides over to the man and starts yelling and waving his arms threateningly.

That's when I see it. Fading in and out of focus, a figure standing over the man in the chair. Almost seven feet tall, with a face like the skull of a dead bird, long twisted arms and fingers like bare branches that poke and scratch at the man's face while he twists and moans. The angry man shouts and flails at the tall stick-thing, and it turns its head toward him, opens its boney beak and hisses. Two orderlies start to move in, but before they can reach him, the man turns and stalks out of the room, and the tall stick-like thing follows him. The orderlies go back to their other tasks, the man in the chair stops muttering; the tension seems to leave his body and he closes his eyes and appears to fall asleep. I sit there, unable to move or understand what I've just seen.

PLEASE. COME GET ME. That's the four-word message I keep typing into my cell phone and deleting—I don't know how many times. I stopped sending texts to Robert a while ago. I couldn't bear to keep looking for his response and not finding it. I still type them. I just don't send them. That way, it doesn't hurt as much when he doesn't answer.

"Why you do that to yourself?"

A gravelly voice speaks close to me. I look up from my phone. The man with the shaved head is sitting right across the table from me, glaring at me with his bright, angry eyes. He nods at the phone in my hand.

"You know he ain't coming back here for you."

How...? I look more closely at him. The bones of his ebony-dark face are sharp and highly defined, proud, even beautiful, and I think of the statue of an Egyptian pharaoh. His eyes that continue to blaze at me have small flecks of gold and green.

"My name's Dean," I offer.

"Carlton." He extends his hand across the table. I take it and feel how strong he is. His skin feels dry and leathery and radiant with heat.

He releases my hand and studies me for a moment. "Dean. Tell me. Why is it you don't want something *better* for yourself?"

The tears that burn my eyes startle me, and I turn to wipe them away. *How does he know?* When I look up at him again, he's glaring at something in the room behind me.

"Look," he says. I turn around and feel my throat close with fear.

They're all here. Fading in and out of my vision like objects appearing and disappearing in a heavy fog. The tall, stick-like thing with the dead bird's beak. The grinning man with teeth like butcher knives. The tall figure with the dead black eyes and the wide snake mouth. A dozen others I've never seen before. They bend low over these poor men and women who are trapped here, scratching and stabbing into their soft flesh, hissing terrible words into their ears that make them moan and weep.

"You see them, don't you?" Carlton says. "Don't tell me you don't see them, 'cause I know you do."

My throat is too tight to speak. All I can do is nod. Carlton glares at the creatures tormenting the patients, and shakes his head.

"You ... you stopped one," I manage to say. "I saw you. You made it go away."

"Not now," he growls. "Too many. Some days there's too many, and you can't do nothing."

"But some days..." I say the words carefully, as if they might break, "...you can."

"That's right. Some days you can." He looks at me for a long moment, then leans closer across the table, eyes burning into mine. "Listen," he says, "I ain't never getting out of here. But you will. When you do, remember something. You got work to do. You got real important work to do. You understand what I'm saying."

I look into his wild, feverish eyes. I don't understand, not yet. But I know it's coming. The understanding. Like a train or a storm, it's coming.

ON THE MORNING when they finally release me, the woman who is filling out my papers asks, "Is there someone you'd like us to contact? Someone you'd like to come and get you?"

"No," I say. "No one." When I see the concerned look in her eyes, I remember to smile and say, "Thanks."

In the end, the world outside is not so different from the one inside. You just have to learn to negotiate them both. That's what I'm doing now. One step at a time.

I did see Robert again. He was standing on the street corner in a crowd of people, waiting for the light to change. I saw the thing that was with him. Looming over him, grim and terrible, it had long, twisted fingers like tangled tree roots that pierced the skin of Robert's back, and were growing inside of him. I knew that Robert suffered, but I didn't know why or how much until now. I didn't approach him or try to help, because I knew he wouldn't believe me. When the light changed, I saw Robert cross the street with the dark thing. And even though Robert was in front, I could see that it was leading him.

THERE ARE SO MANY other people out here who need help. More than I ever knew. I look for the ones who I know can't handle it by themselves. The ones who are too old or too young, not strong enough. Like the little boy in the park. I recognize him the moment I see him, the way he sits by himself with his eyes closed and his lips moving, the same way he did in my classroom. I don't need to see the two monstrous insect-like things bending over him and whispering to know how long this has been going on for him—his mother's strained and weary face tells me all I need to know.

I don't hesitate. Not anymore. I walk right up to the two red things bending over him. "Leave him alone," I say. One of them looks up at me, chittering and hissing, the insect features of his face rearranging themselves into what must be an expression of surprise or resentment.

"Leave him alone!" I say again. I hear the mother call out her boy's name, alarm in her voice. In one more moment, I know she'll stand up and run over to protect her child from this stranger approaching him.

"Come with me," I say to the two ugly red things that are now both staring at me. "Now."

And they come. They follow me away

from the boy and his mother who I know is now on her knees beside him. "What did he say to you?" I hear her asking. "What did he say?" I don't stay to hear him answer. I keep walking through this world with all these things that walk behind me. I don't need to turn around to know how many there are.

I can't slow down now. I've got work to do.

David Surface is the author of the collection Terrible Things *from Black Shuck Books. His stories have appeared in* Shadows & Tall Trees, Supernatural Tales, Nightscript, The Tenth Black Book of Horror, Phantom Drift, Morpheus Tales, Twisted Book of Shadows, Uncertainties III, *and* The Best Horror of the Year, Volume 13. *A YA supernatural suspense novel co-written with Julia Rust,* Angel Falls, *is now available from Haverhill House Publishing's YAP imprint. David is also the author of the newsletter* STRANGE LITTLE STORIES. *To learn more about David and his writing, visit davidsurface.net*

ALLEN K. '02

THE CALM
By James Dorr

IT WAS ON A BRIGHT SUMMER'S DAY, IN THE YEAR OF OUR LORD 1755, THAT THEY CAME TO THE VILLAGE. They had mustered out of Massachusetts, under the flag of Governor-General William Shirley to fight the French, and the wind had pursued them. It had followed them from the well-kept farms and ordered towns that they had grown up in, west and then north as their detachment, commanded by Captain Laurence Pindar, broke off from the main body, up through the Berkshires and into Vermont, a mixed troop of British regular army and raw colonials. It whistled after them through Brattleboro and Newfane and Windham, as they marched up, first, the West River valley, then, hoping to meet with the Battenkill and then the Mettawee and Otter Rivers, either of the latter of which could bring them to Lake Champlain, into the sow-backed ridges and valleys of the east slope of the Taconic Mountains.

Possibly of them all, Philip Latham, himself from the western part of Massachusetts and elected corporal of his town's militia, knew the wind best. *Le vent de la mort*, the French trappers called it, the few that, before, had come down to the lands of the English settlers.

The wind that presages death.

This was a Huron superstition, or so he had been told, brought east from the Great Lakes but shared by the Iroquois tribes as well, that a wind that persisted could only bring ill fate. Especially a wind, as this, that even as they pressed into the mountains, still rustled the treetops. Still lay in wait for them to swirl their hats off whenever they broke to the infrequent clearings, the patches of grass where they fell out and rested while their officers grazed their horses.

He kept this lore to himself, of course—no sense spooking the others. Enough men were being lost to desertion. Enough there was to make men away from their homes for the first time, as most in his group were, to feel uneasy about their own shadows, much less the brooding, patch-shadowed peaks they caught glimpses of from time to time, as, hacking their way through tangles of honeysuckle and wild grape surrounded by forest, they pushed ever upward.

Until, at last, they came out on a ridge-top and saw the village.

The captain halted them. "Lieutenant Barnstone," he called, "bring the maps up." Still well outside the village proper, the men looked down on it, its empty town square with its well in the center, its rough-granite church standing squat on the far side with signs in its churchyard of recent activity, while the officers were conversing. They looked for signs of life, seeing no movement, the houses on its square's three other sides all barred and shuttered tight.

But shuttered against what, Corporal Latham wondered. Perhaps a coming storm? Beyond the small town stood a half-mile high mountain, its peak lost in darkened, fog-like clouds that hugged its cragged sides, not spreading out in the sky as most clouds did, but huddled close to its bare-rocked surface. But as for the wind that would bring a storm to them—he realized now that, for the first time, the wind appeared to be dying.

He looked toward the other men, then to the captain and his lieutenant as the officers called him over with the other non-coms. "This village should not be here," the lieutenant began. "At least it's not on any of our maps, which gives us a problem. Not knowing what this village is, we have no way of knowing which side its inhabitants support. Whether they'd welcome us with open arms, or—"

"Or whether they'd shoot us, if they had the chance to," the captain said for him.

"We may as well be blunt. I know we've lost men every mile of the way once we came in these mountains. The hard march. The unfamiliar surroundings. The men need resting, a chance for cooked rations. And so I propose that we take a risk and make camp in the town here, but not all go in at first. I want some of you men to take the horses—we passed a small meadow not a mile back—and the wagons with them. See that they're hobbled there, then be ready to join back with us the instant there's any sign of trouble...."

And so the captain's orders continued, detailing some of the men as pickets to remain on the ridge-top, at least until given orders to come down, others, including Corporal Latham, to precede the main body into the village, but spreading out into its open places, guarding the dirt paths between its houses, its church and its churchyard. Latham, in point of fact, to take his group and scour the churchyard for any townspeople who might be hiding there, bringing any he found to the square where Captain Pindar would set the main camp up.

And the wind, meanwhile, slackened further, while other sounds now came, sounds of murmuring within the houses as the first troops passed slowly between them, the men with bayonets fixed on their muskets, alert for hostility. Then even these were then drowned out by the sounds of drums, as, the scouts passing through to the square without incident, the doors and the windows remaining shut tight, the main troop descended in battle order, carefully, warily, until they, too, reached the village's center.

"You of the village," the captain then shouted. "You see we are here and that we will not harm you. We ask you to come out—to send someone out to us. We wish to buy provisions from you. To use your well to fill our canteens with. To camp here peaceably only for one night and then be on our way."

And this time several of the doors opened. Latham watched from the churchyard where he and his small group had been inspecting what seemed the signs of a recent funeral, one interrupted before it was finished, as men from the houses came out to the square, but never straying too far from their own front doors. Some of them shouted, short, bent men, as if Aboriginals or else of mixed blood, but not in English. Part French, a few of them. Others in some tongue that seemed like that of the Oneida tribespeople, yet not entirely that, while Latham listened, hearing a snatch now and then that he recognized.

"*Gardez!*" a few shouted—that in a broken French Latham could understand. "*Gardez-vous de la fin du vent! Gardez son éxtremité!*"

And Latham, at least, realized what they were saying. The wind that presages death— *beware its ending!*

But Captain Pindar shouted over them: "*Damme*, is there no one here who speaks English!"

Then there was silence, a moment of silence as the villagers retreated softly back into their houses, closing the doors quietly behind them, and even the wind sank down to a sigh. And then to a whisper.

And then—next to Latham. Practically in his ear, a quiet voice murmured. "*I* speak English."

Latham jumped back, nearly tripping over a shovel—another sign of the ceremony that had, for some reason, been abandoned. Before him a man stood, robed as a village priest.

"I-I'm Corporal Latham," he stammered. Then, regaining his wits, he bowed hurriedly. "Begging your pardon, sir, but I was startled. The sudden silence, after our captain's shout. Then your voice, so near. I did not hear you come out."

"My pardon, then, *Caporal*," the priest answered, leading him with him to the square where the captain waited. "I am Charles Devinette, *curé* of the church where I came out a side door. Here in our village we have become used to moving with little sound, staying inside when our work does not call us out. 'Out of sight, out of mind,' as say you English, yes?"

"Uh, yes," Latham answered. "This is our commander, Captain Pindar, who, as you may have heard, wishes to let your villagers know that we only wish to camp here for the night. To rest and reprovision ourselves."

The priest nodded, then shook hands with the captain. "My children," he said, "the flock of my village, wish you no harm either. With your permission, I will call them out again, but only for the briefest moment. I will explain to them that you must be sheltered, even as they are sheltered themselves, that they must each take one or two of you with them into their houses. To let you wait with them...."

The captain shook his head. "Damme!" he said. "You mean what you wish is to separate us—to get us in small groups where you can kill us. Your language is French, at least what I can make of it. Some of you Indians by the look of you, I would imagine. Likely most of you, even if you live in white men's houses." The captain smiled then, a bitter, tight-lipped smile. "Probably massacred, those that built 'em, eh?"

"*Capitaine, non!*" the priest protested. "We massacre no one. We are on neither side. As for our bodies, our language, our ways, we are, all of us, only what life makes us to be, yes? Here in these mountains there are *êtres*—*things*—much older than French or English. Or even the Iroquois. Things that are even more silent than we are. That strike when the wind dies!"

And the wind was silent as the priest suddenly turned and bolted back into the churchyard, Latham following on his heels at the captain's orders. He ran as quickly as he could, but the priest was faster, dodging gravestones, dodging the long, narrow, wicker basket used to carry the newly deceased—when even funerals were interrupted when the wind showed signs of stopping its constant hum—dodging the shovel that Latham had almost tripped over before, and then disappeared through a stout oaken door in the church's stone side, locking it with a firm *click!* behind him.

And Latham stood, transfixed, as the air became completely calm. As the leaves of the trees outside the town ceased their constant rustling, as every iota of motion was stilled. As even the murmurs inside were halted—until, a sudden scream!

A scream of horses, beyond, in the meadow where they had been taken. The shouts of the men who had been posted with them, followed by the captain's barked orders, to form up in ranks. A defensive square. Riflemen inside, bayonets outside.

Latham turned and ran to join them, seeing, as he did, over the church roof, the fog on the mountain beyond the village streaming downward, tendrils already having reached the plateaued grass where the horses had been tied. He twisted, broken-field dashing through the cluttered churchyard when, with a sharp jolt, he felt the earth drop away beneath him.

He landed in darkness—the newly dug grave, the corpse already in it, but left unfilled when the gravediggers had hastily dropped their shovels to flee the impending calm. He tried to climb out of it, scrambling up its crumbling side, but his foot was caught in the winding cloth of the corpse's shroud, becoming all the more entangled the more he attempted to extricate it.

And overhead the air became heavy, hot with moisture, darkening as the fog rolled in behind him. As—

He tried to scream! To give some warning even if he could not join the others, faced outward in their defensive formation to stave off *whatever* it was that ignored those inside the houses—*out of sight, out of mind,* as the *curé* had said—but oozed on steadily up the pathways between the houses. Converging on the square. While, in the square itself, *behind* the men—he tried to scream, but the words would not come out.

He tried a second time to shout a warning that, in the square's center, out of the well where they had been planning just minutes before to refill their canteens *another* something was rising, haze-like, slowly forming in misted tendrils into some dim *shape.* Into some massing thing long-forgotten, hinting of scales and half-rotted tentacles, of bone and horn-like beak, as if of some race of ancient sea creatures long trapped beneath the ground. Fearing the wind only, the slightest breeze that would tear its damp form apart, scattering its substance into atoms, but, when even that which it feared had become still...

When all that moved were things filled with blood's wetness....

The scream would not come! He felt blood fill his own mouth as, struggling, he trapped himself yet more firmly within the shroud-cloth's vise-like windings, falling now on the corpse, rolling now under it as, in new darkness, he felt in his ears the echoes of other screams.

Then only silence.

And then, again, wind and the murmur of voices as villagers dug him out. Wind that portended death for some, as the French trappers used to say, when it stopped blowing. For others, just graves.

But now, for Philip Latham, neither. Now the villagers took him in, an unwitting orphan, and saw to his hurts, and fed him and clothed him. They made him one of them, working side by side with him in the fields, finding a wife for him, helping him to establish a family. And always, now, he fled indoors with them when the wind began to slack in its blowing, until a time came, scarcely twenty years after, when another war spread to the mountains.

This war, however, was not *with* the British, regular army and raw colonials fighting side by side, but rather was a struggle against them. Except in the village, sides still did not matter.

The priest was long dead by then, unfortunately, when a detachment of New Hampshire volunteers, under Captain Nathaniel Flambard, arrived at a time when the wind once again was beginning to die down. As for the villagers, even their French had become unintelligible by then to anyone but themselves. And so, this time, they could give no warning, not even when this new captain screamed as he stood in the village square, the well behind him, his troops arrayed with him in loose formation, for someone, anyone, who could speak English.

"We wish not to harm you," he shouted. "We wish only for provisions. To fill our canteens here. To rest for the night and then be on our way."

Some who remembered brought Latham out to the square, to stand a moment remembering himself when he, too, was a soldier. He attempted, too, to give them some word or some sign, to make the captain understand that his men were in danger before, with the others, he scurried back inside.

And then, just before the wind stopped completely, one of the other officers turned to this new captain. "What do you make of it, Nate?" he asked.

The captain shrugged. "Whole village is mad, for all I can gather. And that man most of all. Harmless enough now, but something must have happened years back that gave him quite the fright. Did you see the inside of his *mouth* when he tried to talk?"

The other nodded. "That blackened stump? Aye, sir. I wonder if we'll ever know what it was—what could have frightened a man so much—that he'd bite his own tongue off."

"The Calm" first appeared in New Mythos Legends *(Marietta Press, 1999).*

Indiana author James Dorr's most recent book is a novel-in-stories from Elder Signs Press, Tombs: A Chronicle of Latter-Day Times of Earth. *Working mostly in dark fantasy/horror with some forays into SF and mystery, his* The Tears of Isis *was a 2013 Bram Stoker Award® finalist for Superior Achievement in a Fiction Collection, while other books include* Strange Mistresses: Tales of Wonder and Romance, Darker Loves: Tales of Mystery and Regret, *and his all-poetry* Vamps (A Retrospective). *He has also been a technical writer, an editor on a regional magazine, a full-time non-fiction freelancer, and a semi-professional musician, and currently harbors a Goth cat named Triana. An Active Member of SFWA and HWA, Dorr invites readers to visit his blog at:*

jamesdorrwriter.wordpress.com

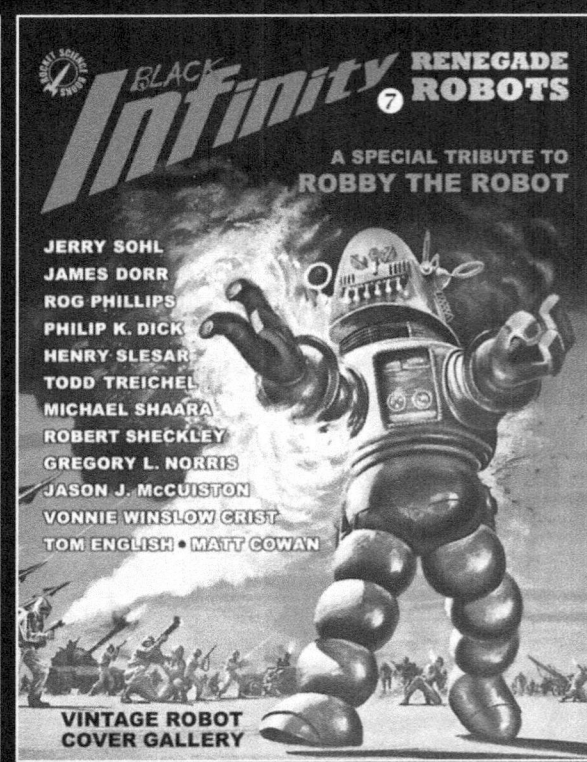

VOICES OF THE DARK

by Gary Fry

For Jamie Turner, an enthusiast from darn unda. Here's something meaty for the barbie, cobber.

WHEN THE THEATRE HAD OFFERED A FLAT WITH THE BOOKING, CHARLES HAD FELT THE WAY HE HAD BACK IN HIS GLORY DAYS. Once upon a time, when he'd been on television, no entertainment commissioner would have dared to approach his agent without also promising five-star accommodation. How the mighty tumble. Now he didn't even have an agent.

Charles produced the key he'd been sent through the post and poked it in a door whose paintwork looked recently applied. The flat occupied the top level of an Edwardian terrace on the grander (if also rundown) side of Scarborough. He'd struggled in the car to find the right street, his ageing satnav on the fritz again. All the same, while letting himself inside the place that would serve as his home for the next few weeks, he told himself that all would work out well.

If only he could say the same about his career. This was the first piece of work he'd been offered in a decade, though partly through choice. Yes, his choice to drink every night (and most of the morning, come to that). His choice to neglect his family: a wife who'd given up on him long ago, and an adult daughter who'd just done the same. And his choice not to keep his impressionist act up to date, as celebrities came and went with bewildering speed. But on this occasion, Charles, once a consummate professional, was determined to get a grip on his self.

On his *selves* might be a more appropriate way of addressing the challenge. Indeed, once he'd closed the door and started to inspect the four-room flat, he riffled through a selection of his alter egos.

"What the feck do we have here?" he asked, his voice adopting the mild Scottish accent of TV chef Gordon Ramsay. "This scullery isnae big enough to fry a moggie in, let alone a whole farmyard."

It was true. The small room, combined with an equally cramped lounge, was nothing like the glossy fitted kitchens he'd enjoyed in earlier life, nor even the serviceable one in his London apartment. Still, he'd need to make use of it during his stay; he could no longer afford to dine out each evening. He'd just have to watch more of profane Ramsay on TV, picking up recipes that, in the absence of anyone to cook for him, went beyond his usual drunken egg and chips routine.

"Jesus Christ," he said, using his home counties voice. But he didn't care for the bitterness he heard there, and so moved to another part of the flat.

The bathroom had been cleaned, but Charles couldn't be sure that anything other than bleach had been used. The room stank of it, as if some unspeakable substance, resistant to water, had been scrubbed off everything. Refusing to lift the toilet lid, he dragged open the shower cubicle door (there was no bath), and then summoned his Alfred Hitchcock impression.

"This ish where the murder was committed, right here—but ... oh, but it's too horrible to deshcribe. Quite dreadful."

The words unsettling him more than they should, Charles headed into the next room, switching on the light as he entered. It bore a carpet so thin he could almost see the floorboards through its fabrics. About ten feet square, the place felt like a prison cell, and it was only after observing how dingy it was that he realized that it boasted no window, just a low doorway and functionally papered walls. The skirting boards were crooked.

Charles was unable to conjure a suitable voice to assess this room—Morgan Freeman in *The Shawshank Redemption* seemed appropriate, but he hadn't learned to impersonate him—and so he shut himself out. With a shudder he ascribed to the autumn chill, he headed for the flat's final offering, at the far end of a narrow hall passage.

At least the bedroom had something going for it—a bed, for one, bearing laundered sheets. Since he'd cut down on booze (from a quantity that would floor a mule to one that might injure only a pony), bed had become his favorite place, a comforting companion, the one thing in life that didn't take more than it demanded.

He checked his wristwatch: two p.m. He'd arranged to give an interview later to a local journalist, but instead of bringing in his luggage from the car, he thought the time until then might be spent catching up on some shuteye. It had been a long drive from the south, and now in his late fifties, he wasn't as sprightly as he'd been in the golden years, when everything he'd touched had turned to that precious metal rather than...

"*Mes excuses, madame,*" he said, dropping onto the mattress while using his once popular Peter Sellars-as-Inspector Clouseau voice, "things have had a tendency lately to become *la merde.*"

Climbing under the sheets fully dressed, he hugged a pillow with all the fondness he'd offer a needy other, and fell soundly asleep.

LATER, REFRESHED FROM a nap in which he'd dreamt about pleasing company, he brought in his suitcase to unpack clothing and toiletries. When that was done, he descended the property's three-level staircase, which gave on to other flats whose tenants seemed to keep their business as private as he hoped he'd be allowed to keep his. He hadn't heard a sound from any of them by the time he reached the front doorway.

Before heading for the town centre, he turned to glance at the end-terrace, trying to figure out which of the upper storey windows corresponded with which of his rooms. The large one facing the sea must give on to the kitchen/lounge combo, and another down the side would belong to the bedroom. The bathroom's would be at the rear, of course. But why wasn't there another at the front, on the side near the corner?

The red brickwork here in one area appeared different from the rest, a smallish square whose edges didn't overlap in the usual jagged fashion, instead forming straight lines. Had the room beyond—surely the gloomy chamber he'd viewed earlier—been deliberately sealed up? But why would anyone do that?

The thought nagged him as he walked into Scarborough, but he pushed it aside when he passed the seafront theatre in which, for the next fortnight, he'd perform a one-man comedy show. Bookings had been "solid," the artistic director had informed Charles by email, and that was "impressive outside of the holiday season." Charles was experienced (aka jaded) enough to realize that this meant the place had hired a show-biz legend for cheap to compensate for low income when it was too cold for tourists to do anything else. But it would be churl-ish to protest. The booking might lead to others, getting him back on the road, and even—stranger things had happened in this business—on TV again.

Feeling sufficiently upbeat that he didn't stop at a pub for a mood-enhancer, Charles strolled to the restaurant in which the local journalist had proposed meeting up.

The Surf n Turf turned out to be a trendy bar. All the same, as he waited for his inquisitor to arrive, he behaved impeccably, ordering only a single pint to take to a table in one corner … along with a whisky chaser, of course, just to shut out the seasonable chill.

Back in the 1980s, when he'd become a household name, he'd been recognized wherever he'd gone. That was far from the case now. As he returned to the bar for an-other drink (the journalist was ten minutes late and he'd grown edgy), none of the youths who let him pass conceded even a flicker of interest, while older drunks on barstools probably saw famous people in their sozzled imaginations all the time. Charles sympa-thized; life was less arduous with booze. He ordered another pint and returned to his seat.

"Charles Guise?"

He'd drunk only half of his beer when the voice—a pleasant young female's—spoke from up ahead. Charles glanced that way, his vision already compromised by the alco-hol he'd consumed on an empty stomach.

"Hi there," he said, standing with old-school courtesy and extending a hand for the shake. "You must be Hilda Greene—from the newspaper, yes? Please, sit."

The newcomer, a blonde, slender woman who didn't look like he'd expected from her formal emails earlier that week, re-turned a confident handshake and then took the chair opposite, placing a handbag on the tabletop.

"Nice to meet you."

This feeling was certainly reciprocated. Hilda could only be in her twenties—early thirties, at tops. Although that was roughly the age of Charles's own daughter, he'd never let social taboos get in the way of a good time.

"May I buy you a drink? I was just going for another for myself."

"A small white wine would be nice. But please, let me pay for them. You're here at my invitation, after all."

Charles couldn't decide whether she'd expressed a desire for gender equality or was alluding to an expense account, but he pooh-poohed her suggestion anyway.

"Please, I insist. A gentleman should always do that for a lady. I'm old-fashioned that way."

She smiled, revealing teeth as white as her lips were red.

"Okay," she replied, reaching for her handbag to part its zippered mouth. "I'll set up my recorder."

Would that mean all his best lines would be captured? In other circumstances his inner egomaniac would be delighted, but in such a potentially intimate one, might he prefer to keep things private? But who was he kidding? After buying two more drinks (well, three, with his usual whisky) and steering his unkempt bulk through a gang of good-looking lads half his age, he slumped again in his seat.

"There you go," he said between need-ful gasps. "One white wine. A large one to … well, to keep us going for a while."

He hadn't planned a double-entendre, but Hilda's look suggested that she'd taken it that way. Suppressing a half-smile, she glanced down at a gadget she'd produced, fingering its buttons.

"Are we ready to start?"

"Fire away, dearest," he said, and now, with alcohol in his blood, he got into character—by which he meant, *out* of it. He opened with an impersonation of Richard Nixon: "I'll confess to anything … except where all the bodies are buried."

Hilda, who'd set her device recording, looked blank.

"Never mind. Before your time, I expect," said Charles, and fell silent to await her first question.

They began by discussing the show he'd perform the next few weeks. It would consist, he explained, of older impressions for which he'd once been famous, along with newer ones to entertain a younger audience. As the interview became less formal, Charles told some of his better jokes, which had Hilda chuckling with less than reverence but more than politeness. It was clear that, outside of whatever research she'd conducted, she was unfamiliar with his work, but he didn't take this personally. The heights of his popularity might have overlapped only briefly with her earliest years.

What a sobering thought, he reflected. Indeed, when she asked about his personal life, a familiar uneasiness kicked in, leading him to drain his third pint (along with the whisky) and point at her empty wine glass.

"Can I get you another?" he asked, his voice vacillating between those of Oliver Reed and George Best, an Anglo-Irish composite, half-plummy, half-brogue.

"I'm fine, thank you." Hilda raised a hand to cover her drink and tilted blue eyes his way. "We're nearly done. I'd just like to get more about *you* into the article. Our readers always enjoy a human angle."

Unless he went to the bar only for himself, he'd have to tackle this bit without alcohol. So be it, he decided, recalling a pledge to straighten out the wrinkles in his life. If Hilda thought he'd been trying to compromise her with booze, she should think again. He'd simply enjoyed her company, the way he enjoyed *any* company these days.

"Perhaps you can tell me something about your childhood."

Suddenly he was Sigmund Freud, adopting a cod German accent. "Vat do you vant to know, meine frau? Perhaps I vill tell you about my mother."

"If you like."

Then he was Norman Bates: "She isn't feeling herself today. I do try to help. She's a boy's best friend."

Hilda smiled but appeared confused by the impressions. A moment later, she sharpened her interrogation. "Maybe you can say something about when you first realized you could make people laugh."

"That would be at school," he replied, a brief lapse into honesty before he summoned another impersonation—on this occasion, Groucho Marx. "They used to laugh at my moustache and glasses and big cigar, but what the hell, ma'am. I wouldn't want to be a member of any club that would have me as a member."

The joke elicited a chuckle from Hilda—it was so well known, she must have heard it before—but then her cross-examination continued.

"I understand that a lot of comics use humor as a way of coping with difficult issues—like bullying, for instance. Is that true of you, Charles?"

"I wouldn't say I was bullied,"—he wouldn't say it and never had in any interview; it was true, however—"but I see what you're driving at. I think someone once described comedy as a *civilized snarl*. That makes sense to me, though I don't know who I've been snarling at."

His father was one candidate, or rather the man's absence during Charles' childhood. But he wasn't about to drag out that family skeleton. He'd consigned it to the back of his mind during his awkward teens and that was where it would remain, no matter how much truth serum he sank.

Hilda responded to his strained comment with a nod. "That's an interesting quotation. May I cite it?"

"Publish and be damned!" he said in a snotty English accent which might or mightn't resemble the Duke of Wellington's, since nobody knew how that great man had spoken. Sensing a break in the interview, Charles departed for another drink.

When he returned with a pint of the strongest ale the place offered, Hilda's questions strayed into safer territory, his early career on the comedy club circuit and then his break into television. That allowed him to focus on successes rather than to lament failures, even though such triumphant periods hadn't lasted long. The interview ended with discussion about his family, chat about his love life (which summoned an impersonation of philanderer Richard Burton), and enquiries about children. That forced him to be serious again, despite so many toxins wrestling within.

"That's one of my regrets," he explained, finally using his own voice and speaking without self-consciousness, probably because booze had taken complete control. "Could you put something specific in your article, Hilda?"

He paused, considered another drink to fortify his resolve, thought better of it, and went on.

"Wendy—that's the name of my daughter—if you're reading this online, or whatever it is you youngsters do these days, will you accept my apology? I've behaved like no kind of father. I know that now. And I want to make it up to you. So please get in touch. I'm back on … back on the straight and narrow. I promise you that."

He slumped in his chair, sensing the bar around him shift and slide. Then he observed Hilda repacking her handbag with a haste he ascribed to time pressures rather than disgust. In the depths of unhappiness, Charles bid her goodbye, and moments later, alone again, he drained his pint.

He soon went for another, however.

HOURS LATER, after eating in a curry house to balance the food and drink in his belly, he belched his way back to his accommodation. Having consumed more beers (and whisky chasers) over his meal, he couldn't remember everything about the interview—had he grown maudlin near the end?—but he hoped young Hilda would write a positive account of him.

He was so distracted by such thoughts that he forgot to reinspect the property's exterior wall, the better to decide whether the small room's window had indeed been bricked up. Not that he'd have seen much in the wan moonlight, he reflected, stumbling upstairs for the top floor, where he slotted the key in two locks which only concentration reduced to one.

Inside the flat, he wondered whether any of the other flats in the building were occupied. He'd assumed that they must be, but with an absence of sound—he heard not so much as a raised voice or TV burbling elsewhere—was he justified in that conclusion?

It didn't matter, little did, except for reorienting his life. He tugged off his clothing in the lounge/kitchen, snatched pajamas from the bedroom, and then entered the bathroom. When he emerged minutes later, his mental focus improved by a sudden application of cold water, he stared at the entrance to the small room he'd observed earlier, the one lacking a window.

The door was shut tight, just as he'd left it, and for a reason he promptly disowned, he believed it would be unwise to go inside. That was irrational, he realized—anathema to the materialist mindset he'd upheld since youth—but the impulse remained all the same. Something wasn't right about that place; he felt it in his aging bones, in the recesses of a psyche deeply troubled for as long as he could remember. It was as if the room, or perhaps whatever it contained, were attempting to communicate with him.

THEN, IN THE MIDDLE of the night, it did.

Surely this was just a combination of his current ruminations spiked by so much booze. Indeed, the voice he heard—boasting a Glaswegian accent and clearly belonging to some nervous man—had to be projected by his subconscious, and only seemed to come through the wall beyond the foot of his bed, where that windowless room was situated at the front of the property.

Charles sat up, one hand scrabbling for the nearby lamp. The sudden shock of illumination hurt his head, forcing him to clench shut his eyes while hearing remained unhampered.

Despite expecting wakefulness to eliminate his delusion, he heard the speaker continue to mutter words so faint they sounded muffled by the wall directly ahead of him.

"...he doesnae believe me ... thinks I've sold the stash on for me own gain ... I'm scunnered trying tae convince the psycho otherwise..."

As concentration aided reason, did Charles believe that what he experienced was real? If speech by another person inside the flat wasn't alone alarming enough, the choice of words that followed only heightened his fear.

"...nobody kens what I'm going through ... got nae missus or wee bairns tae worry about ... might as well blow me 'ead clean off..."

Before the intruder had chance to do such a terrible thing, Charles was off the mattress and through the bedroom's doorway. He hurtled along the hall passage and yanked open the spare room's door, thrusting himself through, hoping all the while, however frightening he considered the prospect, to catch whoever was inside.

After switching on a bulb hanging on a wire, however, he found nobody there—nobody at all. Only the walls glared implacably back.

It had been a trick of his mind, then—what was the technical name? Yes, an *auditory hallucination*. Heavy drinkers experienced them, even though he never had in the past.

"F-First time for everything," he said, his voice, one of the few things he could usually control, floundering as he reached full conscious awareness. Feeling suddenly focused, he realized that all he'd experienced must have been a nightmare bleeding into real life, so many toxins in his body adding to his confusion.

As his breathing slowed to a less punishing rate, he drifted into the lounge/kitchen and made himself a strong coffee. The luggage he'd brought held no booze; at least one of his selves was wise enough not to trust his present one. He sniggered, calling to mind Homer Simpson's pithy line about this problem.

"Alcohol," he said out loud, a solid impersonation of the TV character, and certainly the only voice to occupy the flat that night. "The cause of, and solution to, all of life's problems."

He raised his mug in the direction of the room that wasn't haunted after all, and slurped its contents, the caffeine encouraging even greater confidence in his conclusion. Then, after supping up, he returned to bed, cautiously passing the empty room's door, which he'd closed after exiting, good and tight.

THE FOLLOWING DAY, ahead of his premiere that weekend, he had a rehearsal at the theatre. He'd previously talked over the phone to Alan Benson, the man who'd commissioned ten evening performances, and meeting him held no surprises. Middle-aged, flamboyant, playfully giddy, he was every artistic director Charles had ever worked with. They got on well together before lunch, Alan expressing such enthusiasm for Charles's work that when Charles left to eat in a nearby café, he was happy for the guy to join him.

They'd tucked into fish, chips, and mushy peas before Charles plucked up the nerve to ask the question he'd planned since his arrival.

"So tell me, how did you chance upon the flat you've put me up in?"

"Is it okay? I do hope so." Alan looked briefly uneasy, as if he'd made an error. "I'd heard on the showbiz grapevine that you preferred not to stay in hotels. I trust that's still true."

"I like my own space, yes," Charles reassured the director, but then returned to his original question. "I just wondered how you'd managed to lease somewhere for such a short period."

Alan's smile grew canny. "I have a contact at a holiday letting agency. They help us out by providing accommodation for artists appearing in our productions. It's more economical than alternatives. It's not like the West End up here, however much—and I include your good self in this category—I think our acts are as worthy as any in the Smoke."

Charles sensed that this very substance was being blown up his ass, but then, as casually as possible, he asked for the letting agency's name. Later that afternoon, assisted by directions on the smartphone his daughter had bought him the previous Christmas, he located the town centre office of this business and went inside. The young woman on reception was unable to help but summoned an older man who immediately recognized him.

"Charles Guise," he said, shaking his hand with gusto. "Christ, I used to watch you on TV as a kid. Side-splitting stuff. It's a pleasure to meet you."

Charles felt flattered for the second time that day, and even became a little less self-loathing. All the same, he'd come to discuss quite another matter. He asked about the flat he occupied.

"We were very proud to cater for you," the man explained, his balding head gleaming under the showroom's lights. "I personally selected a newish property on our books. I trust it's to your satisfaction?"

"It's … fine, thanks. It has all I need." Charles sucked in his belly while trying to think of a way of learning more without arousing suspicion. "I was just curious about the house's history. It's an interest of mine. Aren't they all Edwardian terraces up there? There must be some fascinating stories attached."

"Nothing I've ever heard about that one. What about you, Alyssa? You're more likely to be familiar with tittle-tattle in the town."

"Don't be cheeky," Alyssa said from behind her desk, where she'd been working on a computer while the two men talked. "As it happens, I've just searched for that house online. Before the owner renovated it last year—she's a property developer from the south—the building appears to have been derelict for some time."

"Does it say why?" Charles leaned towards the screen, rebuking himself for not having accessed the internet himself earlier. Wasn't just about everything available there?

"Nothing that I can … Ah. Oh dear," said Alyssa. She couldn't be much above school leaving age, boasting an innocence that Charles would never wish to blemish.

"What's wrong?"

"Ugh. That's not very nice at all."

"What *is* it?"

She glanced up, startled to observe that he'd moved in close.

"Look," she said, indicating an article she'd highlighted in the search results.

Charles identified its source: the archives of Scarborough's only newspaper (for which Hilda Greene worked). The report was dated 1984, and if its text was too small to read, a digitized photo of the building—more specifically, the top of it, revealing that bricked up window—convinced him that his investigations hadn't been in vain.

SCOTTISH DRUG COURIER
COMMITS SUICIDE WITH SHOTGUN

… read the headline, and at that moment, it was as much as Charles wanted to know.

HE RETURNED TO THE FLAT, not without some trepidation, at six p.m. He'd dined out again, at a Chinese restaurant, the limited selection of alcohol there more agreeable than similar temptations at French or Italian alternatives. If, prior to his arrival in Yorkshire, he'd somehow chanced upon the information he'd learnt at the letting agency, he must minimize the possibility of more frights overnight, and that meant staying sober.

Re-entering the moonlit house, he wondered whether, during a boozy session back in London, he'd gone online to research the place he'd call home for a fortnight. Could he have read that same article? Perhaps he'd blocked the story from memory, in case he used it as an excuse to avoid this attempt to reinvent himself... As he climbed beyond the silent flats, he realized how desperate his reasoning had grown.

Charles unlocked the door and entered, half-expecting a man to step out of the hall passage, most of his face missing after inflicting upon himself a gunshot wound. But the place was empty, and once he'd switched on the television to take his mind off its stillness, he relaxed in a way he'd found difficult lately.

New acts—young, attractive men and women—blustered onscreen, telling jokes more profane than during Charles' day. Maybe his old-fashioned style was what some people missed, the reason they'd booked to see him the next few weeks. He belonged to a more restrained age, when only a handful of TV channels had been available. His family-focused humor had once drawn people together, which was ironic given how fractured he himself had felt and what a mess his life had become.

He removed his smartphone and stared at it, imagining billions of voices online, each representing different aspects of countless people's personalities, shrinking into insignificance the modest number of impressions he himself could perform. When had the world become so obsessed with self-expression? He wondered whether it had begun during his own youth back in the 1960s, when individualism had taken precedence over other considerations. Maybe people born earlier were less bewitched by modern phenomena as social media and the like. Was a simple, private life preferable?

Sensing himself reaching nebulously for an understanding of his perverse identity— he as much as anyone had succumbed to the hedonism of modern culture—he heard a sound from elsewhere in the flat.

He stood, snapping off the TV, and listened carefully. There it came again, a muffled scratching from—oh, wouldn't he know it—that windowless room.

His heart rate accelerated, prompting him to move to the hall. He'd once read that adrenalin mobilized the body, preparing for fight or flight. He'd experienced similar sensations in front of cameras or while performing to theatres full of fans. He needn't be afraid here, even without much booze in his blood.

Once he reached the door, he took hold of the handle, gripping it tight, and then, drawing in a breath that reinforced his resolve, turned and pushed.

Light from the rest of the flat tumbled through the gap. For one panicky second, Charles believed that he saw a thin figure in one corner, its unclothed frame malnourished … But then he snapped on the naked lightbulb and, blinking, observed nothing at all. It had been just a feverish fancy, perhaps arising from a TV program he'd watched earlier about unfed foreigners. Moments later, wilfully adjusting his focus, he spotted the true source of the disturbance.

A mouse. Just a tiny mouse scuttling around on the worn carpet. Charles stooped, rubbing together his fingertips as if brandishing food. The creature ignored this bogus offering, whirled around, and vanished through a hole in the room's aged skirting board.

Charles stood again, relief running through him like a chilled drink. He'd sleep tonight, after all; his fears had been without source.

THE VOICE, quite a different one this time, woke him just before dawn.

"…d-doctor says n-nothing can be d-done … p-p-people are cruel … I j-just want to c-c-c-communicate well…"

Charles flung back the sheets and edged fretfully to the bedroom entrance. He listened again as a woman with a stuttering Yorkshire accent spoke from next door.

"…so sc-scared of b-be-being alone … ending it all s-seems less fr-frightening … s-so which method sh-shall I choose … r-rope or g-g-gas?"

Remnants of sleep preventing him from marshalling his mind, Charles lost all composure.

"Stop!" he cried with mounting desperation. Hurrying out into the hall passage, he frantically added, "Am I going mad here? Am I losing my mind?"

Though he continued to listen, the young woman's voice fell silent. Even snatching open the room's door and pacing inside did nothing to satisfy his bewildered psyche.

The room under the naked lightbulb was empty, its windowless walls returning only blankness. The mouse was absent, too, leaving Charles with nothing to do but repeat his questions, the ones plaguing him lately. His voice quieter now, he spoke aloud, as if some listener might even care.

"Am I going mad here? Am I losing my mind?"

AFTER WAKING in the early hours, he dressed without washing, snatched up his keys, and fled the building for the town centre. Not many people were out this early. He found a café near the railway station, ordered a coffee, and sat at a table in an alcove.

Then he produced his phone.

First, he revisited the website the letting agency's receptionist had located yesterday. He hadn't wished to do so the previous evening but now considered this necessary. He speed-read the article in fragments:

"...James McCourt ... out of work ... living in a small flat ... involved with local drug dealers ... took his own life at home ... an illegal firearm acquired on the black market ... suspected betrayal of a gang leader ... twenty-five years old ... June 20th, 1984..."

Alongside the text was a photo of the man: pale, wiry, and dressed in dark garments. For long seconds, Charles simply stared at him, wondering whether this was the source of the ghost that undoubtedly occupied his temporary home. But then he carried out a new internet search that dismantled his theory.

Were there rather *two* ghosts in the flat? After reading a second article from the same archive, this conclusion seemed most likely. The Scarborough News, established in 2012, was a relaunch of a newspaper dating back to the 1880s. Its slick website offered scanned versions of old paper editions or digitized renderings of recent ones. Charles found material reaching back to the 1950s, using a search function identifying information after he inputted specific terms. To discover the history of the property he'd currently occupied, he typed in its street name and then hit return. Only one other article appeared.

Without glancing again at the picture of a girl about the age of Charles' daughter, he read the accompanying text, registering its chilling phrases:

"...Sarah Gibson ... a history of psychological disorder ... hanged herself from a roof beam ... living in rented accommodation ... thirty-two years old ... family claimed she had few friends ... oversensitive about a stutter ... December 21st, 1964..."

It was reference to a stutter that made Charles's hands suddenly shake. His phone fell to his lap as he struggled to control himself with an insufficiently toxic drink. Once another influx of caffeine had stabilized his thoughts, however, he returned to the investigation.

Two ghosts. Was that possible? Had the house been supernaturally active since its construction, collecting the spirits of people who'd taken their own lives there? Worse, had it actually driven them to such brutal acts?

Charles returned to the search engine and tried going even further back in time. But this proved impossible. The archive was incomplete, dating back to only 1951. A message claimed that the site was under construction and that earlier editions of the newspaper would be available in the future. Anyone interested in such material could arrange for hard copies to be sent from the business' offices just outside Scarborough.

At that moment, Charles recalled his contact at the press. He opened his email account and scrolled through an inbox lacking desirable communications. Nobody had been in touch to offer further employment, and there was no message from the one person he wanted most to hear from: his daughter. All the same, between items of spam, he located the email he sought: Hilda Greene's invitation to their interview.

After transferring her mobile number to his phone, he made the call. The line buzzed for nearly a minute before a voice spoke.

"Hilda Greene. How may I help?"

Charles reintroduced himself, hoping that the journalist wouldn't hold his embarrassing drunkenness the other evening against him. In the event, she seemed untroubled by him getting in touch, and so he told her about the articles on the newspaper's website, offering the same story he'd used at the letting agency: he was interested in the history of his current accommodation, just something to amuse him while he performed in the area. Perhaps he'd sounded unconvincing, however; after he'd asked if she could acquire material from before the 1950s, Hilda interrupted him.

"You don't sound very well, Charles? Is there more to this request than you're letting on?"

What had given him away? The frantic speed at which he'd issued his request?

"I'm okay. It's just that ... well, I haven't been sleeping lately." That was true, but what followed wasn't. "It must be just nervousness ahead of my first show. It's been a while since I performed live."

"Or could it be caused by all the alcohol you're drinking?"

The statement took him by surprise, and for long seconds he was unable to respond. But then Hilda saved him the trouble.

"I'm sorry to be so blunt, Charles. But I was shocked by how much you knocked back the other night. At the end of our interview, you seemed really unhappy—all that stuff about your family. To be honest, I was a bit concerned."

And so there it was: the way someone with her life in order perceived the once king of TV comedy. Was this what Charles Guise had been reduced to, a subject of pity rather than of admiration? How had he let things get this way? More significantly, how might he turn it around?

Finding a stranger's sympathy too much to bear, he lapsed into silence, every anxiety he'd suffered lately oozing out like rejected poisons. At that very moment, he resolved never to take another drink. He'd sort himself out, he truly would … but first, after blinking tears from his aging eyes, he had to understand what was going on back at that house.

As the journalist had allowed him to compose himself without interruption, Charles told her about all he'd experienced since arriving in the town. When he'd finished, there was a long silence, to such a degree that Charles assumed Hilda had hung up, no longer wishing to be associated with a washed-up crank. But then she drew a breath and asked a question.

"Just how big a problem do you have with drink, Charles?"

If it stills all the voices in my head, none whatsoever, was one response, but that would hardly convince her that he was in his right mind. Instead, he said, "If you're suggesting that I might have *imagined* those voices, Hilda, it surely can't explain *both.* Yes, I was quite drunk the night you and I met—when I heard the guy with the Glaswegian accent. But the following evening, when the stuttering young woman spoke, I was as sober as … as … well, I'd only had a *few* beers—at a Chinese restaurant while I

ate dinner. And, okay, a few whiskies. But no more than that."

Having spoken in his normal voice, he suddenly heard himself as the journalist must, his words as convincing as a charlatan's. Just then, he considered drawing on another impression—Cary Grant in *North by Northwest* perhaps, persuading a judge that he'd been forced to drink alcohol rather than willingly consumed it—but he decided not to bother. He simply made a concession.

"You think these are withdrawal symptoms, don't you? That maybe I'd read the articles before leaving for Yorkshire and then forgotten—no, what's the term used by quacks?—*repressed* this knowledge."

Hilda exhaled audibly, as if feeling guilty about prompting the truth. Her voice sounding defensive, she said, "I merely asked a question, Charles. But for what it's worth, you're not far off the mark. It makes sense, doesn't it? The other things you referred to—the *weird* things—well, they just *don't.*"

How could he argue with her when, at least until he'd experienced a second uncanny episode, he'd entertained similar thoughts? After swallowing more lukewarm coffee, he apologized for involving the journalist in his private concerns, but Hilda claimed to have been happy to help. Before ending the call, Charles made a final request.

"Perhaps I'm coming around to your way of thinking, but all the same, I wonder whether you'd satisfy my curiosity."

"How can I do that?"

He hesitated, drew in an anxious breath, and then said, "I wondered if you'd be good enough to search the newspaper's archives, the ones that aren't available online, to see what you can find out about the house at earlier periods."

"Oh, Charles—"

"Please, just humor me. I know it sounds crazy. But I'm the kind of person who likes to get things straight in my head."

He pictured her over the line, her young face heartbreakingly innocent. Then she relented.

"Okay, I'll do it. But on one condition."

"Name it, me lass," he replied, lapsing into a new impersonation, that of Yorkshire thespian and *Star Trek* legend Patrick

Stewart. "I'll do owt in me power t' mek it so."

She laughed, sending a ripple of pleasure right through Charles. Moments later, she spoke again.

"I demand two tickets to see your show this weekend. Front row seats!"

"Would these be for you and a boyfriend?"

"No, they're actually for my daughter and me. She's seven. If your jokes aren't too adult in nature, I'd like to introduce you to the next generation."

He felt suddenly inspired in a way he hadn't in years.

"In that case, I'll definitely clean up my act," he said, and then, after exchanging farewells, he rang off.

HE SPENT THE REST of the day in the town, moving from one place to another and none of them a pub. After eating in a seafront diner, he took a stroll on the beach, watching parents and children play in the sand.

Sitting on a bench at the end of a pier, Charles removed his phone and considered calling Wendy, his daughter. The truth was that he'd missed out on much of her upbringing. Touring and filming had been a convenient way of avoiding the restrictions on his recreational life that bringing up a child necessitated. His wife had grown impatient with his behaviour sooner than the girl had, and it was only after he'd chatted up a woman half his age—one of his daughter's closest friends, in fact—that Wendy threatened to give up on him, too.

Would he be forgiven if he swore off the booze, promising to behave with dignity in the future? Charles doubted he'd be taken seriously, however; he'd already caused too much damage. In which case, he'd have to deal with the dilemma later, working his way back into the young woman's life only after he'd proved he could remain sober.

He got up and walked on, knowing that he ought to be rehearsing his act ahead of its premiere the following day, but unable to settle his restless mind. Had he recently experienced the sudden onset of serious health problems? Hallucinations couldn't be dismissed as harmless, could they ... if that was indeed what he'd suffered.

Shaking his head with confusion, he advanced for the clifftop where the town's famous castle overlooked the harbour. Why had he suspected that the house might be haunted by *two* ghosts? On reflection, it seemed unlikely, particularly as both deceased people had lived in the building more than twenty years apart. Did they keep each other company, Charles wondered with a snigger? Had they formed a double act like Laurel and Hardy, specializing in terror rather than amusement? He laughed aloud, wondering whether he might salvage some new material from the experience, a more mature form of comedy focused on aging and the ridiculous things one could be persuaded to believe.

"This is another fine mess you've got me in to," he said, addressing only himself on the windswept hillside. A moment later, evoking Stanley in response to the Ollie he'd just impersonated, he added with feigned sobs, "I didn't mean to ... it wasn't my fault ... I couldn't help it."

A woman walking down the path up ahead looked on as if he were mad. Her eyes unblinking with disquiet, she turned away and hurried off.

No matter how hard he tried, Charles was unable to find much humor in this episode. His problems, commonly masked by comedy, were much too serious for that.

A FEW HOURS LATER, he was back at the house. With daylight lingering in the sky, it was possible to see that the small room's only window had indeed been bricked up. Why had this been done, and more crucially, *when*? Charles mentally recalled the two photographs of tenants who'd taken their lives on dates more recent than the place's Edwardian architecture suggested it had been built. Others had surely occupied the property, during its original incarnation as a single home—accommodating affluent families—as well as after it had been converted into flats.

He hoped before long to understand more about the house's past, once Hilda had fulfilled her half of their deal. He smiled at the prospect of her attending his show with her daughter. In the meantime, he must get over his silly fear of this house. He advanced to its front door, producing the key to let himself inside. He hadn't paid much attention before, but now he noticed that the lobby was functionally decorated, boasting a hardwearing carpet and nondescript wallpaper. The ground floor flat's entrance stood to the right, but he knew there was no point in knocking. What would he say if someone did live there?

"Nothing I can think of. So much for putting on an act."

His words resounded up the stairwell as he climbed, as if to warn listeners that he was on his way. But as he reached the next level, which boasted a similarly soundless flat, he was reluctant to say more. His heart hammering hard, he ascended the final flight.

Stop being so foolish, he told himself, in a voice very much like his own. Once he unlocked and opened the door, something hurried to greet him, but it was just a cool draft from all the unheated rooms. He stepped forwards and then closed himself in. The flat's silence was dismaying, but that could be overruled by more TV.

After making a coffee, he switched on the set and sat to watch. The absence of alcohol in his blood helped him to feel confident, as if he were in control of his surroundings. As darkness gathered at the window, he tugged on the curtains without anxiety. A stroll to the toilet to relieve himself of all the caffeine he'd consumed was effortlessly handled; the closed door to the windowless room he passed hardly registered in his mind. A few hours later, after watching a documentary about the development of children and the crucial role language played in the process, Charles decided to go to bed.

He tackled his evening routine with habitual speed: stripped, washed, donned nightwear, cleaned teeth, exited the bathroom, entered the bedroom, climbed under the sheets, switched out the light, closed his eyes, and finally reflected on his day.

It had been a good one, especially by recent standards. For once, he felt positive about himself. The sad truth was that this was the first twenty-four hours in over a decade he'd gone without booze. His tiredness was different from the tetchy sluggishness induced by drink. All the walking he'd done earlier made his body pleasantly ache. At that moment, he resolved to call his daughter tomorrow, just before his show's premiere. He'd try to convince her of his genuine desire to change, hoping she'd hear this in a voice none other than his own.

Perhaps this would herald a new self, the resurrection of Charles Guise. If he was unlikely to achieve former glories, he might at least gain self-respect. And to prove these goals were realistic, all he needed was to get through the next night without chemical assistance.

His body relaxed, he drifted into a snooze. His dreams when they came were full of success, of audience applause and wild celebrations. He was again loved by the public, his act timely and appealing. It felt wonderful ... but then, as he shuffled in bed, his mind tilted into darker territory. The world changed, commissions dried up, nobody returned his calls. He dealt with the crisis the only way he knew how: by seeking fulfilment elsewhere. Then his marriage fell apart, his wife moving out with their child. He turned to drink, a spiral of gloom that eventually led him here, to this flat, on the eve of an out-of-season gig which, he had to be honest, wasn't even fully booked.

Charles snapped open his eyes, the grip he'd gained earlier on his surroundings squirming away. It was pitch dark. He sat up, shaking his head. What had conspired to transform his optimism into renewed misery? He glanced around, his vision adjusting to the dimness. He observed grey humps of furniture, half-lit by what little moonlight pushed through the curtains.

At that moment, he heard the noise, the one he must have detected during sleep, which had tipped his thoughts into a negative realm and wakened him.

It came from the room next door.

Charles could identify no voice this time, just the sound of something physical in motion halfway along the hall passage. Could it be the mouse, scratching at the walls in the hope of escape? Indeed, that very act was achieved a second later: the spare room's door arced open, its hinges exuding a vermin squeak.

Charles shifted forwards on the bed, his brain running fast. What animal could open a door, he thought as he began to shake? More crucially, if he'd assigned the previous disturbances—the Scottish man's voice, and then the stuttering woman's—to intoxicated imagination, how could that account for this latest one? He was completely sober.

Something passed through the jaws of the room's exit.

Charles felt his heart rate accelerate, blood rushing into his skull. While continuing to listen, he realized that his limbs had frozen, locking him half-in and half-out of the bed. All he could do was look, his eyes failing to blink, even though tears of terror had formed there.

Whatever had emerged into the hall passage began to advance his way.

"No ... go away," Charles hissed, wondering whether visual hallucinations commonly followed auditory ones. But such a deluded hope didn't last: the windowless room had been sealed the previous evening; the only thing that could open the door must be tall enough to reach the handle.

Here it came, an ineffectual figure heading into crisscrossing shadows. It had yet to reach the bedroom's threshold, but even so Charles detected its joints creaking, smelled its crypt-like stench. As it shuffled on, growing closer to the bedroom entrance, the unseen newcomer began to speak.

It used many voices—the Glaswegian's for sure, and yet also the faltering one of his other recent intruder. But here came more: a few male, the rest female; some elderly, others younger; most sounded white-British, but at least one belonged to a member of an ethnic minority group. In short, it was a cacophony of speakers emerging from just one newcomer, so many rapid-fire impressions that they rendered Charles's own repertoire paltry by comparison.

"...och aye...

...n-n-nice to have c-c-c-company...

...not everyone who lived here died...

...I do like to be beside the seaside...

...I can see for miles from the windows...

...the sun todaaay reminds me of me yoof in Trinidad...

...such a charming town...

...there are worse places to spend one's retirement...

...I think I'll go to the beach today...

...it's cool being a student in Scarborough...

...you'd never believe, looking at this grotty flat, how splendid the house might once have been...

...I think the building might have a ghost, you know..."

As Charles attempted to assimilate all he'd heard, the speaker stepped into what little light the curtained window allowed inside the bedroom.

It was emaciated to the point of malnutrition, its legs no thicker than the arms, and each protruding from the filthy rag of a dress. It had to be female, if only to judge by this lengthy garment, though the thatch of wiry hair sprouting from a scalp more bone than skin similarly hinted at that gender. Its face was long gone to dehydration, its flaking cheeks sunken beneath eye sockets crammed with orbs that lacked any glisten. Only the mouth, perhaps regularly operated, retained any of the life its host had once enjoyed, each lip incongruously firm amid such a catastrophe of flesh.

Rickety fingertips wagging just as broken toenails snatched at the carpet, the hideously decayed woman-thing stared across the room.

"Am I going mad here?" she said, and her voice was a serviceable impersonation of Charles Guise, even incorporating an intoxicated slur. "Am I losing my mind?"

Charles thought he really must be, and only seconds later, despite being alcohol-free for the first time in years, he tumbled into merciful unconsciousness.

HE WAS AWAKENED by a shriek which forced him to jerk away from whatever was about to attack. But when he threw out his hands and encountered no retaliation, just the soft fabric of sheets, he realized all danger was over.

He opened his eyes, and his surroundings bloomed into focus. He was in the same bedroom in which he'd collapsed the previous night, but the place was now filled with light: curtains at the window admitting the morning. Everything was starkly visible—the wardrobe alongside the open door; drawers in the far corner; a small table beside his pillows. It was from the table that the shrilling sound came: his phone ringing on top.

He reached for the handset, using his other hand to massage tension from his neck as he sat up. *The flat's empty*, he told himself as savage memories returned with unforgiving speed. *It was just a nightmare. All in my head. Alcohol still affecting my blood.*

Fumbling the screen's functions, he answered the call.

"Morning, Charles," said a voice he promptly identified. It couldn't be copied by any impersonator; the journalist had surely never visited this house.

"H-Hello, Hilda," he replied, his own speech uncertain. He was still coming to terms with the disturbing episode he recalled, however imaginary its source might be. "I was … was half-expecting you to get in touch."

"I'm sorry it couldn't have been sooner. I intended to call last night but got engrossed in what I was reading."

Charles sat up straighter in the bed.

"Engrossed?" he said, looking through the room's doorway and into the hall passage, only some of whose span he could presently observe. "Do you mean relating to … well, to my *mystery*?"

"I do indeed," said Hilda, but sounded a little troubled. "I can't speak for long. I have a meeting in ten minutes. I just wanted to let you know that I spent a few hours after work yesterday going through our paper archives. In light of what you told me over the phone, I found some, shall we say, *interesting* material."

"That sounds … ominous."

Charles sensed his pulse accelerate, but then the young woman spoke again.

"I think the best way to handle this is if I send you a scanned copy of an article I located which dates back to the 1930s. If you'd like to discuss how it might relate to your … *experiences* in that house, we can talk later."

He didn't care for some of her phrases, let alone the emphasis she'd placed on "experiences." All the same, confident that he was alone in the flat, he replied without apprehension.

"Do send over the article. I expect it deals with when the place was built?"

"Uh, yeah," said Hilda, sounding eager to hang up—to attend her meeting, of course. Before terminating the call, however, she added, "Something like that."

Less than a minute later, his phone gave another ping: an incoming email. He accessed it at once, noticing that the journalist hadn't included a message, only an attachment which he opened at once.

If he heard any sound elsewhere in the flat, it must come from behind a closed door: the entrance to the windowless room, perhaps, still sealed the way he'd left it. Maybe the mouse was out again, skittering across the aged carpet. Whatever the truth was, Charles calmly read the article.

SCARBOROUGH EVENING NEWS
13th October, 1934

SCANDAL AS PHYSICIAN LOCKS UP
DAUGHTER FOR SIXTEEN YEARS

Local physician, Alfred Marks, 58, has been arrested after police discovered that he had been conducting unethical experiments at his seafront home. Suspicions were raised by neighbors, who heard voices through dividing walls they could assign to neither Dr. Marks nor his wife, Patricia.

A search of the building revealed a room on the top floor sealed with a locked door. Dr. Marks had told the few friends he and his wife entertained at home that an interest in photography had led him to create a darkroom, including bricking up one upstairs window.

The truth proved more disturbing. When police entered the room, they discovered a young woman, later confirmed to be the Markses' daughter, only sixteen years of age. She was starved to the point of emaciation and struggled to understand what was said to her. Experts later determined that both indispositions arose from having been locked up in isolation since infancy.

The young woman (who, following a birth at home, had not been named) died from injuries soon after being released from her makeshift cell. An autopsy revealed that, in addition to insufficient musculature and other bodily problems, her eyes had been ill-adjusted to light and her vocal cords barely developed at all.

Further investigation revealed that Dr. Marks, an independent scholar, had been using his daughter as an experimental subject, exploring the relative roles of nature and nurture in human development. He made a full confession, after claiming, with no regret, that sense deprivation and lack of social contact result in irreversible damage.

Dr. Marks and his wife will appear in court next month and are expected to be sentenced soon after.

The local community has expressed shock and sympathy. One neighbor said, "It's tragic. I'm just glad that the poor lass is at peace now. Lord knows how she summoned the ability to talk through the walls. I guess she mimicked people who visited the house down the years, while she was held captive."

"It gives me hope about the endurance of the human spirit," said one of Dr Marks' former medical colleagues. "I hope wherever the girl is now, she can speak freely there."

Charles glanced away from his phone and then climbed out of bed. He was in tears, but they were not of terror, only sorrow and compassion. He paced into the hall passage, knowing what he'd see there: the door to the windowless room standing wide open. He hadn't left it that way the previous evening. The mouse was indeed inside, watching and waiting, its glossy eyes shining with uncanny knowingness.

Crossing the threshold into a place in which a father had once behaved as badly as any could, Charles no longer felt sorry for his foolish self. He no longer experienced the fears he'd projected into a world stranger than he could ever hope to understand. Instead, simply regretting his previous, cowardly attempt to get back in touch with her, he hoisted his phone again and dialed a single number.

His daughter Wendy's.

Gary Fry is a semi-retired academic who lives in coastal countryside in the northeast of England. He has had published around 100 short stories, a bunch of novellas, and several novels. He was the first author in PS Publishing's Showcase range, and none other than Ramsey Campbell has described him as a "master of philosophical horror." He plays piano, loves dogs, and reads a frightening number of books each year. His web presence can be found at:

https://garyfrytalks.blogspot.com

MATT COWAN'S
HORROR DELVE:

WELCOME TO HORROR DELVE,
A SPECTER–HAUNTED PLACE DEDICATED TO THE CELEBRATION OF ALL THINGS THAT RESIDE WITHIN THE SUPERNATURAL HORROR REALM!

10 TALES FOR A GOOD NIGHT'S REST:
DREAMS AND NIGHTMARES IN SHORT HORROR FICTION

DREAMS, THAT SURREAL nether-realm our unconscious minds abduct us to each night, have long been the subject of humanity's collective curiosity and imagination. The question of what purpose their enigmatic imagery is meant to convey has endured throughout the ages. Conventional belief espouses dreams to simply be a byproduct of our mind's cataloging of the day's events, but other theories abound as well. Some insist they serve as a psychic conduit conveying messages from deities, ancestors, extra-dimensional entities, or some other form of supernatural intellect, if only their peculiar symbology can be deciphered. I like to think of it as the imaginative corners of our brains, having been held helplessly captive throughout our monotonous workaday routines, unleashing the full fury of their pent-up, creative frustrations upon our slumbering forms.

Whatever the case may be, dreams, especially of the nightmare variety, have shown a remarkable propensity of escaping the confines of their shadowy, nocturnal environs to walk amidst the bright, sunlit streets of the waking world. They have successfully managed to emerge from their misty, transitory existence to attain immortality within the pages of countless books, upon household television screens, or inside packed movie theaters to spread their terror to the masses for years to come. Hollywood brought us Freddy Krueger, the iconic dream-stalking murderer from *The Nightmare on Elm Street* film franchise, who

subsequently became the patron saint of nightmares. There have also been several movies of people using technology to enter the dreams of others through scientific

Beaumont's "Perchance to Dream" (1959), from *The Twilight Zone*. (Copyright © CBS Television)
Below: Data (Brent Spiner) prepares to slice up Deanna Troy (Mirina Sirtis) in "Phantasms" ('93), from *Star Trek: The Next Generation*. (Copyright © Paramount Pictures and CBS Television)

means, exemplified by both *Dreamscape (1984)* and *The Cell (2000)*.

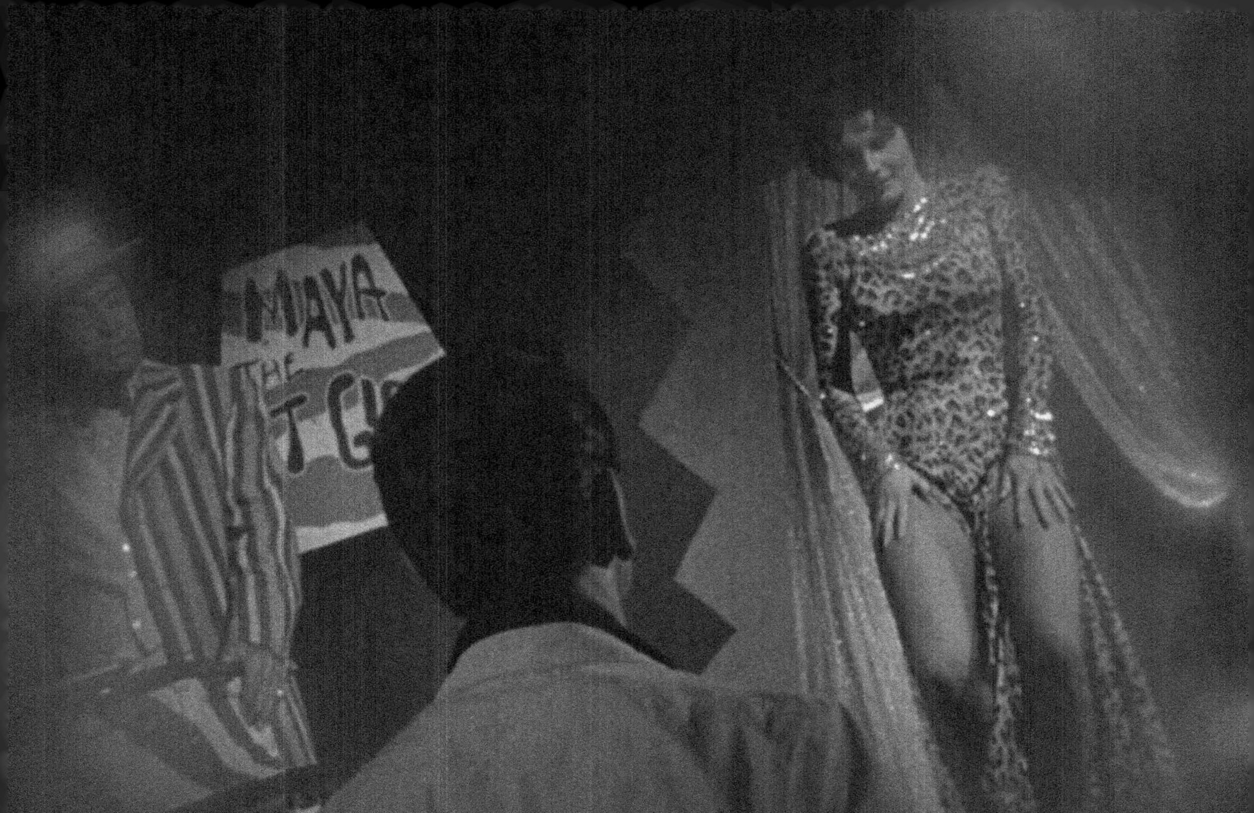

Television has produced plenty of standout dream-centric episodes as well. The series *Twin Peaks* may be the most prominent among them, but others have put themselves on the board, as well. *Star Trek: The Next Generation* had a few in "Night Terrors" ('91, Season 4, Episode 17) and "Phantasms" ('93, Season 7, Episode 6—Who can forget Data using a large knife to cut into a Deanna Troy whose body had somehow been transformed into a cake?). The original *Twilight Zone* series doled out a real heavy-hitter in adapting the excellent Charles Beaumont short story by the same name in "Perchance to Dream" ('59, Season 1, Episode 9). We'll take a look at that story below. The recent Netflix series *The Sandman* does a great job adapting Neil Gaiman's popular comic book series that follows the travails of the personification of dreams and similar unrealities. It even has a literal walking nightmare milling about causing trouble as well. Both the series and the comics are well worth checking out.

THE PRIMARY FOCUS of this column, however, will be on dreams and nightmares in literature. There have been plenty of great longer form fiction offerings reliant on the theme, including one of my all-time favorite novels, *Incarnate* (1983) by Ramsey Campbell, in which a prophetic dream-study group inadvertently triggers supernatural events which begin affecting reality. H. P. Lovecraft, the creator of Cthulhu and The Necronomicon, obviously enjoyed exploring the concept

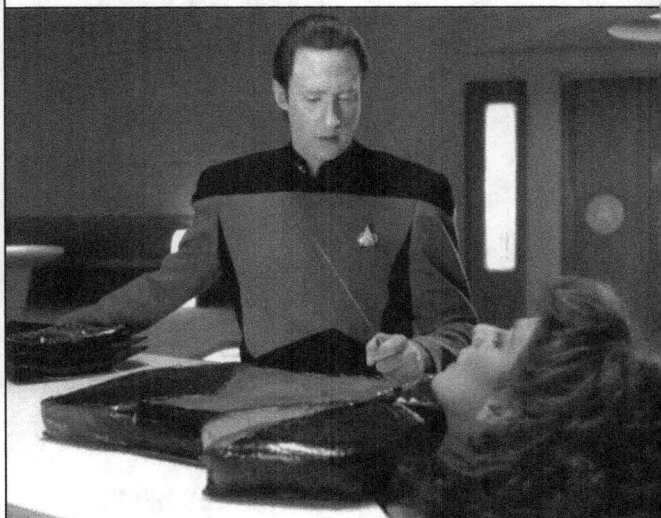

given his *Dream Cycle* series of tales about an alternate dimension which can only be accessed through dreams, highlighted by his novella *The Dream-Quest of Unknown Kadath*. (Just as a sidenote: listening to the album *Sleep* by Mac of BIOnighT while reading that one enhances the experience.)

I still feel short fiction is the form which best suits the swiftly shifting, transitory nature of dreams by perfectly lending its quick-hitting brevity to the task at hand. More than once I've found myself crafting nightmare scenarios in my own stories, one of which is "Dead Hands Clapping."[1]

With all this in mind, I thought it would be fun to assemble a list of some of my personal favorite short weird/horror tales which utilize dreams memorably in their narratives. I could easily have included a lot more, but in the interest of keeping things concise, I'm limiting this list to just ten stories, all published before the year 2000, and am only allowing one story per author—otherwise, Ramsey Campbell and Thomas Ligotti would likely have garnered multiple listings).

So without further ado, let the parade of nightmares begin:

10 Nightmare Tales
(Listed in Order of Publication)

1. **"The House of the Nightmare"**
Edward Lucas White (1905)

While driving down an unfamiliar road, a man becomes distracted by a standing stone near an old house which keeps shifting location. This causes him to have an accident which totals his transportation. Upon emerging from the wreckage, he finds a young boy standing nearby. As night is falling and with nowhere else to go, he asks if he can stay at the boy's house for the night. The boy agrees and while leading him there talks about a recurring nightmare he has inside the house about a carnivorous sow. That night, while sleeping in the house, the man likewise has a terrifying nightmare similar to that of the boy. He's in for more unpleasant surprises when the next day

ALLEN H. 84

[1] Included in this issue.

arrives. A free audio version of this story is available at the *From the Great Library of Dreams* podcast as read by Jim Moon: https://hypnogoria.blogspot.com/2022/09/from-great-library-of-dreams-060-house.html

2. **"Branch Line to Benceston"**
Sir Andrew Caldecott (1946)

A man dreams he's murdered an associate he secretly hates. That associate actually dies at the same time. The man also dreams he's set to hang for this dream crime which he didn't really commit. He begins to fear what will become of him in the waking world.

3. **"The Professor's Teddy Bear"**
Theodore Sturgeon (1948)

This fascinating tale begins with a four-year-old boy talking with his diabolical sounding teddy bear about the dreams he has of himself in the future. In them he's become a college professor. The bear encourages him to try and psychically shape the people and events in his dreams to terrible ends. Later, we readers are shown things from the professor's point of view. This is a marvelous tale that twists whimsy into eeriness and terror.

4. **"Perchance to Dream"**
Charles Beaumont (1958)

A man goes to see a psychiatrist because he's terrified of falling asleep. He explains how he has a bad heart condition which has forced him to avoid anything which would put extra-strain upon it, such as being frightened. Recently he's been having a series of episodic dreams where a woman is trying to literally scare him to death.

5. **"The Janissaries of Emilion"**
Basil Copper (1967)

This novelette is told by the friend of a brilliant scientist who began experiencing a series of interconnected dreams where he washes ashore on a beach in ancient times. Each time the dream finds him closer inland headed toward a beautiful city in the distance which he inexplicably knows is called Emilion. Although he doesn't know her name, he knows there's a woman who lives there who is his lover, and that he needs to go to her. The first time he wakens from the dream, he's damp with seawater and has sand all over him. As the dreams draw him nearer to the city, a horde of warriors calling themselves *The Janissaries of Emilion* come into view between him and the city. He believes if they reach him in the dream, they'll kill him both there and in the real world.

6. **"3.47"**
David Langford (1983)

A man is plagued by a constant, horrendous nightmare where he sees a foreign woman just before insect-like feelers sprout from his arms, and his teeth become like chalk and break apart. Every time he wakes up, his digital alarm clock is displaying the same time, 3:47 a.m. It worsens to a point where he becomes terrified of going to sleep and wonders if he has somehow become the subject of a curse.

7. **"What Dreams May Come"**
Brad Strickland (1988)

A divorced man has an encounter with a stranger while taking his teenage daughter and her friend to *Six Flags Over Georgia*. The stranger asks him what kind of dreams he has before touching him on the shoulder and fleeing with an unexplained apology. After the incident, the divorcée dreams about a murder which he later learns actually happened. He also starts to feel a dark influence infesting his soul as he struggles to find a way to combat what's happening to him. I found the concept of passing off a homicidal nightmare to someone else, à la M. R. James' 1911 novelette *Casting the Runes*, intriguing.

8. **"The Night Before Christmas"**
Roger Johnson (1989)

A young woman is routinely terrorized by a horrible dream which she can never recall when she wakens but which always leaves her in a traumatized state. When staying at a wealthy friend's estate for Christmas one year, she faints upon seeing the family's uncle come in dressed as Santa Clause. This allows her to finally recall her dream. It involves her being stalked by a morbidly obese man who looks like a demonic Santa Clause. This remembrance leads to more unsettling discoveries as to the nature of this mysterious nightmare.

9. **"The Dreaming in Nortown"**
Thomas Ligotti (1991)

A college student relates the bizarre events he experienced upon discovering his old roommate had become involved with an esoteric group experimenting with psychic dreaming. When the roommate's dreams begin seeping into his own, he decides to follow him to learn more about what's happening. Ligotti is a brilliant, unique writer, and this is my favorite of his stories. It's a masterfully crafted tale of surreal horror which is tied to dreams!

10. **"The Alternative"**
Ramsey Campbell (1994)

A successful accountant with a happy family life suffers from recurring dreams where he lives a different version of his life. There he and his family suffer through extreme poverty and despair. In the real world, he finds the downtrodden housing complex where he dreamed his unfortunate alternative-self resides and recognizes things inside it as identical from his dreams. He begins to try and secretly assist this divergent family, often at the expense of his own. This is another in a long line of excellent tales by Ramsey Campbell.

I know there are many more stories that deserve a place on this list, and hopefully I'll discover them as I continue to seek out more examples of nightmares in fiction.
Pleasant dreams!

THE HOUSE OF THE NIGHTMARE

BY EDWARD LUCAS WHITE · ART BY ALLEN K.

I **FIRST CAUGHT SIGHT OF THE HOUSE FROM THE BROW OF THE MOUNTAIN** as I cleared the woods and looked across the broad valley several hundred feet below me, to the low sun sinking toward the far blue hills. From that momentary viewpoint I had an exaggerated sense of looking almost vertically down. I seemed to be hanging over the checkerboard of roads and fields, dotted with farm buildings, and felt the familiar deception that I could almost throw a stone upon the house. I barely glimpsed its slate roof.

What caught my eyes was the bit of road in front of it, between the mass of dark-green trees about the house and the orchard opposite. Perfectly straight it was, bordered by an even row of trees, through which I made out a cinder side path and a low stone wall.

Conspicuous on the orchard side between two of the flanking trees was a white object, which I took to be a tall stone, a vertical splinter of one of the tilted lime-stone reefs with which the fields of the region are scarred.

The road itself I saw plain as a box-wood ruler on a green baize table. It gave me a pleasurable anticipation of a chance for a burst of speed. I had been painfully traversing closely forested, semi-mountainous hills. Not a farmhouse had I passed, only wretched cabins by the road, more than twenty miles of which I had found very bad and hindering. Now, when I was not many miles from my expected stopping-place, I looked forward to better going, and to that straight, level bit, in particular.

As I sped cautiously down the sharp beginning of the long descent, the trees engulfed me again, and I lost sight of the valley. I dipped into a hollow, rose on the crest of the next hill, and again saw the house, nearer, and not so far below.

The tall stone caught my eye with a shock of surprise. Had I not thought it was opposite the house next the orchard? Clearly it was on the left-hand side of the road toward the house. My self-questioning lasted only the moment as I passed the crest. Then the outlook was cut off again; but I found myself gazing ahead, watching for the next chance at the same view.

At the end of the second hill, I only saw the bit of road obliquely and could not be sure, but, as at first, the tall stone seemed on the right of the road.

At the top of the third and last hill I looked down the stretch of road under the over-arching trees, almost as one would look through a tube. There was a line of whiteness which I took for the tall stone. It was on the right.

I dipped into the last hollow. As I mounted the farther slope I kept my eyes on the top of the road ahead of me. When my line of sight surmounted the rise, I marked the tall stone on my right hand among the serried maples. I leaned over, first on one side, then on the other, to inspect my tires, then I threw the lever.

As I flew forward, I looked ahead. There was the tall stone—on the left of the road! I was really scared and almost dazed. I meant to stop dead, take a good look at the stone, and make up my mind beyond peradventure whether it was on the right or the left—if not, indeed, in the middle of the road.

In my bewilderment I put on the highest speed. The machine leaped forward; everything I touched went wrong; I steered wildly, slewed to the left, and crashed into a big maple.

When I came to my senses, I was flat on my back in the dry ditch. The last rays of the sun sent shafts of golden-green light through the maple boughs overhead. My first thought was an odd mixture of appreciation of the beauties of nature and disapproval of my own conduct in touring without a companion—a fad I had regretted more than once. Then my mind cleared and I sat up. I felt myself from the head down. I was not bleeding; no bones were broken; and, while much shaken, I had suffered no serious bruises.

Then I saw the boy. He was standing at the edge of the cinder path, near the ditch. He was so stocky and solidly built; barefoot, with his trousers rolled up to his knees; wore a sort of butternut shirt, open at the throat; and was coatless and hatless. He was tow-headed, with a shock of tousled hair; was much freckled, and had a hideous harelip. He shifted from one foot to the other, twiddled his toes, and said nothing whatever, though he stared at me intently.

I scrambled to my feet and proceeded to survey the wreck. It seemed distressingly complete. It had not blown up, nor even caught fire; but otherwise the ruin appeared hopelessly thorough. Everything I examined seemed worse smashed than the rest. My two hampers, alone, by one of those cynical jokes of chance, had escaped—both had pitched clear of the wreckage and were unhurt, not even a bottle broken.

During my investigations the boy's faded eyes followed me continuously, but he uttered no word. When I had convinced myself of my helplessness I straightened up and addressed him:

"How far is it to a blacksmith's shop?"

"Eight mile," he answered. He had a distressing case of cleft palate and was scarcely intelligible.

"Can you drive me there?" I inquired.

"Nary team on the place," he replied; "nary horse, nary cow."

"How far to the next house?" I continued.

"Six mile," he responded.

I glanced at the sky. The sun had set already. I looked at my watch: it was going—seven thirty-six.

"May I sleep in your house tonight?" I asked.

"You can come in if you want to," he said, "and sleep if you can. House all messy; ma's been dead three year, and dad's away. Nothin' to eat but buckwheat flour and rusty bacon."

"I've plenty to eat," I answered, picking up a hamper. "Just take that hamper, will you?"

"You can come in if you've a mind to," he said, "but you got to carry your own stuff." He did not speak gruffly or rudely, but appeared mildly stating an inoffensive fact.

"All right," I said, picking up the other hamper; "lead the way."

The yard in front of the house was dark under a dozen or more immense ailanthus trees. Below them many smaller trees had grown up, and beneath these a dank under-wood of tall, rank suckers out of the deep, shaggy, matted grass. What had once been, apparently, a carriage-drive, left a narrow, curved track, disused and grass-grown, leading to the house. Even here were some shoots of the ailanthus, and the air was unpleasant with the vile smell of the roots and suckers and the insistent odor of their flowers.

The house was of grey stone, with green shutters faded almost as grey as the stone. Along its front was a veranda, not much raised from the ground, and with no balus-trade or railing. On it were several hickory splint rockers.

There were eight shuttered windows to-ward the porch, and midway of them a wide door, with small violet panes on either side of it and a fan-light above.

"Open the door," I said to the boy.

"Open it yourself," he replied, not un-pleasantly nor disagreeably, but in such a tone that one could not but take the suggestion as a matter of course.

I put down the two hampers and tried the door. It was latched but not locked, and opened with a rusty grind of its hinges, on which it sagged crazily, scraping the floor as it turned. The passage smelt moldy and damp. There were several doors on either side; the boy pointed to the first on the right.

"You can have that room," he said.

I opened the door. What with the dusk, the interlacing trees outside, the piazza roof, and the closed shutters, I could make out little.

"Better get a lamp," I said to the boy.

"Nary lamp," he declared cheerfully. "Nary candle. Mostly I get abed before dark."

I returned to the remains of my convey-ance. All four of my lamps were merely scrap metal and splintered glass. My lantern was mashed flat. I always, however, carried candles in my valise. This I found split and crushed, but still holding together. I carried it to the porch, opened it, and took out three candles.

Entering the room, where I found the boy standing just where I had left him, I lit the candle. The walls were whitewashed, the floor bare. There was a mildewed, chilly smell, but the bed looked freshly made up and clean, although it felt clammy.

With a few drops of its own grease I stuck the candle on the corner of a mean, rickety little bureau. There was nothing else in the room save two rush-bottomed chairs and a small table. I went out on the porch, brought in my valise, and put it on the bed. I raised the sash of each window and pushed open the shutter. Then I asked the boy, who had not moved or spoken, to show me the way to the kitchen. He led me straight through the hall to the back of the house. The kitchen was large, and had no furniture save some pine chairs, a pine bench, and a pine table.

I stuck two candles on opposite corners of the table. There was no stove or range in the kitchen, only a big hearth, the ashes in which smelt and looked a month old. The wood in the woodshed was dry enough, but even it had a cellary, stale smell. The axe and hatchet were both rusty and dull, but usable, and I quickly made a big fire. To my amazement, for the mid-June evening was hot and still, the boy, a wry smile on his ugly face, almost leaned over the flame, hands and arms spread out, and fairly roasted himself.

"Are you cold?" I inquired.

"I'm allus cold," he replied, hugging the fire closer than ever, till I thought he must scorch.

I left him toasting himself while I went in search of water. I discovered the pump, which was in working order and not dry on the valves; but I had a furious struggle to fill the two leaky pails I had found. When I had put water to boil I fetched my hampers from the porch.

I brushed the table and set out my meal —cold fowl, cold ham, white and brown bread, olives, jam, and cake. When the can of soup was hot and the coffee made I drew up two chairs to the table and invited the boy to join me.

"I ain't hungry," he said; "I've had supper."

He was a new sort of boy to me; all the boys I knew were hearty eaters and always ready. I had felt hungry myself, but somehow when I came to eat I had little appetite and hardly relished the food. I soon made an end of my meal, covered the fire, blew out the candles, and returned to the porch, where I dropped into one of the hickory rockers to smoke. The boy followed me silently and seated himself on the porch floor, leaning against a pillar, his feet on the grass outside.

"What do you do," I asked, "when your father is away?"

"Just loaf 'round," he said. "Just fool 'round."

"How far off are your nearest neighbors?" I asked.

"Don't no neighbors never come here," he stated. "Say they're afeared of the ghosts."

I was not at all startled; the place had all those aspects which lead to a house being called haunted. I was struck by his odd matter-of-fact way of speaking—it was as if he had said they were afraid of a cross dog.

"Do you ever see any ghosts around here?" I continued.

"Never see 'em," he answered, as if I had mentioned tramps or partridges. "Never hear 'em. Sort o' feel 'em 'round sometimes."

"Are you afraid of them?" I asked.

"Nope," he declared. "I ain't skeered o' ghosts; I'm skeered o' nightmares. Ever have nightmares?"

"Very seldom," I replied.

"I do," he returned. "Allus have the same nightmare—big sow, big as a steer, trying to eat me up. Wake up so skeered I could run to never. Nowheres to run to. Go to sleep, and have it again. Wake up worse skeered than ever. Dad says it's buckwheat cakes in summer."

"You must have teased a sow some time," I said.

"Yep," he answered. "Teased a big sow wunst, holding up one of her pigs by the hind leg. Teased her too long. Fell in the pen and got bit up some. Wisht I hadn't a' teased her. Have that nightmare three times a week sometimes. Worse'n being burnt out. Worse'n ghosts. Say, I sorter feel ghosts around now."

He was not trying to frighten me. He was as simply stating an opinion as if he had spoken of bats or mosquitoes. I made no reply, and found myself listening involuntarily. My pipe went out. I did not really want another, but felt disinclined for bed as yet, and was comfortable where I was, while the smell of the ailanthus blossoms was very disagreeable. I filled my pipe again, lit it, and then, as I puffed, somehow dozed off for a moment.

I awoke with a sensation of some light fabric trailed across my face. The boy's position was unchanged.

"Did you do that?" I asked sharply.

"Ain't done nary thing," he rejoined. "What was it?"

"It was like a piece of mosquito-netting brushed over my face."

"That ain't netting," he asserted; "that's a veil. That's one of the ghosts. Some blow on you; some touch you with their long, cold fingers. That one with the veil she drags acrosst your face—well, mostly I think it's ma."

He spoke with the unassailable conviction of the child in *We Are Seven*. I found no words to reply, and rose to go to bed.

"Good night," I said.

"Good night," he echoed. "I'll sit out here a spell yet."

I lit a match, found the candle I had stuck on the corner of the shabby little bureau, and undressed. The bed had a comfortable husk mattress, and I was soon asleep.

I had the sensation of having slept some time when I had a nightmare—the very nightmare the boy had described. A huge sow, big as a dray horse, was reared up with her forelegs over the footboard of the bed, trying to scramble over to me. She grunted and puffed, and I felt I was the food she craved. I knew in the dream that it was only a dream, and strove to wake up.

Then the gigantic dream-beast floundered over the footboard, fell across my shins, and I awoke.

I was in darkness as absolute as if I were sealed in a jet vault, yet the shudder of the nightmare instantly subsided, my nerves quieted; I realized where I was, and felt not the least panic. I turned over and was asleep again almost at once. Then I had a real nightmare, not recognizable as a dream, but appallingly real—an unutterable agony of reasonless horror.

There was a Thing in the room; not a sow, nor any other nameable creature, but a Thing. It was as big as an elephant, filled the room to the ceiling, was shaped like a wild boar, seated on its haunches, with its forelegs braced stiffly in front of it. It had a hot, slobbering, red mouth, full of big tusks, and its jaws worked hungrily. It shuffled and hunched itself forward, inch by inch, till its vast forelegs straddled the bed.

The bed crushed up like wet blotting-paper, and I felt the weight of the Thing on my feet, on my legs, on my body, on my chest. It was hungry, and I was what it was hungry for, and it meant to begin on my face. Its dripping mouth was nearer and nearer.

Then the dream-helplessness that made me unable to call or move suddenly gave way, and I yelled and awoke. This time my terror was positive and not to be shaken off.

It was near dawn: I could descry dimly the cracked, dirty windowpanes. I got up, lit the stump of my candle and two fresh ones, dressed hastily, strapped my ruined valise, and put it on the porch against the wall near the door. Then I called the boy. I realized quite suddenly that I had not told him my name or asked his.

I shouted, "Hallo!" a few times, but won no answer. I had had enough of that house. I was still permeated with the panic of the nightmare. I desisted from shouting, made no search, but with two candles went out to the kitchen. I took a swallow of cold coffee and munched a biscuit as I hustled my belongings into my hampers. Then, leaving a silver dollar on the table, I carried the hampers out on the porch and dumped them by my valise.

It was now light enough to see the walk, and I went out to the road. Already the night-dew had rusted much of the wreck, making it look more hopeless than before. It was, however, entirely undisturbed. There was not so much as a wheel-track or a hoof-print on the road. The tall, white stone, uncertainty about which had caused my disaster, stood like a sentinel opposite where I had upset.

I set out to find that blacksmith shop. Before I had gone far the sun rose clear from the horizon, and was almost at once scorching. As I footed it along I grew very much heated, and it seemed more like ten miles than six before I reached the first house. It was a new frame house, neatly painted and close to the road, with a whitewashed fence along its garden front.

I was about to open the gate when a big black dog with a curly tail bounded out of the bushes. He did not bark but stood inside the gate wagging his tail and regarding me with a friendly eye; yet I hesitated with my hand on the latch and considered. The dog might not be as friendly as he looked, and the sight of him made me realize that except for the boy I had seen no creature about the house where I had spent the night; no dog or cat; not even a toad or bird. While I was ruminating upon this a man came from behind the house.

"Will your dog bite?" I asked.

"Naw," he answered; "he don't bite. Come in."

I told him I had had an accident to my automobile, and asked if he could drive me to the blacksmith shop and back to my wreckage.

"Cert," he said. "Happy to help you. I'll hitch up foreshortly. Wher'd you smash?"

"In front of the grey house about six miles back," I answered.

"That big stone-built house?" he queried.

"The same," I assented.

"Did you go a-past here?" he inquired, astonished. "I didn't hear ye."

"No," I said; "I came from the other direction."

"Why," he meditated, "you must'a' smashed about sun-up. Did you come over them mountains in the dark?"

"No," I replied; "I came over them yesterday evening. I smashed up about sunset."

"Sundown!" he exclaimed. "Where in thunder've ye been all night?"

"I slept in the house where I broke down."

"In that big stone-built house in the trees?" he demanded.

"Yes," I agreed.

"Why," he quavered excitedly, "that there house is haunted! They say if you have to drive past it after dark, you can't tell which side of the road the big white stone is on."

"I couldn't tell even before sunset," I said.

"There!" he exclaimed. "Look at that, now! And you slep' in that house! Did you sleep, honest?"

"I slept pretty well," I said. "Except for a nightmare, I slept all night."

"Well," he commented, "I wouldn't go in that there house for a farm, nor sleep in it for my salvation. And you slep'! How in thunder did you get in?"

"The boy took me in," I said.

"What sort of boy?" he queried, his eyes fixed on me with a queer, countrified look of absorbed interest.

"A thick-set, freckle-faced boy with a harelip," I said.

"Talk like his mouth was full of mush?" he demanded.

"Yes," I said; "bad case of cleft palate."

"Well!" he exclaimed. "I never did believe in ghosts, and I never did half believe that house was haunted, but I know it now. And you slep'!"

"I didn't see any ghosts," I retorted irritably.

"You seen a ghost for sure," he rejoined solemnly. "That there harelip boy's been dead six months."

"The House of the Nightmare" first appeared in the September 1906 issue of Smith's Magazine.

Although American author and poet Edward Lucas White (1866–1934) wrote several hugely successful historical novels, including El Supremo: A Romance of the Great Dictator of Paraguay *(1916), he is best remembered today for his dark fantasy stories, many of which, according to Lucas, were inspired by the author's own dreams. One such story, in addition to the one reprinted here, is the celebrated terror tale "Lukundoo" (1925), about a British explorer cursed by an African Shaman. The story was published in the November 1925 issue of* Weird Tales *and has been reprinted close to four dozen times in various anthologies.*

ALLEN K. '84

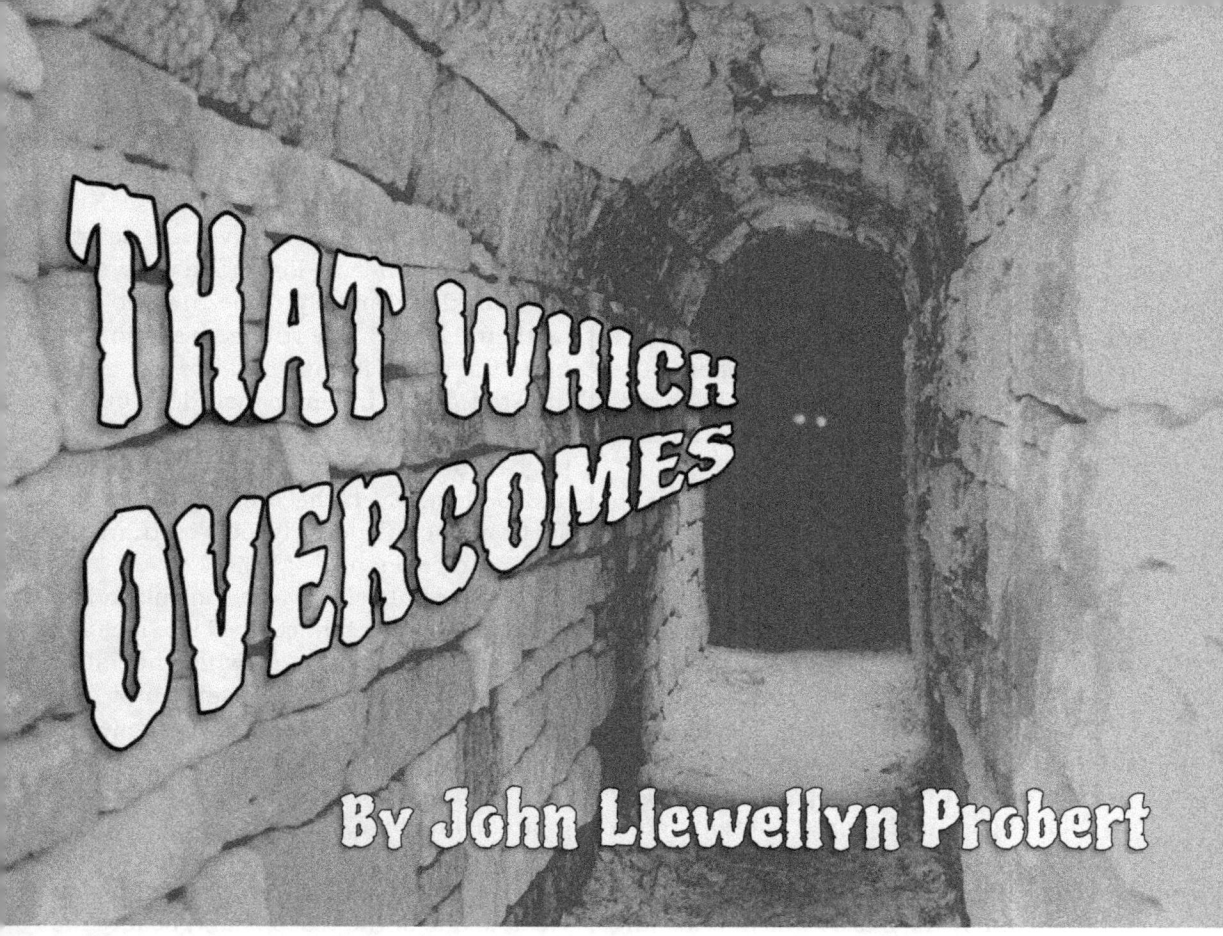

THAT WHICH OVERCOMES

By John Llewellyn Probert

"**I WANT TO SHOW YOU SOMETHING.**"
WE WERE SITTING IN THE STUDY OF MY FRIEND JEREMY BENNETT.
Book-lined and comfortably warm on this chill November night, with its oak paneling dancing with flickering shadows cast by the fire, it was the perfect environment in which to settle oneself of a wintry evening. I stayed seated in my wingback oxblood leather armchair as Jeremy rose and crossed to his immense desk, whereupon lay an ungainly volume of size and shape not unlike one of those Times Atlases of the World. He passed it over to me and I squinted at the gold letters embossed on its covering of red buckram.

"'Partington's Encyclopaedia of Mazes'," I read aloud. I gave him a questioning look.

He returned to his seat by the fire. "Open it."

I did as instructed. The paper was coarse, old, and at that point where it was threatening to crumble if treated too harshly. "'A Gazetteer of England's Most Famous and Infamous Mazes & Labyrinths'." Again I was reading aloud, this time from the title page.

He nodded. "Carry on."

With infinite care I began to peruse the volume. Each entry within the encyclopaedia had been granted a page or two each. Name and location was printed at the top, in a copperplate script so overly elegant as to be almost indecipherable. Beneath this text was a woodcut-style diagram of the maze in question, and beneath that, in varying sizes of print depending on how much needed to be said, a brief description of any interesting attributes, quirks, or peculiarities specific to that maze.

"Quite a lovely old volume." I closed it as gently as I could. Even so a puff of dust erupted from its pages, suggesting either that it was rarely looked at, or that the paper had reached a worse state of disintegration than I had previously surmised.

"I would prefer to call it 'interesting'." He

leaned forward. "For the period in which it was printed the artwork is perfunctory, and the descriptions are superficial to the point of being flippant."

"So you've brought me here on this foul night..." I paused for effect. The sound of the rain hammering against the windows did not let me down. "...to show me a book you don't consider to be terribly good?" I proffered the volume back to him but he shook his head.

"I said it was 'interesting', and I stand by it. Turn to page 452."

The book didn't look thick enough to boast that many entries. However, as I leafed through the volume I found its pages becoming progressively, and almost imperceptibly, thinner. The four hundred and fifty second page was very close to the back, and it was tissue thin compared with the heavy, parchment-like bond on which the foreword had been printed.

"There aren't many people I would allow to touch those final pages," Jeremy continued. "But I know I can trust you."

I was only half listening to him, my attention taken by the maze I was now looking at. Or rather, the heading that described its location. I looked at my friend in disbelief.

"'The Maze at Gressingham House'?" Jeremy nodded. "You mean this Gressingham House?" Another nod. "The one in which you have been living all these years?" My friend's nodding became more enthusiastic. "But I've visited you here many times, and while I know you have some lovely gardens, you've never shown me a maze."

He leaned back and folded his arms. "That's because according to that book there isn't one here for me to show you ... most of the time."

Now I was confused and I must have looked it. He pointed to the volume once more. "Read the description."

I did as I was told. "'A most peculiar and enthralling legend, the maze at Gressingham House is one of the hardest to find. Not because of the building itself, this is easily located. The maze, however, is considerably more difficult, as it is rumored to manifest only under certain specific conditions.'"

Now this was too much! "Are you telling me your house has a ghost maze?"

My friend was now gripping the armrests of his chair, his eyes afire with enthusiasm. "Isn't it fascinating?" He pointed with a finger fairly quivering with delight. "All those tissue-thin pages at the rear of the volume describe mazes that either no longer exist, or which are considered merely to be the subject of myth and legend." He rubbed his chin. "Perhaps the paper is thin because the author insisted on their being included, but the publisher was against it, and hoped those pages would quickly fall from the volume and be lost. Even the binding of the final section is considerably poorer than that which precedes it."

"Or the publisher was a sensible individual who was somehow coerced into including some arrant nonsense in what they otherwise considered to be a useful and intriguing volume." I gave him a wry smile. "I'm presuming part of the reason you asked me here was to provide that sort of sober, grounded opinion?"

"Yes indeed!" My attitude did not seem to have dampened Jeremy's ardor a jot. "That is one of the reasons and believe me I am grateful you are here. However, I would urge you to read on."

"'The maze at Gressingham House is rumored to appear on only one night of the year'," I raised an eyebrow, sure that the other was soon to follow in response to yet more ludicrousness. "'The night when the seventh Earl of Gressingham, having gained knowledge of his wife's repeated indiscretions with a servant, led her to the very center of one of the most impenetrable labyrinths of its day and left her there, sealing her fate with a ritual that caused the structure to henceforth exist outside of natural space and recorded time. Only on that night do the dimensions align so that the maze can appear, lasting in our reality only for as long as her cries may be heard.'" I could not resist a snort at the point. "Honestly, Jeremy, I think in all the time we've known each other I have never heard of anything so silly."

But now my friend looked deadly serious. "Perhaps not as silly as you think. The other reason I asked you here tonight is that shortly I believe we are going to be provided with a chance to see for ourselves whether what is written in that book is true."

"True?" I resisted the urge to bark a disparaging laugh. We had been friends too long for that. "How could it be true? You've lived here for years and never found the thing, why should now be any different?"

There was a rumble of thunder from outside.

"Because until now I had never heard of it, until now I had never known the story of the seventh Earl, and until now I had never known the right time to look."

The book was still open on my lap at page 452 as realization dawned and I began shaking my head. "Oh good grief. It's supposed to be tonight, isn't it?"

My friend nodded and looked at the carriage clock on the mantelpiece. "We have a little more time before the maze is supposed to manifest, enough for me to tell you that I acquired the book a few months back at an auction. There were several other rare volumes included in the lot." Now he was gazing into the fire as he spoke. "I thought the books would simply provide some interesting background to this house in which I have always lived. I never thought it would reveal such a secret."

"Such a load of nonsense more like." I ignored his glare, the first of the evening and from the way things seemed to be going, likely not the last. "And what is this bit, here?" I tapped at the bottom of the page. "This saying, written in a different script, a larger font, almost like a kind of warning."

"'Quod vincit'." He said it before I could. "'That which overcomes.' I don't know why that's there, but I hope to find out, with your help."

I agreed that he needed help, just not necessarily of the kind he was thinking. I assumed the air of the medical professional that I was. "Tell me more," I said. That seemed to silence him, most likely, I suspect, because he didn't know quite where to start. So I decided to help him along. "Did you really come across a set of volumes as a job lot that just happened to describe this house and its history?"

That seemed to do the trick.

"No." Jeremy slumped back in his chair.

"Of course not. But it seemed the quickest explanation to offer you. I have been searching for writings pertaining to this rambling old place of mine for as long as I can remember, as long as I have had the ability to do so."

"You mean since you were much younger?" His eyes brightened at that so I persevered. "Since you were a child?"

"That was when it all started." I could see he was on the verge of opening up. Then he went silent again. In my profession it is of course important to allow the patient to talk, but it's also important to prompt them at points so they don't get distracted or lost. "Are you talking about when your father left home?"

We had discussed this before. One morning when he was eight years old, my friend had woken to find his father gone and his mother with no idea what had happened to the man. The front door was still bolted from the inside and there was nothing to suggest some form of reckless escape out of the first-floor window. As far as Jeremy could tell me the marital relationship had been satisfactory and there had been no reason for Graham Bennett to have any financial worries. The police were duly called and, after the appropriate amount of time allowed for a missing person to return home of their own accord had elapsed, a search of the surrounding countryside had been instigated, all to no avail. It was as if Jeremy's father had simply vanished off the face of the earth.

"I'm talking about before that."

"You mean it's helped you remember something?"

He shook his head. "No, it's made something I remember all too well just seem more important."

And so he told me about the nightmares. About how he remembered being awoken once when he was very small by the sound of sobbing, coming from what sounded like far beneath his bedroom.

"I assumed it was my parents having a fight," he said. "And when you're that age you don't think about investigating it, all you want is for it to stop. And it didn't happen very often. In fact, now I think about it, it didn't happen very often at all."

I tapped the book. "You mean this has now made you believe it only happened once a year?"

"It could have, couldn't it? Suppose my bedroom was above where the maze is supposed to appear. That could have accounted for my parents not hearing it. Except for the time when my father did. Perhaps he was late home from work, or went downstairs for something and found himself ... drawn towards it."

"And he found the maze and disappeared into it and that's where he is?" Now I saw where this was all going. "Jeremy I think this has all gone a bit far. I think you've spent far too much time overthinking things you can hardly remember, and then combined your conclusions with nothing but some dusty old nonsense you've found through secondhand book dealers. While it may seem the most logical explanation to you now, I can assure you it's just your mind trying desperately to explain things that happened to you as a child, things for which you are likely to find no explanation. Ever."

It went quiet after that, the only sounds the crackling of the flames in the grate, and the tapping of the rain against the windows. Despite the fire the atmosphere in the study had grown cold. I regretted my outburst and found myself at a loss for words. Eventually it was my friend who broke the silence.

"They found me once, you know."

"Found you?"

He gestured to the door. "Out there. In the hallway. I was crouched next to the stairs. I don't honestly remember. It somehow came up in conversation when I was about to leave for university and my mother said how glad she was that there hadn't been any more of those 'events', especially now I was going away and she wouldn't be there to keep an eye on me."

"And you don't remember?"

"Not a thing. Apparently it was a couple of years after my father disappeared, which means I must have been around ten or eleven. And it only happened the once. Now that I think of it, I wonder if my mother started to pay closer attention to me after that. She was probably worried about me sleepwalking and injuring myself."

"Looking for your father?"

"Subconsciously perhaps. It's a funny thing now I think of it, but as far as I'm aware I never physically searched for my father. I only looked for him, or rather clues as to what might have happened to him, in books."

"Did you suffer any sleepwalking episodes while you were at university?" He shook his head. "And what about when you came back here?"

"No. But after my mother died something made me take the bedroom furthest from the one I occupied as a child." He held up his hands and offered a hapless smile. "And here I am, still alive, definitely not disappeared, but with a growing body of information to suggest what might have happened to my father, that I might also have been at risk of the same thing, and that for all I know I still might be."

"It may be information, but it's hardly evidence." Nevertheless what he had been saying intrigued me. Was it his persuasive tone, the atmosphere in the study, or the fact that the dust I now noticed had settled on my trousers from that volume reminded me of desiccated skin, that was beginning to make me wonder if there was something in what he was saying? "You're suggesting that many years ago this house had a maze, that the seventh Earl imprisoned his wife within it, did some sort of ... ritual to make the maze disappear, but left it as a potential trap for other residents of this house once a year?" Saying it all out loud like that helped to make it sound like the nonsense it so plainly was. Perhaps. But it was also starting to sound chilling.

"Maybe it was part of the eternal torment he intended for his wife," Jeremy looked thoughtful.

"How so?"

"Maybe she wasn't meant to die. And if we assume that to have been the case, surely she, or whatever she had become, would need ... something, from time to time, to keep her alive."

A spark popped from the fire and I jumped. I hadn't realized I was so tense. What Jeremy said next didn't help.

"It looks like it's time."

And with that the clock on the mantelpiece began to chime, hollow tones ringing out what felt like a death knell against the background of the storm outside. Suddenly I had no wish whatsoever to leave that room.

We both remained seated once the clock had finished its tolling. I was about to say something when Jeremy held up a hand for silence. I strained to listen, but could hear nothing.

Could I?

Because as we sat there, the fire subsiding and the rain quietening down, I imagined there was another sound, behind the occasional crackle of a spark and the pattering of water, another sound that was far more disquieting that either of those, on this night.

At first it was so distant I could barely make it out. An animal perhaps? A cow caught out in the rain and miles away, lowing to be led back into the shelter and warmth of the barn. A low moaning of distress ever so faint, ever so distant.

As if to help me better hear it, the rain stopped altogether.

Was that the reason it seemed louder, that crying that could almost be mistaken for that of a human being, one in great distress? That had to be it, for there was only one other reason.

That the sound was moving closer.

"What is that?" I could not help but speak in a tone of irritation brought on by fear. "An animal out in the rain? What a wretched thing to do, leaving the poor thing out there."

"It's not out there." Jeremy's voice was devoid of emotion. He, too was listening carefully. "It sounds far away but it's not out there."

"What do you mean?"

He didn't respond with words. Instead he extended the long index finger of his right hand and pointed directly down at the ground.

"Beneath us?"

He nodded. I was incredulous. But now he had pointed it out, I realized he was right. The sound was not coming from a field far away but from underneath us, from some distant subterranean enclosure where

perhaps light had never shone. I tried hard to dismiss the image of a white, shapeless, eyeless thing flopping around in the dark, its lipless mouth calling for the sustenance it craved.

"Do you have cellars here?"

Jeremy nodded, and produced a sturdy satchel from beneath his chair. He tossed me the first torch he took from it and then reached in to get one for himself. "They would seem a good place to start, don't you think?"

Right then for me a good place to start would have been several miles away in the local pub, with a couple of decent brandies and perhaps a sleeping pill inside me to stave off any nocturnal hallucinations that might disturb a good night's sleep. But I didn't say that, because I, too, could hear the thing, and I, too, had read the tale of Gressingham Hall's ghost maze in that rotting volume, including those final words that I was now sure had been intended as a warning.

Quod vincit.

"You're actually going to look for it? For this ghost maze?" And for what it might contain. I lacked the courage to speak that last part aloud.

Jeremy was already on his feet. "Of course! And you're going to come with me, aren't you?"

"I don't want to." At least I could be honest with him. "But I can't imagine I'm going to be able to dissuade you, and I cannot possibly let you go by yourself." And so I stood, more shakily and with far less determination than my friend. I checked the torch, which I found was capable of delivering a searingly bright light, thank goodness. I switched it off again to save the battery. Now we had stopped talking I could hear the sobbing again, louder still, and definitely coming from beneath us.

The door to the cellars was in the kitchen, accessed through what once must have been a large pantry the storage space of which was no longer needed. This chill, bare, poorly lit room was in stark contrast to the cosy warmth from which we had just emerged. However, if I thought the pantry was uninviting, the narrow flight of stone steps leading down to the cellar was positively forbidding.

"I'll go first."

Yes, you will, I thought, as Jeremy led the way, torch held before him. So preoccupied was I with what hidden terror might be waiting for us that I had forgotten to switch mine on. I swiftly corrected that omission. Was it my imagination, or did the beam now seem significantly weaker than when I had checked it in the study?

"When were you last down here?" My words echoed off the walls of the narrow passageway. The descent took longer than I was expecting and I had to hurry to keep sight of my friend's back.

"No idea," came the reply from somewhere in front. "I can't remember ever needing to come down here."

Finally the steps stopped and we reached flagstones so cold I could feel the chill through my shoe leather. I shone my torch around.

"This place is huge!"

"This is just part of it." Jeremy's torch flashed ahead of us to reveal a broad vaulted corridor leading off into the distance. "The house is old, remember? They would have stored all kinds of things down here. Wine, and food, old junk. For all I know these passages may have acted as an escape tunnel in the old days."

"Escape for whom?" I didn't want to ask from what.

"Priests, heretics, individuals of the wrong religion, who can say?" Once again Jeremy was moving quickly. I suddenly wished we had copied Ariadne of old and tied a thread to our entrance in case we could not find our way back. I had no desire to spend any longer in this chill damp atmosphere than I had to. I coughed but managed to suppress a sneeze.

"Are you all right?"

I replied that I was. "How long do you want to give this?"

We had reached a crossroads. An equally broad and high vaulted tunnel now ran east to west across our path. Jeremy shone his torch in one direction and I the other. Both ways stretched to the limit of our beams.

Jeremy sniffed. I was glad the air wasn't just affecting me. "I don't know. These tunnels could stretch on for miles."

"Miles?" My outburst was cut off by Jeremy's raised hand. We both listened.

The crying, louder than it was in the study, could now be discerned more easily.

And it was coming from straight ahead.

"Come on!" Jeremy was off again before I could stop him. By the time I caught up I was pleading with him to slow down, to stop.

"Why?" Now he sounded exasperated. "What's the matter?"

"Listen!"

As the beams from our torches crossed and melded and created demons from shadow in the darkness we both concentrated.

Now the crying was coming from behind us.

"That's impossible!"

I knew that, as strongly as I now believed that we should turn back, but Jeremy was already running in the direction of the sound.

When we arrived back at the crossroads the sound seemed to be coming from a different direction, this time off to the left. Jeremy was off in pursuit of it while I shouted in his wake that if we weren't careful we were going to get lost. I shone my torch back the way we had come to get my bearings.

I could not see the steps that led out of this place.

This filled me with the urge to panic, but I did my best to remain calm, and rational. The way back to the kitchen was likely just out of sight. To prove it I left Jeremy to his search for a moment and began to retrace my steps, shining my torch along the right-hand wall in the hope I would see our way out at any moment.

Twenty steps on and I had still not come to any stairs.

Thirty.

Fifty.

I was still convinced that they had to be close, my overconfidence acting as a barrier to the possibility that I just might be going in the wrong direction. I was promising myself

I would just take ten more steps before going back to find Jeremy when I heard my friend give the most terrible scream.

I whirled and began to run in the direction of that sound, the light from my torch bobbing before me. I came to the crossroads. He had turned right from here hadn't he?

Hadn't he?

Another scream reverberated against the crumbling brickwork. It came from the left. I followed, confused about the direction in which I thought Jeremy had gone but trusting my ears.

It wasn't long before I came to another crossroads. I called my friend's name.

Silence.

"Jeremy!"

For a moment, nothing. Then another cry, still sounding like my friend, but weaker this time. So much weaker. This, too, came from the left.

I turned to run in that direction when there was a further, sharper, more desperate cry that also sounded like Jeremy's voice, only this time it was coming from the right. So I turned in that direction, only to find myself confronted by a solid wall.

One of the most impenetrable labyrinths of its day.

Oh no.

I turned back the way I had come and shone the torch ahead of me. The passageway curved round to the right. Was that where Jeremy had got to? I was no longer certain of what to do, only knowing that to remain still would be to condemn Jeremy to certain death. I set off down the curving corridor.

As I came round the corner I found my friend.

And the thing that had him in its grasp.

Even now I find it difficult to describe what I saw, partly because the memory of it fills me with a terror that makes my hands shake and my heart hammer against my chest, but also because the flickering, weakening beam of the torch could only reveal fractured segments of it at any one time.

It resembled something between a spider and a centipede, taller than a man and of a length I did not stay long enough to

ascertain. The thing gleamed white in the torchlight. At first I assumed this to be a consequence of the albinism common to so many creatures that spend all their days in darkness. However, the clacking of the hideous beast soon made me realize that each of its myriad, multi-segmented limbs shone so brightly because they had been made from the bones of those it had consumed.

Those it had overcome.

This horrific observation was confirmed as, in the shaking torchlight, I saw my friend consumed and added to the horrific concatenation before me.

I think he saw me before he died. I think he knew I would have helped if I could.

I turned to run, and as I did so I observed a most peculiar thing. The walls of the labyrinth in which Jeremy and I had found ourselves were shifting, shimmering, as if the creature, so distracted, so intent upon the consumption of its latest victim, was unable to maintain the concentration seemingly required to keep up the illusion of the maze that was its lair. I could see the steps that led up to the kitchen just ahead of me. As I made for them I heard a terrible, sobbing shriek from behind. The walls of the maze began to solidify once more. Determined that this horrific creation should not enjoy a second meal I forged onwards, pushing myself through shimmering edifices of stone until I reached the cellar stairs, still dimly visible ahead of me. Once I was upon them I did not stop until I was safely back in Jeremy's study.

It was an hour before I could summon the courage to return to the kitchen pantry and check the cellar door.

That door led to a broader, shorter set of wooden steps, rather than the stone ones my friend and I had descended. The cellar they opened into would have held a decent quantity of wine bottles but little more than that.

What could I do? I telephoned the police and told them my friend had gone down to the cellar and hadn't come back. That was all I could sensibly tell them and in a way it was the truth.

As for me, I have developed a mortal fear

of spiders and centipedes and other wriggling things, and my sleep ever since has been fractured and of poor quality. I keep hearing crying in the night, not just of the Earl's wife, or what she had become, but of her many victims, including my friend. I know I cannot save him, that I could not have saved him, and yet still I feel myself being drawn back to that place. Whether it is to face the beast that took my friend, or merely to prove that I myself have not gone insane I cannot tell. There is only one thing of which I can be sure.

I only have five more months to wait.

John Llewellyn Probert is the published author of nine novellas, six short story collections, two novels and two non-fiction film books, all horror-related. He is the winner of the British Fantasy Award and the Children of the Night Award. He has two new short story collections due out in late 2022 (from NewCon Press and Black Shuck Books respectively). He writes about new film releases at his site, House of Mortal Cinema, and has a major new film book planned to launch in August 2023.

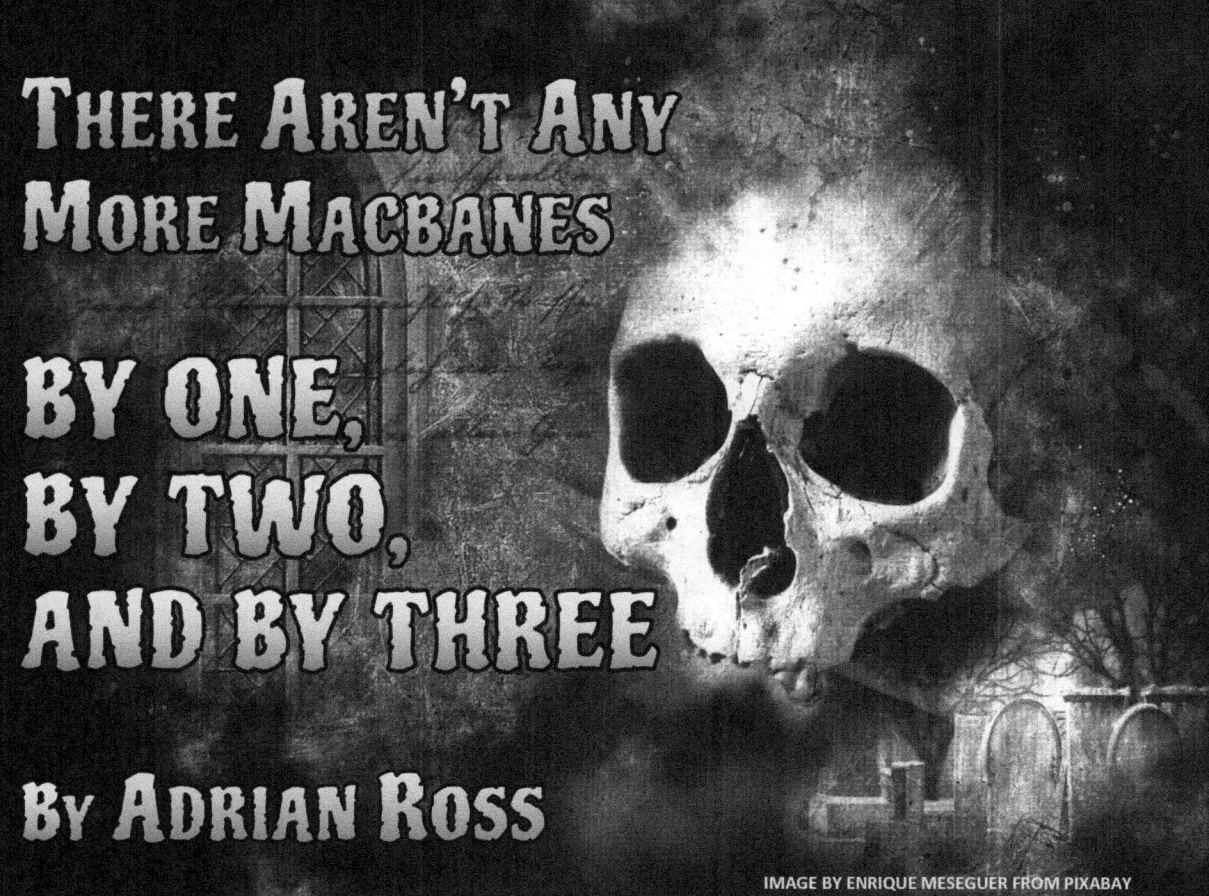

THERE AREN'T ANY MORE MACBANES

BY ONE, BY TWO, AND BY THREE

BY ADRIAN ROSS

IMAGE BY ENRIQUE MESEGUER FROM PIXABAY

IT WAS WHILE I WAS AT CAMBRIDGE THAT I FIRST CAME TO KNOW ANGUS MACBANE. We met casually, as undergraduates do, at the breakfast table of a mutual friend, or rather acquaintance; and I remember being struck with the odd cynical remarks my neighbor threw out at rare intervals, as he watched the argument we had started, about Heaven knows what or what not, and were maintaining on either side with the boundless confidence and almost boundless ignorance peculiar to freshmen. I seem to see him now, leaning back after the meal in a deep armchair, with his host's cat purring her contentment on his knee. He never looked at the semicircle of disputants round the fire, but blew beautiful rings of cigarette smoke into the air, or gazed with a critical expression, under half-shut lids, at the photographs of actresses forming a galaxy of popular beauty above the mantlepiece. Then he would emit some sentence, sometimes sensible, oftener wildly nonsensical; but always original, unexpected—a stone dropped with a splash and a ripple into the stream of conversation.

I do not think that he showed any very particular power of mind at the breakfast-party, or indeed afterwards. What made one notice him was the faint aroma of oddity that seemed to cling to him, and all his ways and doings. He was incalculable, indefinable; this was what made a good many dislike him, and made me, with one or two others, conceive a queer liking for him. I always had a taste, secret or confessed, for those delicate degrees of oddity which require a certain natural bent to appreciate them at all. Extravagance of any kind commands notice and compels a choice between admiration and contempt; moreover, it generally (and not least at a University) invites imitation. No one ever either admired or despised Macbane, as far as I know; and no one could ever have imitated him. The singularity lay rather in the man himself than in any special habit. For Macbane was not definably different from other young men. He was of medium height, slightly made, but not spare; his face had hardly any color, and his hair and moustache were light. His eyes were of a tint difficult to define—sometimes they seemed blue, sometimes grey, sometimes greenish; and he had a trick of keeping them half-shut, and of looking away from anyone who was with him. This peculiarity is popularly supposed to be the sign of a knave; in his case it was merely a part of the man's general oddity, and did not create any special distrust.

Our acquaintance, thus casually begun, ripened into a strange sort of friendship. Macbane and I saw very little of each other; we did not talk much, nor go for walks and rows together, nor confide to each other our doings and plans, as friends are supposed to do. On rainy afternoons I would stroll round to his rooms and enter, to find him generally seated before the fire, caressing his cat. We did not greet each other; but I generally took up one of the numerous strange and rare books that he contrived to accumulate, though he spent very little money. This I would read, occasionally dropping a remark which he would answer with some cynical, curt sentence; and then both of us relapsed into silence. Tea would be made and drunk, and we sometimes sat thus till dinnertime, or later. Yet though I always felt as if I bored Macbane, I still went to his rooms; and when I did not go for some time, he would generally, with an air of extreme lassitude and reluctance, come round to my quarters, there to sit and smoke and turn over my books in much the same way as I did when I visited him.

Angus Macbane never told me anything much about himself or his family; he was one of the most reticent of mortals. All he ever did in that way was to say once in an abrupt manner that some of his ancestors had been executed for witchcraft; and when I vented some of the usual commonplaces on the barbarous ignorance and cruelty of those times, he cut me short by remarking in a tone of profound conviction that he thought his ancestors thoroughly deserved their fate, and that their condemnation was the only oasis of justice in a desert of judicial infamy.

From other sources, however, I discovered that Angus Macbane was an only son, whose parents had both died soon after his birth, leaving nothing behind them but their child. An uncle, a rich Glasgow merchant, had provided in no very lavish way for the boy's education, and was supposed to be intending to leave him a large share of his property. This was all I gathered from those people who made a point of knowing everything about everybody; and there is no lack of them at Universities.

TWO STRIKING PECULIARITIES there were about Macbane, which stood out from the general oddity of the man. The first was his fondness for cats, or, to speak more accurately, the fondness of cats for him. He had always one pet cat—generally a black one—in his rooms, and sometimes more; and when he had two, they were invariably jealous of each other. But he seemed to have an irresistible attraction for cats in general: they would come to him uncalled and show the greatest pleasure when he noticed or caressed them. He did not stroke a cat often, but when he did, it was with a certain delicate and sensitive action of the hand that seemed to delight the animal above everything. So marked was the attraction he exercised, that a scientific acquaintance accused him of carrying valerian in his pockets.

The other peculiarity was in his books. He had picked up, in ways only known to himself, a very fine collection of early works on demonology and witchcraft. A more complete account, from all sides, of "Satan's invisible world" was seldom accumulated. There were books, pamphlets and broadsheets in Latin, French, German, English, Italian and Spanish, and some old family manuscripts relating to the arts or trials of warlocks and witches. There was even an old Arabic manual of sorcery, though this I am sure he could not read. Most of these works were of the sixteenth and seventeenth centuries, since which period, indeed, civilization has ordained a "close time" for witches; and any treatises on the black art dated after that time Macbane not only did not buy, but as a rule refused to accept as gifts. "Early in the eighteenth century," he once remarked, "men lost their faith in the devil; and they have not as yet recovered it sufficiently to produce any witchcraft worthy of the name." And indeed he had the greatest abhorrence and contempt for modern Spiritualism, mesmerism, esoteric Buddhism, etc.; and the only occasion during his Cambridge life on which I saw him really lose his temper was when a mild youth, destined to holy orders, called on him and asked him to join a society for investigating ghostly and occult phenomena. He turned on the intruder with something like ferocity, saying that he did not see why people wanted to be wiser than their ancestors, and that the old way of selling oneself to the devil, and getting the price duly paid, was far better both in its financial and moral aspects than paying foreign impostors to show the way to his place of business. "Though what the devil wants at all with such souls as yours," he added meditatively, "is the one point in his character that I have never been able to understand. It is a weakness on his part—I am afraid it is a weakness!" The incipient curate turned and fled.

A few sayings of this kind, reported and distorted in many little social circles, gave Angus Macbane an evil reputation which he hardly deserved. The College authorities looked askance on him, and some of them, I believe, would have been thankful if his conduct had given them a pretext for "sending him down," whether for a term or for ever. But no offense or glaring irregularity could be even plausibly alleged against him. He attended the College chapel frequently, and never lost an opportunity of hearing the Athanasian Creed. "When I hear all those worthy people mumbling their singsong formulas, without attaching any meaning to them, and chanting forth vague curses into the air," he once said to me, "I close my eyes, and can sometimes almost fancy myself on the Brocken, in the midst of the Witches' Sabbath."

This devout assiduity was only reckoned as one point more against him; for Angus Macbane belonged by birth to the very straitest of Scotch Presbyterians, and evinced no desire to quit them, or to dispute the harshest and most repulsive of the doctrines handed down from his ancestors.

Yet to my knowledge he never went near any Presbyterian chapel, but preferred, as his worthy uncle said, "to bow in the house of Rimmon."

This uncle, as I gradually divined, was the one being whom my friend regarded with something like hatred. Mr. Duncan Macdonald was the brother of Macbane's mother. He was a big, red, sandy man, rich, unmarried, and not unkindly in nature; and an ordinary person with a little tact could have managed him, if not with complete satisfaction, at any rate to no small profit. It is true, the manufacturer was one of those self-made men who think that no man has any business to be otherwise than self-made; but by flattering his pride, he could easily have been induced to support his nephew in ease, and even in luxury and extravagance, if enough show were made for the money. But he was a Philistine of the Philistines, two-thirds of his life dominated by gain, and the rest by a rigid sense of duty. Material success and respectability were his two golden calves; and to both of these his nephew's every thought and act did dishonor.

Angus Macbane could not have been made a successful man by any process less summary and complete than the creation of a world for his needs alone; and not even this would have given him respectability. He could not live without aid from his uncle; but he accepted from him a mere pittance, which, grudgingly taken, soon came to be as grudgingly given. Yet when he forced himself to compete for scholarships and prizes, which would have made him partly independent, he missed them in a way which would have been willful in any other man. His essays were a byword among examiners for their cynical originality, perverse ability, and instinctive avoidance of the obvious avenues to success. Thus he was constrained to depend on that scanty income of which every coin seemed flung in his face. With his developed misanthropy and contempt for ordinary men, he would at all times have been intolerant of the mere existence of such a man as his uncle; and that he himself should be hopelessly indebted to such a creature for every morsel he ate, for every book he read, was a sheer monstrosity to his mind—or so I should conjecture from what I knew of the two. Angus seldom willingly mentioned his uncle; and when he did so, it was with a deadly intensity of contempt in his tone—not his words—such as I never heard before or since.

II

AN END COMES to all things; and my time at Cambridge, which had passed as swiftly for me as for most men, and left me with the usual abundant third year's crop of unfulfilled purposes, came to its end in due course. Angus Macbane had "gone down" before I did, with a high second-class degree in mathematics, chiefly gained, as I happened to hear from an examiner, by a very few problems which hardly anyone else solved. A serious quarrel with his uncle followed on this ill-success; but from motives of family duty and respectability Mr. Macdonald continued to pay his nephew enough to maintain life. No relation of his, he felt, must come to the workhouse.

For a year or two I lost sight of Macbane; and when I saw him again, he was living in lodgings in an obscure street of a London suburb. I had learnt his address from another old college friend, Frank Standish by name, who had kept up relations with Angus. Frank was a complete contrast to Macbane; he was a tall, hearty, handsome, athletic fellow, successful in everything he undertook, and was now making his way as an engineer, and likely to do well. It was this opposition in their natures that had begotten their friendship. I have seen them sitting together at Cambridge, Standish chatting on by the hour, and Macbane watching him in contented silence. As someone remarked, it was like the famous friendship of a racehorse and a cat.

I was myself now an under-master at a large day-school, and my evenings were in general free; so one night I called for Standish at his lodging, and together we trudged off to find Macbane. Our path led through one of those strange uncanny wildernesses that lie about the outskirts of every great and growing town. Skeletons of unfinished houses, bristling with scaffolding poles, loomed on us at intervals through the rainy mist; the roads were long heaps of brickbats and loose stones, already varied with blades of coarse grass. The path we followed was seamed across with the ruts of heavy carts that had gone to and from the half-built houses; and we stumbled over posts and through plashy pools, along the ghostly highway, completely deserted now that the workmen were gone, and stretching its miles of raw ruin through the autumn mist.

Standish whistled cheerily as he strode on through the desolation, and I was comforted to have him with me—I think I should almost have felt afraid but for his presence. We crossed the No Man's Land of chaotic brick and mortar, and found ourselves in a street of mean new houses. At No. 21, Wolseley Road, Standish paused and rang; a slatternly maid-of-all-work answered the bell, and ushered us into the presence of Angus Macbane.

HE WAS SITTING by a poor little fire, in a shabby armchair, with his black cat on his knee as usual, and a volume of demonology in his hand; and, save that the room was small, cheaply furnished and hideously papered, and the occupant looked thinner and wearier, we could have fancied ourselves at Cambridge again. But after the first greetings, I soon noticed that Macbane was changed for the worse since I had seen him last. He did not seem at all dissipated, nor had he acquired the air of meanness and shiftiness that marks the needy adventurer; but there was a genuineness, almost a desperation, in his cynical utterances, which they had not had before—a hopelessness of expression and an irritability which I did not like. The misanthropy at which he had played before was now in grim earnest.

He told us a little—very little, and that reluctantly—of his own way of life. He was doing nothing of any moment—a struggling unknown writer, spasmodically trying to secure some literary foothold, and failing always, whether by the fatality which attended him specially, or by the same chances as befall any author. Added to this misery was the consciousness of his dependence on his uncle, which was bitterer to him, I could see, than ever. He began to talk about Mr. Macdonald of his own accord, and that was always a bad sign.

"Do you know," he said, with a bitter laugh, "my worthy relative is coming out here before long? He writes me that he is due in London on business in a fortnight or so, and will pay me a visit to see if I am still given over to the same reprobate mind as before, and opposed to what *he* calls my duty. Won't you come and see the fun, you two? I think I know how to aggravate him now, perfectly well. I assure you, at my last interview with him, I made him swear within three minutes—and he an elder!"

"I say, Macbane," Standish put in, in his good-natured way, "don't carry that game too far. The old chap is good for a lot if only you don't rub him up the wrong way. If you rile him this time, ten to one he cuts you off with a shilling—and then where will you be?"

"If he only would die!" Macbane went on, not seeming to hear his friend's remonstrance. "Fellows like that have no sense of fitness. When I saw him last he reminded me of one of those big fat coarse speckled spiders, that you want to kill, only they make such a mess. I should so like to murder him, if I could do it by deputy."

He was joking, of course, but there was more earnestness than I liked in his manner. I looked at Standish, and he at me, before I spoke.

"If those are your sentiments," I said, echoing his light tone, "we had better come to prevent bloodshed."

"Yes, do come," Angus resumed; "and if you will kindly take off his head outside, I shall be greatly obliged to you. Bring a delightful rusty old axe, Standish, with plenty of notches in the blade. It will be so nice to be like one of those dear Italian despots, and get one's assassination done for one. Though there are better than hiring a bravo, even. An ancestor of mine——" and here he stopped suddenly.

"Well, what did your ancestor do?" asked I.

"Oh," said Macbane coolly, "he raised a devil of some sort and got scragged by it himself."

As he spoke these trivial words, there came a faint sound at the door as of something scratching very gently on the panels.

I turned to Macbane and asked—

"Is that your dog, Mac?"

"My dog!" he said with a shudder, "why, I *hate* dogs. I never have one near my room by any chance—except when the landlady sends me up sausages."

"Perhaps it is another cat come to make friends with you," suggested Standish. "There it is again. I will let it in, whatever it is."

He flung the door open, and the chill air rushed in from the drafty passage and stairs. There was nothing outside or in sight, and he shut the door again with a bang.

"I heard it distinctly," he said, in the aggrieved tone of one who fancies he has made himself ridiculous. "What could it have been?"

"Wind, perhaps, or a rat," said Macbane lightly. "There are plenty of rats in the place, and I am glad of it, for it is the only thing that prevents me from expecting the house to fall every moment. When it is going to fall the rats will all run out, and my cat Mephistopheles will run out after them, and I shall run out after Mephistopheles; and the landlady and the first-floor lodgers, and the landlady's cat that eats my tea and sugar, will all be squelched together, to the joy of all good cats and men—eh, Mephisto? Why, what ails the cat?"

For Mephistopheles was standing upon his master's lap, with back arched and tail rigid and bristling, glaring into the darkest corner of the little room, and hissing in a passion of mingled rage and fear. Then, before anyone could stop him, the cat made one leap at the window, with a yell and a great crash of glass, and was gone, leaving us staring at each other.

Angus Macbane spoke first, with a forced laugh.

"There goes my cat," he said, "and there goes one-and-nine for broken glass. Cats I may get again, but one-and-ninepence—never. A cat with nine lives, a shilling with nine pence—all lost, all lost!"—and he went on laughing in a shrill hysterical way that I did not at all like. During the pause that followed, Standish looked at his watch.

"It is pretty late now," he said, "and I have a lot of working drawings to prepare tomorrow. Goodnight, Macbane. If I come across your cat, I'll remonstrate with him for quitting us so rudely. But no doubt he will come back of himself."

As Standish said this, the rest of the large pane through which the cat had leaped suddenly fell out with a startling crash into the street, making us all wince.

"It was cracked already," remarked Angus; "and the glazier does not allow for the pieces. Goodnight, both of you. I fancy I have something to do myself, too."

I was surprised, and a little hurt, at being thus practically turned out by my friend (for I had expressed no intention of departing, and it was not really very late); but I was not sorry to go now, and have the solace of Standish's cheery company home. A curious undefined feeling of apprehension was creeping over me, and I wanted to be out in the night air, and shake off my uneasiness by a brisk walk.

We went downstairs, leaving Macbane brooding in his chair. As the landlady saw us out, I slipped a half-crown into her hand.

"Mr. Macbane's window got broken tonight," I said. "Will you have it mended, and not say anything about it to him?"

I knew that he would probably forget the occurrence if not reminded of it. Standish nodded approval, and we went out into the mist. We walked on in silence till we turned out of the lamp-lit and inhabited part, and then my companion remarked abruptly—

"That makes one-and-threepence I owe you, Eliot"—and relapsed into silence, not even whistling as he strode along.

WE HAD REACHED nearly the middle of the long artificial desert, where a street was someday to be, when Standish stopped and caught me by the arm.

"Eliot, what is that?" he whispered.

We both stood still and listened. From the waste land beyond one of the skeleton houses came a fearful cry, whether of a child or an animal we could not tell—a scream of mere pain and terror, intense and thrilling, neither human nor bestial. Then there was a deep snarling growl, and the yell died into a choking gurgle, and suddenly fell silent.

"Come on," Standish gasped, and ran with all his speed in the direction of the sound.

I followed as fast as my shorter legs and wind would take me over the stiff slimy clay of the waste land, and after a few minutes found him bending over a little dark heap on the ground at the edge of a puddle.

"Have you got a match?" he said.

I nodded—I was too much out of breath to speak—and pulled out my matchbox. I struck a light, screening it with my hand, and we both looked earnestly at the black lump at our feet.

"Bah!" said Standish, as he mopped the perspiration from his face. "Why, it's only a cat, and it sounded like a baby!"

It was the body of a large black cat, still warm and quivering, but quite dead. The throat was almost entirely severed, and the blood had streamed out, darkly streaking the thick yellow water of the pool. Of what had killed it there was no sign or sound, only, in the soft clay beside the puddle, there were marks which seemed those of the poor cat's feet, and other footprints like these, but larger. I pointed them out to Standish.

"I see what it was," he said, as we trudged laboriously back to the road. "The cat was out there, and some beast of a dog caught it and killed it—though what cat or dog should be doing there is more than I can say. What teeth the brute must have! Ugh! I hope he's not waiting round to take another bite!"

We got back to the road unbitten, and went on our way in silence, till I said—

"Standish, do you know, that cat was very like Macbane's?"

"Do you know, Eliot," was his answer, "that is just what I was going to tell you?"

And not another word did he utter, till I left him at his door and said goodnight.

III

MACBANE WAS NEVER a good correspondent, but he duly informed us of the date of his uncle's expected visit; and when the day came, I called for Standish in the evening as before, and we trudged off through another sloppy mist. Standish, good thoughtful fellow, had brought with him, in his overcoat pocket, a bottle of very fine old Irish whiskey, which he had long been treasuring up for some festal occasion, but now intended to devote to the mollifying, if possible, of Mr. Macdonald.

"Every glass he takes of this," he solemnly assured me as we went on, "will be worth a hundred a year to Macbane."

We did not go by the same dreary road that we had taken before. Frank declared, with a shudder, that the last cry of that cat was still ringing in his ears, and that he could not stand the ghastly place again. I was rather surprised at his unwonted nervousness, but readily acquiesced in it. So we went a mile or so out of our way, keeping along endless streets of shabby-genteel houses, which were sufficiently hideous, but not appalling; and about nine in the evening we reached Wolseley Road.

I was surprised and almost shocked to notice the change that had passed over Macbane in the few weeks since I had seen him last. He did not seem worse in health —on the contrary, there was at times a nervous alacrity about his movements which I had not remarked before. But his face and expression seemed to have darkened, as it were, and grown evil. His college cynicism had already turned into misanthropy; and now, I thought, it had developed into a positive malevolence. He still was silent and brooding, after the first greetings; but he no longer seemed dejected. Altogether a transformation of some kind had come to him, such that I—though not very impressionable—was rather inclined to fear than to pity him.

The conversation, as was natural, turned on the uncle, who might appear at any moment now. Standish and I joined in urging on our friend the necessity of attempting conciliation, of showing some semblance of submission. We had more than once induced him to do so before, though his perverse temper generally made him unable to do more than avert an instant stoppage of the supplies; but tonight he was obstinate, and even spoke as if he were the aggrieved party, and his uncle the one to make advances.

"If the old fool cares to be civil," he said fiercely, "then there's an end of it; and if not, there's an end too. I am tired of humoring him."

As he spoke, the "old fool's" heavy tread was heard on the stairs, and in another minute he entered. He was a big, strong, red-faced, coarse-looking fellow, with sandy whiskers and grizzled hair, who nodded awkwardly to us, and gave a surly greeting to his nephew, who sat still in his armchair, looking into the fire with half-shut eyes.

Mr. Duncan Macdonald seemed disconcerted by our presence, and I offered to withdraw; but Macbane would not let us.

"You see, uncle," he remarked, still keeping his eyes averted, and using the familiar title solely, I am convinced, because he knew the uncle did not like it, "these gentlemen know all about our little affairs, and they had better hear your version of matters now than my version afterwards. Besides, one of them is going to be a literary man and write a tale with Scotch characters in it; and you will be quite a godsend for him, as raw material for a study. If you want to swear at me, pray don't mind him; there is nothing that tells more in literature than a little aboriginal profanity, properly accented."

This was a bad beginning for an interview; and would have been worse still had Mr. Macdonald been able fully to understand his nephew's speech. What he did understand, however, obviously offended him; and he began to address Macbane in no very conciliatory tones, though at first with a forced moderation of language and strained English accent which were evidently the result of the young man's taunt. Then, as Macbane did not answer, but sat still looking into the fire, his uncle began to lose temper. His language grew broader and stronger, both as Scotch and as reproach. He addressed us with a sort of rough eloquence: on the subject of his nephew's miserable laziness, shiftlessness, effeminacy—pointing at him, and showering down vigorous epithets on him. In the midst of his tirade, as he paused for breath, came a low sound of scratching at the door.

"There's that confounded rat again!" cried Standish, glad of any pretext for interrupting the miserable business. "Dead, for a ducat, this time!" He dashed open the door as he spoke, but there was nothing to be seen. Only the gaslight in the passage, flickering and flaring in the draft, sent strange shadows flitting across the walls.

Frank came back and sat down, and busied himself in uncorking his bottle of whiskey, and setting the kettle on to boil. I took up a book, so as not to seem to observe a scene which I knew must be so painful and humiliating for Macbane. The uncle again plunged into the stream of his invective, and I kept my eyes on the nephew. I knew that he was really quite as passionate as the elder man, and I was afraid of what he might do if he once lost his self-control; but though a little shiver passed over him sometimes, he was quite silent, leaning back in the armchair, with his head resting on his right hand, and his left arm hanging listlessly over the side of the chair. Presently he began to move the hands languidly to and fro, with the fingers outstretched, and the palm horizontal and slightly hollowed, keeping it more than a foot from the carpet. It was a curious gesture, but he had many odd tricks of the kind.

At last Mr. Macdonald, having spent his store of abuse without any response, began, I fancy, to feel a little ashamed of himself, and became more conciliatory, letting fall some hints as to the terms on which he might even yet receive his prodigal nephew back to favor. The manner of his overtures was far more offensive than their substance, and to one who could make allowance for the man's coarse nature, there was even a trace of a feeling that might be called kindness. But Macbane was always far more sensitive to externals than other men, and his uncle's condescension, I could see, irritated him far more than his anger. He left off moving his hand to and fro, sat up and clutched the arms of his chair. Then, when the older man had done, he cast one deadly look at him, and shook his head as if he would not trust himself to speak.

"Winna ye speak, ye feckless pauper loon?" roared his uncle, with a string of oaths.

Macbane was silent, but that good fellow Standish interposed at what he thought was the right moment.

"Come, Mr. Macdonald," he said frankly, "I don't think you should talk like that. After all, Macbane is your own sister's son, and he is not well now, and you must not come down on him too heavily. Let us have a glass of toddy all round now and part friends, and we three will talk it all over, and make matters smooth tomorrow. We can't do any good tonight."

As he spoke, he got out some tumblers from the cupboard and wiped them clean. The Glasgow manufacturer seemed a little mollified; nobody could help liking Standish or his whiskey, and all might yet have been well if the devil had not seemed to enter suddenly into Angus Macbane. Standish had poured out a generous measure of the fragrant spirit, and was turning to take the kettle off the hob, when Macbane sprang up like a cat, in a white heat of rage, took the tumbler from the table and flung it right into the grate. The glass rang and crashed, and the flame leapt out blue like a tongue of hellfire; and Angus stood at the table, quivering all over, with his right hand opening and shutting as if feeling for a weapon. Standish caught him by the arm and pulled him back into his chair.

"Are you mad, Mac?" he exclaimed. Macbane did not seem to hear, but sat glowering at his uncle. As for Mr. Duncan Macdonald, he turned purple with anger. The complicated atrocity of the insult—an outrage at once on kinship, hospitality, thrift and good whiskey—had smitten him dumb for a moment with surprise and rage. He clenched his fist and struck blindly at his nephew, who was fortunately out of reach; then he spoke in a husky but distinct voice, slowly, as if registering a vow.

"De'il throttle me," he said, "if ever you see bawbee[2] of mine again." And he took up

---

[2] A coin of low value; a silver coin worth 3 Scottish pennies.

his hat and umbrella and turned to the door.

"Done with you, in the devil's name!" cried Macbane.

Without another word the uncle flung the door open, and shut it after him with a crash that shook the house. Then we heard him heavily stamping down the stairs and along the passage, till another great bang proclaimed that he had left the house. This last noise seemed to rouse Macbane from a sort of trance. He sprang up again and rushed to the door and threw it open, as if to pursue his uncle. We were going to stop him, for he looked murderous enough; but instead of dashing downstairs, he stopped, flung out his hand with a strange gesture, as if he were pointing at something, and muttered a few words that I could not catch. Then he shut the door and came back slowly to his old seat, as pale as a dead man.

In the excitement of the scene, we had none of us noticed the time; but now the cheap little clock on the mantelpiece struck twelve and recalled the fact that two of us were far away from our lodgings. Standish and I looked at each other; we neither of us liked to leave Macbane alone yet. The man's expression as he flung the glass into the fire —still more his look as he pointed down the stairs—was black enough for anything; and if we went now, he seemed quite capable of going out and murdering his uncle, or staying and murdering himself. Standish winked at me, and went out quietly. In ten minutes he came back and addressed Macbane, who was sunk in one of his reveries again.

"All right, old fellow," he said cheerily, "your landlady tells me her first floor is vacant, and she will put us two up for the night. So cheer up, Mac. It is a bad business, but we will see you through it, never fear. Now let's brew some punch and be jolly tonight at any rate, as we needn't go."

Macbane woke up again at this, with a sudden feverish gaiety. He eagerly took the steaming tumbler Frank prepared for him, and drained it at a draught—he whose strongest stimulant was coffee. The whiskey did not seem to affect his head, however. More than this, he hunted out a soiled pack of cards from an obscure drawer, and proposed—he who hated all games—that we should play to pass the time. Dummy whist he thought too slow, and I proposed three-handed euchre, generally called "cut-throat." The name seemed to amuse our friend vastly. He insisted on learning the game, and we started at once, His spirits were almost uproarious; I had never seen him like this before. Yet his gaiety was very unequal. Sometimes he would cut the wildest jokes, till in spite of our uneasiness about him we shrieked with laughter; and again he would sink back in his chair, forgetting to play his hand, and seeming as if he listened for some sound. After some time he went to the door and flung it open, declaring that he was "stifling in this hole of a room." Then he sat down again to play, but fidgeted about in his chair impatiently. He was studying his cards, which he held up in his left hand, when I happened to look at the other arm hanging down by his chair.

"For goodness sake!" I exclaimed, "what have you done to your hand, Macbane?"

He held up his right hand as I spoke, and looked at it. Palm and fingers were dabbled and smeared with watery blood, fresh and wet. For a moment we stared at each other with pale faces.

"I must have cut my hand over that confounded tumbler or something," said Macbane at last with an evident effort. "I will go and wash it off in my bedroom and be back in a moment."

He slipped out as he spoke, and we heard him washing his hand, muttering to himself all the time.

Then in a few minutes he came back, keeping his hand in his pocket, and resumed the game. But his former high spirits were gone, and another tumbler of punch failed to recall them. He made constant mistakes, played his hand at random, and at last suddenly threw all his cards down on the table, laid his head on them, and burst into a terrible fit of hysterical sobbing.

We did not know what to do with him, but Standish laid him on the hard sofa, and in a little time he seemed better, though greatly shaken, and managed to control himself. He thanked us in a whisper, and told us to go, and he would get to bed alone. We were still rather anxious about him, but there seemed no reason for staying with him now against his will. The natural reaction had followed on all the strain and excitement, and I, for one, was glad that it was no worse. So we left him beginning, in a slow and dazed way, to get to bed, and descended to try and snatch a little sleep in the genteel misery of the first-floor lodgings.

IV

WE PASSED A RATHER disturbed night in our strange quarters. There were rats in the walls, the windows rattled, and altogether there were more queer noises than one generally hears in houses so new. However, we did get to sleep, and did not wake again till the grey dull sodden dawn was making ghastly the little strip of sky visible over the grimy roof of the house opposite. We rose and dressed quickly and went up to Macbane's room. I peered in, but he was still sleeping heavily; so we busied ourselves, as quietly as we could, in preparing breakfast, intending, if our friend did not wake, to go off to our own work for the day, leaving a message for him. We purposed, in a rather vague manner, to do something for poor Macbane. Standish hoped to work on the better feelings of his uncle; I had resolved to devote some of my little savings to keeping my friend out of the workhouse.

We were half through our scanty and silent meal, when a heavy tread was heard on the stairs, making apparently for the room where we were. "What luck!" said the sanguine Standish; "here's the penitent uncle, come back after the whiskey. Now leave me alone to manage him. There is half the bottle left."

The steps came up to the door and paused: then there was a single sharp rap, and in walked—not Mr. Macdonald, but a policeman. If Standish and I had been thieves or coiners taken in the act, we could hardly have shown more confusion. My first thought was that perhaps Macbane had done something wrong; and this suspicion was confirmed by the officer's first words.

"Beg your pardon, gentlemen," he said; "but is either of you Mr. A. Macbane?"

"No," said Standish; "Mr. Macbane is asleep in the next room. What do you want with him?"

"I want him to come with me to the station, as soon as convenient, sir," was the reply.

"What for?" persisted Standish. "Nothing wrong, I hope?"

"Nothing wrong about him; leastways, I don't suppose so, sir," said the man. "But there's been foul play somewhere. There's been a body found in the road out a mile off, and a card in the pocket with Mr. Macbane's name and address on it; and we want him to come and identify the corpse."

"Do you know the man's name?" I demanded, divining, as I asked, what the answer would be.

"His linen was marked 'Macdonald,' sir," was the cautious reply.

"And how had he been killed?" asked Standish breathlessly.

"Throat cut from ear to ear," said the constable, with terrible conciseness.

We looked at each other and shuddered. Neither of us had any kind feelings for the man thus suddenly cut off; in fact, we had been thoroughly disgusted with his coarse and sordid temper, and had hoped—in jest, it is true—that he might break his neck over the dismal road he had to traverse. But this sudden, mysterious, hideous murder—for such it must be—struck us with a chill of horror. My first collected thought, I believe, was a feeling of intense thankfulness that we had not left Macbane alone the night before. Now, at any rate, no suspicion could attach to him.

The policeman looked curiously from one to the other of us.

"Perhaps," he said at length, "one of you two gentlemen would know him?"

"If it is the man I suppose," answered Standish, "we certainly do know him. Mr. Macdonald is Mr. Macbane's uncle, and was here last night. We both saw him leave before twelve o'clock and have not seen him since."

"Then, sir," said the policeman, "perhaps one of you will wake Mr. Macbane and bring him along as soon as he can come, and the other will go to the station at once, for there is never any time to lose in these cases."

I went into Macbane's bedroom, and Standish took up his hat and followed the policeman out. I touched my friend on the shoulder. He gasped, yawned, then sat up, rubbed his eyes, and stared wildly round him, till his gaze rested on me. Then the recollection of what had happened seemed to come back on him in a flash, and he laid his head back on the pillow.

"Is that you, Eliot?" he said. "I have had such a horrible dream. Thank you for waking me. Must I get up now?"

"Yes, you must, Macbane," I replied gravely. "I will tell you why afterwards."

"Moralities and mysteries!" said he, in his cynical way. "Well, I shall soon hear, if I am a good boy, and don't take long over my dressing. Reach me my trousers, there's a good fellow."

As I did so, I saw that his right hand was again streaked thinly with dried blood, and I could not help an exclamation.

"Ah!" said he, as I called his attention to it. That thing has been bleeding again, I see. Well, I can soon wash it off." And he sprang up in his nightshirt, and ran to his washing stand.

"Look here!" he cried, as he plunged his hand into the water; "shouldn't I make a lovely Lady Macbeth? 'Here's the smell of the blood yet. Oh! oh! oh! All the perfumes of Araby—' How does it go? 'Yet who would have thought the old man had so much blood in him?'"

"For God's sake, be quiet!" I screamed. "Your uncle is lying at the police-station with his throat cut! Be thankful you had nothing to do with killing him!"

Macbane turned faint and sick, and sat down on his bed again; but he bore the news much better than I had thought he would. To be sure, he had no love for his uncle, and could not be expected to sorrow for him; but the shock did not seem somehow to affect him greatly, except by a mere physical repulsion at the horrid manner of his uncle's death. He soon got up again, and went on dressing, listening meanwhile as I told him all I yet knew about the matter; and as soon as he was ready, we went out together.

THE POLICE-STATION was soon reached, and we were admitted into a back room where Mr. Macdonald's body lay on a table, covered with a piece of sacking. There was no difficulty in identifying the corpse. The throat was cut, or rather, as it seemed to me, torn almost through with a frightful wound; but the face was uninjured, and still bore an expression of sudden horror and surprise that was very ghastly. We did not care to look on the sight long. When the covering had been replaced, the constables told us all they knew.

Some workmen, coming to their work at one of the unfinished houses in the new road, had found the body, lying on its back in a pool of clotted blood. There were no marks of a struggle that they noticed. They had put the corpse on a short ladder left in one of the houses, and carried it to the police-station. The nearest surgeon had been called in, and had pronounced that life had been extinct for some hours. A purse and gold watch were found in the pockets. As to the hand or the weapon that had done the deed, neither the surgeon nor the police would offer any suggestion; and we could not help them. Only, as we left the station, the police-sergeant remarked that he thought he had a clue to the murderer. "Do you hear that, Standish?" said Macbane in a mocking tone; "*he* thinks he has a clue."

We walked back to Wolseley Road and left Macbane there; and then Standish and I trudged off to our work—for work must be done, whoever has died. And all that afternoon and evening, whenever I was within sight or sound of a main street, my eyes were greeted with sensational placards, and my ears deafened with the shouts of newsboys, reiterating the same burden—"Third Edition! Awful Murder in Craddock Park! A Glasgow Merchant Murdered!" and over every placard I seemed to see the vision of the dead face, and that gash in the throat.

The inquest was held a few days afterwards, and of course we all attended it. The story of the quarrel with Angus Macbane came out, in its main outlines, from his evidence and ours; and I could tell from the Coroner's pointed questions, that he suspected our friend. But there was no reasonable doubt that Duncan Macdonald had been killed within an hour after he left the lodging-house; and it was perfectly clear from our evidence and the landlady's that Angus Macbane had been in his room long after this, and practically certain that he had never left the house at all that night.

The medical evidence, when it came, was conclusive; the distinguished surgeon who had made the postmortem examination gave it as his opinion that the wound in the throat could have been inflicted with no species of weapon with which he was acquainted; and as far as he could venture to form a hypothesis, death had been caused by the bite of some animal armed with exceedingly large and powerful cutting teeth. This unexpected statement caused quite a sensation in court; and Standish jumped up.

"By Jove, I forgot the cat!" he said to me; and then, advancing to the Coroner, he informed him that he had an addition to make to his former statement. He was sworn again, and told the story of the mysterious death of poor Mephistopheles in a straightforward way that evidently impressed the jury. I confirmed his tale in every particular.

There were no more witnesses, and the Coroner summed up. He began by stating that all the evidence that could be collected still left this terrible affair in a very mysterious state. So far as he could see, however, there was happily no reason for regarding it as a murder. There had been no robbery of the body, though robbery would have been perfectly easy; and though there might have seemed some *prima facie* grounds for suspecting one person of complicity in the act—here the worthy Coroner glanced at Macbane, who smiled slightly—yet it had been proved by reputable witnesses, whose testimony had not been impugned (here Standish blushed, and I think I did, too), that the person in question could not possibly have been present on the scene of Mr. Macdonald's death at the hour when it took place, and had apparently confined the expression of his ill-will to mere words, which it would be unfair to invest with any special significance—and so on, in the usual moralizing vein of coroners.

The medical evidence, he went on to say, pointed to the theory that the death of the deceased was caused by some savage animal; and the further statement of two of the witnesses seemed to indicate that some such ferocious beast, perhaps a dog, was loose in the neighborhood. It would be for the jury, however, to review all the facts, and return a just and impartial verdict upon the case.

The jury deliberated for some time, and finally determined that the deceased died from the bite of some savage animal, but what animal they were unable to say. A rider to the verdict directed the police to use all possible diligence to track out and destroy so dangerous a beast, and suggested that a reward should be offered for its capture or death. This was done by the local authorities, but with no result; and as weeks went on, and no fresh victim fell to the "ravenous beast or beasts unknown," men ceased to go armed, or to apprehend attacks, and the Craddock Park Mystery was forgotten.

Mr. Duncan Macdonald had left no will; and though he had torn up a testament providing for his nephew, he had not yet executed his threat of disinheriting him. So Macbane, as the only near relative, came in for the manufacturer's very considerable fortune. He sold out his uncle's share in his business, and his first act, almost, was to purchase an old, half-ruinous place, called Dullas Tower, which had been (as I gathered from the scanty letter he wrote me about it) the ancestral seat of the Macbanes before the family fell into poverty and ill repute in the old witchcraft days.

I was prevented by my school duties from seeing Macbane, now that he had gone north; and about this time Standish got a good appointment on an Indian railway in course of construction, and had to sail at once. Thus we three friends were parted for long, and it might be for ever. I was sorry enough to lose Standish; I think it was rather a relief to see no more of Macbane. He was stranger than ever, now that his sudden prosperity had come upon him— alternately gay and sullen, exulted and depressed, and disquieting enough in either mood. I occasionally sent him a line, and at still rarer intervals received an answer; but, on the whole, I thought he had dropped out of my life permanently, and I was not sorry to have it so, now that he needed no help. I did not dream of the strange way in which we were once again to be brought together.

V

IT WAS SOME MONTHS after Standish had left for India, and I had already received one letter from him, when I was startled by a brief paragraph among the Indian telegrams in the *Times*. It ran thus—"I regret to state that Mr. F. Standish, the young and talented engineer superintending the construction of the Salampore Junction Railway, has been killed, it is supposed by a tiger." This was all—terribly simple, brief and direct, as messages of evil are now. I was greatly shocked and grieved at this sudden death of my old friend; for though I was not likely to see him again for many years, and college friendships fade sadly when college life is over, yet we had been much together before he left, and my remembrance of him was still warm and affectionate. As soon as I recovered from the blow of the news, I wrote at once to Lieutenant Johnson, a young officer whom Standish had mentioned as being stationed near his quarters, and as being an acquaintance of his, to ask for some particulars of my friend's death.

The answer was forwarded to me about the end of August. I was not at the time in London, but had been invited by an old friend of my family to stay with him and have some shooting (though this was mere pretence on my part) at his place in Yorkshire. Lieutenant Johnson's letter was sent on from my lodgings to Darton Manor, where I was. It was a good letter, showing in its tone of manly regret how familiar and dear Standish had grown in the short time of intercourse with his new neighbors; but what I turned to most eagerly was of course the account of my poor friend's death. It was brief and rather mysterious. Standish had gone out for an early walk in the cool of the morning, taking his gun with him, as was his custom. He had walked along the line of the new railway a little distance, and then turned off into the country. As he did not come back at his usual time, two of his servants had gone out to look for him, and

found him lying on his back in a path, quite dead. His throat was fearfully torn, but there was no other wound on him. There had been no struggle, and the gun was still loaded. Footprints of some animal were observed in a patch of soft ground near by, but it was not certain whether this was the beast that had killed Standish; for while the footmarks were like those of a small panther, the wound seemed rather as if inflicted by the teeth of a tiger. A large hunting-party had beaten the neighboring country without finding any dangerous wild animal.

This narrative set me on a very gloomy train of thought. The details of Standish's end were horribly like those of Mr. Duncan Macdonald's—the suddenness, the stealth, the mystery, the ferocity of the attack were the same in both cases. Yet, what possible connection could there be between the Craddock Park mystery and the death of an engineer on the Salampore railway? Still, I could not keep this haunting feeling of some impending doom from shadowing my mind. Four men had met in that little room in Wolseley Road on that memorable night in November; two of the four had already perished by the same mysterious and horrible death. Was it possible that the same end was reserved for the other two, and, if so, who would be the next victim? It was a wild idea, I felt; but I simply could not get it out of my head, and it made me very gloomy and depressed at the dinner-table that night.

My kindly old host noticed this, and his genial nature could not rest satisfied till all around him were as cheery as himself. So when our *tête-à-tête* dinner was done —we had been very late in dining that day— he resolved to have up a bottle of a certain very rare old wine, which he kept under special lock and key for great occasions. This precious liquor he was now resolved to devote to clearing away my melancholy.

He would never trust a butler with the key of his cellar—least of all would he let a servant touch this priceless vintage. He was going to fetch the bottle himself, but of course I interposed and insisted on going for him. With a sigh of resignation, he gave me his bunch of cellar-keys, carefully instructing me as to their particular uses, and the treasures to which they respectively gave access. Then he dismissed me, and I went down to the cellar.

The cellar of Darton Manor was far older than the house. It was hewn out of the rock on which the hall stood, and was large and lofty. I think that when the old castle, whose walls are still to be traced in the Manor garden, was standing, the vaults beneath must have been the storehouse of the garrison. When the modern house was built, two windows were cut up through the rock to give light to the cellars; but the present owner had protected these openings with double gratings, and put an iron-plated door, with a strong and cunning lock, to defend his precious wines.

I took up a candle, lit it, and went down the winding stair that led to the cellar. The vault below was so lofty and so far beneath the floor of the hall, that the staircase, cut in the rock, seemed as if it would never end; I felt like one descending into a sepulchre.

The clash of the keys swinging from my hand was the only sound in the chilly silence, except when noises came, muffled and faint, from the house above. At last I reached the heavy door of the cellar, and, with some labor, unlocked it and swung it back. Then I drew out the key, as I wanted another on the bunch for releasing the precious bottle I had been sent to fetch. For a moment I stood in the doorway, holding my light high, and gazing round me into the great cavernous room. I could not see all of it; but the long rows of casks and the racks of bottles were very impressive in their silent array of potential conviviality. Then I glanced up at the windows, whose gratings were now and then made visible by a flicker of summer lightning across the sky; and as I did so, I suddenly heard a crash as of glass, far up in the house above. Then, as I still listened, came a faint sound of footfalls rapidly growing louder, as if something was coming down the winding stair with long leaps.

I did not stop to face whatever this might be; I did not pause to think what I should do. In a blind and fortunate impulse of overpowering terror, I flung the heavy door to, plunged the key into the lock and shot the bolt home. How I managed to do it in the one instant left to me, I never could understand; I had found the door hard enough to open before. As I gave the key a last turn, something came against the iron outside with a thud that almost shook the hinges loose. Then there was a moment of quiet, and I, listening behind the door, could catch a quick, hoarse, heavy panting, as of some beast of prey. Then came another great shock, and another; and at every blow the good door creaked and shook, but held firm. Next there was a grating, rending sound, as if teeth and claws were tearing at this last obstacle between my life and its destroyer —and still I stood silent, transfixed with horror, as in a nightmare, expecting to feel the fangs of the unseen Thing close through my throat.

How long I stood thus, tasting all the bitterness of death, I cannot tell. It was years in agony—it may have been only minutes of time. To feel that something fiendish, brutal and merciless was slowly tearing its way to me, and to know nothing of It save that It was death, this was the deadly and overmastering terror. My trance cannot have lasted long. With a start, I awoke to the consciousness that life was still mine, and that a chance of escape yet remained. The frozen blood again coursed through my veins, and my dead courage revived. I sprang to the nearest large barrel that lay on its side and rolled it close against the door, to keep the panels from giving way. Then I took up an iron bar that I found lying on the floor— perhaps a lever for moving the casks—and stood ready to give one last blow for my life. The sound of tearing ceased; I heard one deep snarling growl of disappointed rage; and then the quick steps seemed to recede up the stair. I stood there delivered, for a moment.

Only for a moment, however. My candle, which was a mere stump, suddenly flared, flickered, and left me in total darkness, made darker by the little patch of sky seen through the nearer window, across which still ran an occasional flicker of summer lightning. In trying to strike a light, I dropped the matchbox on the rock floor. While I was groping for it, I suddenly looked up and saw two eyes.

Two eyes, I say, but they were rather two flames, or two burning coals. For a moment I stood glaring, fascinated, at the orbs that glared into mine. Then, as the Thing turned what seemed its head, and the eyes were averted for a moment, I saw, or thought I saw, a dim phosphorescent mass obscuring the faint light of the window. Then the eyes were on me again, and I heard the sound of tearing and wrenching at the outer grating— for there were two, one above the window and one inside. The outer bars were old and rusty—strong enough to resist any common shocks, but not to hold against the unknown might that was rending at them. I heard them creaking, cracking, and then—oh heaven! the whole grating gave way, and I heard it ring as it was hurled aloft and fell far out on the stones.

The next instant the strong glass of the window flew in shivers on the floor—and there were those awful eyes looking into mine now, with only a few bars between us. Then the wrenching began once more at the last barrier. It bent—it shifted—I thought it was giving way, and in a frenzy I rushed forward, whirling the iron bar round my head, and struck with all my force through the grating. Another horrible growl answered the blow, and the bar was seized and dragged from my grasp. It was found next day, deeply indented, on the ground, a hundred yards away.

But now that the prey seemed given over disarmed to its teeth, the devilish fury of the Thing seemed to triumph over the devilish cunning that had directed it. It gave up the persistent assault on the grating, and writhed against the bars in a transport of hissing rage, biting the air, grinding its jaws on the tough iron. And yet—this was the horror of it—I could see nothing distinctly— only a phosphorescent shadow, twisted and tortured with agonies of rage, and turning upon me sometimes those eyes which seemed to redden with the growing frenzy of the Thing, till they were like blood-red lamps. I think I had lost all fear for my life now. I did not think of danger or resistance; but so mighty was the sheer horror of that bestial rage, that I groveled down in the darkest corner of the vault, and hid my eyes and stopped my ears, and cried to Heaven to deliver me from the presence of the Thing.

Suddenly, as I crouched there, the end came. The noise ceased. I turned and saw that the eyes were gone. I stood up and stretched out my arms, and a cool air blew through the shattered window on my streaming forehead. Then every tense fiber of my body seemed to give way, and I fell like one dead on the floor.

I WAS WAKENED from my swoon by a thundering at the door, and the sound of voices—human voices once more. I staggered to the door, pushed away the cask, and after long wrenching—for my hands seemed to have lost all strength—got the lock open, and stumbled into the arms of my good host. Above him, on the stairs, were two or three of the manservants, their pale frightened faces looking ghastly in the light of the flaring candles.

"My dear boy!" he cried. "Thank God you are alive! We have been so frightened about you."

I told him faintly that I had fallen in a swoon. I could not yet speak of what I had gone through, and, indeed, it now seemed like a hideous dream.

"Well, do you know," he said, as he took my arm, and helped me up the stair, "we had such a scare upstairs! Just a few minutes after you had gone, when I was wondering whether you would find the right wine, *smash* came something right through the dining-room window, and over went the big candlestick, and we were in the dark. And when we got a light again, you never saw such a scared set as we were; but there was nothing to be seen. Did you have a visit, too?"

"Something did come down here," I managed to articulate; "but don't ask me about it—not tonight. I want to sleep first."

"I think we all want that," he said briefly, as we reached the lighted hall again; and I, for one, felt as if I had come up from the grave alive.

VI

I SLEPT LATE INTO the following morning, and should have slept later still had I not been aroused about ten o'clock by the butler, who held in his hand a yellow telegram envelope. As soon as I could shake off my drowsiness in part, I tore open the missive, and unfolding the paper, found to my surprise that it was from Macbane. He knew my address, indeed, from a letter that I had sent him; but knowing his ways, I never expected even a note from him, much less a telegram. When I read the message, my surprise was not diminished.

"If safe, and wishing to see me alive," it ran, "come at once. If unable, forget me. Nearest station, Kilburgh."

What could this mean? Could Macbane know anything of my mysterious danger of last night? and if so, was the doom that had missed me impending over him? Or was it merely that he was ill and desponding, and thought himself dying? Turn and twist the message as I could, it puzzled me; but one thing was plain—Macbane was, or thought himself to be, in deadly need of me, his only friend, as far as I knew; and if I did not go, it was possible that he might lose the last chance of any friendly human care in his solitary life. I resolved at once, shaken and weary as I still felt, to start for Dullas Tower. I rose and dressed hurriedly, and snatched some breakfast alone—for my good old host was too much exhausted by the excitement of the last night to come down yet. While eating, I was studying a railway guide, and discovered that by driving to the nearest station at once, I could catch a train which would enable me by devious junction lines to make my way to Kilburgh (a little place in a wild part of a Lowland county) by the evening. While the horse was being put into the dogcart, I scribbled a note to my host, explaining the reason for my speedy departure, and promising to return as soon as possible; and then I stepped into the cart and was driven off, arriving just in time to catch the train.

* * *

MY JOURNEY WAS of the exasperatingly tedious character known to all who have ever tried to go any distance by means of crosslines and local lines and junctions. Twice I got some food during my long intervals of waiting at stations; and all the time, whether traveling or resting, I was possessed with a haunting perplexity, a shadowy fear. Through my brain incessantly beat, keeping time to the pulsating roar of the wheels, a text, or something like one—I know not how or why it suggested itself—"One woe is past; behold another woe cometh." The mysterious peril of the last night seemed already to have happened years ago; the dim terror of the future would be ages in coming; and between them, and in the shadow of both, I was still going on and on, slowly but endlessly— a dream myself, and in a dream.

It was about eight in the evening, I think, when I reached Kilburgh station; but my watch had stopped, and I could not be sure. As I stepped out on the platform, I was conscious of an intense sultry heat in the dense night air, and a sudden little gust of wind smote on my cheek like a breath from a furnace. The train went on again, plunged with a doleful wailing shriek into a tunnel, and was lost to sight; and when its rumble died away, the utter stillness was strange after the noise and rattle in which I had passed the day. I cast a hasty glance round me, and could just make out the lights of a few houses in the valley below the station, and the dark outlines of hills around, some of them serrated with black pines, and the sky dense with cloud, and with a denser mass of gloom laboring slowly up from the west. There was the weight of a coming storm in the air.

I asked the stationmaster where Dullas Tower was, and how I was to reach it.

"Dullas Tower?" he said meditatively; and then, with a sudden flash of comprehension—"Oh, it's the De'il's Tower ye'll be meaning, sir—Macbane's?"

I nodded acquiescence; this popular corruption of the name seemed ominous, but somehow natural.

"Then ye've a matter of ten miles to go," he said deliberately; "and gin I might offer an opeenion, ye'll do better to tak' Jimmy Brown's bit giggie. The man frae Macbane's tauld him to be ready the morn."

Guided by the cautious "opeenion" of the stationmaster, I found Brown's trap waiting outside the station. He was English, as I could tell by his accent; and this perhaps accounted for the slight tinge of contempt in the worthy official's reference to him and his vehicle. His horse, as far as I could tell by the station lamp, seemed a poor one; but it showed a remarkably vicious temper when I tried to get in—kicking and backing, and seeming possessed by an irrational desire to do me some bodily harm.

"Whoa, then, will ye, ye beast?" called Brown, as he caught hold of the rein and dexterously foiled the brute's instant attempt to bite him. "You're a harm to others and no good to your owner. You're just like Macbane's muckle cat, that killed two men, and the third was Macbane."

I had gained my place on the seat at last, but this remark nearly shook me off it again.

"What do you mean by that?" I almost screamed at the man, He turned a puzzled face up to mine, as he climbed into his place and took the reins.

"Oh, I don't know, sir," he answered, as we rattled off. "It's just a saying the folks have about here. It's some story about an old warlock Macbane that had the Tower long ago, I believe. Nothing to do with this one, sir—of course not. I got into the way of saying it from hearing it often, that's all."

I did not answer him, as we drove on between high banks of earth and rock, with now and then a tree nodding threateningly above us. I was faint and tired, and unable to think in a connected manner. The grim old proverb, like the Scriptural or quasi-Scriptural phrase, transformed itself into a dreary refrain, which rang in time to the beat of the horse-hoofs on the dry road: "*Killed* two *men* and the *third* was Mac*bane*— *killed* two men and the *third* was Mac*bane*" —it seemed a part of me, a pulse in my very brain, till it grew meaningless with incessant repetition.

We drove on westward, toiling up hills, rattling down them, always moving towards the storm, as the storm moved towards us.

Now and then I heard the muttering of thunder—now and then a livid gleam of lightning glanced across the face of the cloud, or a moaning gust of hot wind swept up the dust, and fell silent again. I took little note of the scenery on either side; and indeed I could see but little of it in the darkness. The lightning, growing brighter and nearer, occasionally revealed some bare cliff-face, some solemn black row of pines, some thread or sheet of water—I hardly saw anything. It was all a part of my dream still, and it seemed natural to me when a black grove of tall trees, and in the midst a denser black mass, with one or two lights twinkling in it, rose up before us, and the driver told me this was the De'il's Tower.

AS WE CAME UP to it, and I roused myself from my lethargy a little to observe my journey's end, I could see that part of the building seemed ruinous and broken down; the walls ended in a slope bristling with bushes. One grim-looking tower at the corner loomed high above us, apparently uninjured, and half-way up it shone a faint light.

I alighted, paid the driver, who seemed in a hurry to get away, rang, and when an old woman came to the door, asked if Macbane was at home. She said in reply that he was ill, and could see no one; but when I gave my name she conducted me through a long passage—part of it almost ruinous, part in better repair—to the foot of a winding stair. Here she told me to go up and knock at the first door I came to, and stood at the foot of the steps with her candle to light me up. When I reached the door—which was some way up—I could hear her hobble away, leaving me in darkness, only relieved by an occasional gleam of lightning through the narrow slits that let in light and air to the staircase.

I knocked gently, and a voice said "Come in." I felt along the iron-studded door till I found and turned the handle of the latch. As I entered I saw Macbane sitting back in an old chair with a shaded lamp on the table beside him, and some books and papers in its circle of light. The room was small and circular, and was, as I conjectured, half-way up the tower that had given its name to the building. A window, made visible from time to time by the lightning, opened on the outer air; and I noticed with a sort of dull wonder that there seemed to be a set of strong bars defending it—perhaps a relic of old times when the room was a prison; I cannot tell.

My friend did not rise from his chair to greet me. He motioned languidly to a seat near him, and for some minutes I sat and looked at him, and he stared at the door. I noticed a new and alarming change in him, since I had seen him last. Then, his look had been almost malevolent, instinct with a positive hatred for men; now all passion, all life, good or bad, seemed extinct in him. He looked worn and wasted; but it was the settled stony hopelessness of his face that struck me most: and the pity that I had felt for him in his old days of poverty now revived tenfold.

After a long pause, only broken by the muffled growls of the nearer thunder, he spoke.

"I hardly thought you would come," he said; "but now you are here, you had better read this. There is not much time to explain"—and he pointed to a yellow and torn old manuscript lying on the table.

I was perplexed by this—for why should I have been sent for in hot haste to read an ancient document of this sort? But I did not inquire or object. It all seemed part of the inexplicable dream in which I was moving. I took up the roll and began to look into it.

It was crabbed and quaint in writing and style, and it would only be perplexing to give its antique phraseology and obsolete Scotch law-terms and phrases, even if I remembered them. But the substance of it was plain. It was a record of the trial and condemnation of Alexander Macbane of Dullas Tower for witchcraft, early in the seventeenth century. After many preliminaries over which I passed hastily, the narrative came to the confession of the wizard. This was apparently volunteered, and not extorted by any torture; but such cases were by no means rare at that time, I think.

The peculiarity of this confession was that it was clear, consistent, rational even (if so wild a tale could be called rational), and did not involve any one besides the wizard himself. Actual torture was applied, it would seem, to make Alexander Macbane implicate an old crone tried at the same time, but in vain. "The devil," he had said, "was no fool; he had better servants than these poor women." These particulars, petty though they may be, struck my attention at the time; and I have never been able to forget them since.

Briefly put, the gist of Alexander Macbane's confession was as follows: He admitted that he had, by certain magic processes which he refused to reveal (because their very simplicity might lead others to use them), secured the services of a strange familiar. This Thing owned him as master and did his bidding, though only in one way —it could slay, and nothing more. He had killed by it two men, kinsmen of his, one his enemy and one his friend, who had in fact (a marginal note stated) died in a sudden and strange manner. But that which he had regarded as his servant (the confession went on to say) had become his master, and he a bondslave to its devilish power. It was jealous of all he did; it had cut off any beast for which he showed a fondness, and it had driven him to cast off all his friends, and to give up all friendly feeling for men. One man, whom he loved, he had bidden it slay, or else it would have slain himself. The Thing needed to have victims pointed out to it at certain intervals, or it turned on its master. Being asked how he knew the intentions of his familiar, the wizard answered that he could not tell how, but he divined its thoughts, even as, he felt sure, it read his. To the inquiry what form his demon assumed, he said that at first it was invisible to him as to others, but could be felt; and that gradually it took visible form as a beast black and catlike, with a great mouth.

The judges here asked the reason why Alexander Macbane had turned against his demon; the answer, given in quaint but still pathetic language, was that he had married a woman whom he loved, and had been happy with her for some months, and now he knew that he must choose between her and himself as a sacrifice to his familiar. In making his confession, he knew that he was devoting himself to death the same night; but he was resolved to do this. Better, he said, was it to die horribly thus, than to live alone with his sin and its punishment. "And so," the record concisely ended, "the said Alexander Macbane, being remanded to his prison, was there found dead the next day, with his throat rent through, and the bars of the window broken. Whereby it was thought that he had said the truth as to himself."

As I read the last words, I dropped the roll; for the lightning glared into my very face, and a moment after, a ringing crash of thunder burst over the building as if sky and earth were coming together. Then the roar leaped and rolled through the clouds, and died muttering far away; and through the rush of rain and wind I heard Macbane's voice.

"You understand now," he said, with that dreadful hollow sameness in his tone; "I am glad anyway that you will be left, and not I; I always liked you better than Standish. Perhaps it was a tiger after all that killed him, poor fellow. You are quite safe now; it is coming for me tonight. I thought it would have killed me last night, when I called it back—" a crash of thunder drowned his last words.

"Macbane!" I cried, finding my power of speech at last; "it shall not be! Whether it is real or a dream, I do not know; but you shall not die that way. I kept the Thing out; cannot you do it? Never give up hope. Cannot you save yourself?"

Macbane smiled hopelessly. "Listen," said he, and held up his hand; and in a pause of the rain I heard, low and distinct, *a scratching on the door.*

"Open it, Eliot," he said calmly. "It must come, and the sooner the better. Then go down and wait; for it will not be a pleasant thing to see."

I sprang to the door, but not to open it. With frenzied speed I locked and double-locked it, and drove the heavy bolts into their sockets. But no rush came against the door—no tearing or grinding of teeth. I could hear nothing—not even a breath; and the stillness was more terrifying than any sound.

"It is no use," said my friend; "you could

keep yourself safe; you cannot save me. It will have help tonight."

A gust of wind swept round the tower as he spoke; and mingling in its wail I seemed to hear—or was it but my fancy?—the long deadly howl of the Thing that I felt was so near us. For a few moments there was silence. Then, with a crash, the lightning fell close to the tower, and a great pine, shattered by the stroke, rushed down right against the window, and its top crashed into the room, rending away the iron bars like rotten sticks. The wind of the fall extinguished the lamp; but in the darkness and the roar of thunder I could *feel* something pass by me with a mighty leap: and next moment a fainter flash showed me a picture which was but for an instant, but in that instant was branded on my memory. Macbane stood upright with arms folded, gazing calmly forward and upward—and before him crouched, as if for a spring, a black mass with blood-red burning eyes—the same eyes that had glared on me the night before.

So much I saw; then, suddenly, the world was one blinding flame, one rending crash around me, and I fell stunned and senseless.

When I lived again, the dawn's grey glimmer was dimly lighting the tower; and outside the blackened and shattered window a bird was singing. As I opened my eyes, my glance fell on something lying in the center of the room; it was Macbane's body. I crawled to him and looked into the dead face. There was no wound or mark on him, and there even seemed a faint smile on his lips; and near his feet lay a little heap of grey ash.

"By One, by Two, and by Three" was first published, uncredited, in the December 1887 issue of Temble Bar. *When it was reprinted in the March 1913 issue of* The Strand Magazine, *the novellete was credited to "Stephen Hall," a pseudonym of British author Adrian Ross (1859–1933). Ross, whose legal name was Arthur Reed Ropes, published only three pieces of fantastic fiction, the short novel* The Hole of the Pit *(1914), the poem "The Pipes of Pan" (1889), and the story reprinted here— which was adapted for the small screen in 1972 as "There Aren't Any More Macbanes," a second-season episode of Rod Serling's* Night Gallery *(1970–1973).*

HEH HEH. THE EDITOR OF THIS GLOOMY GAZETTE WAS SPENDING TOO MUCH TIME SLOUCHING OVER THE KEYBOARD. HE WAS STARTING TO LOOK LIKE MY BROTHER-IN-LAW, THE HUNCHBACK OF NOTRE DAME. I FELT HE COULD BENEFIT FROM A FEW *STRETCHING* EXERCISES . . . ON THE RACK I KEEP IN THE . . . *er* . . . RECREATION ROOM! HE WAS SO THANKFUL! IN FACT, I CAN HEAR HIM NOW. WHAT'S THAT? HELP? BUT I'M NOT A MEMBER OF THE EDITORS' LEAGUE—I COULD BE TARGETED WITH A *UNION SUIT!* OH WELL, WHILE HE'S GOOFING OFF I'LL SHARE THIS *BRIEF* ITEM, A HAUNTING SHORT ABOUT SOME HAUNTED SHORTS. I THINK IT'S A TOP-*DRAWER(S)* TALE. HEH HEH! IT'S CALLED . . .

OUR FATHER'S UNDERWEAR

BY KURT NEWTON

WE WERE ALL SCARED OF OUR FATHER'S UNDERWEAR.
There were times when our father would come stomping up the stairs in the middle of the night, the light would come on and there he stood, like an Exorcist ready to shout down whatever demons were possessing us.

"How many times do I have to tell you kids to go to sleep? Whoever's running around, whoever's laughing, whoever's knocking things over—cut it out! If I have to come up here again, you'll all be in trouble! I have to work in the morning! *Now, go to bed!*"

It didn't matter what our father said, it was his underwear that instilled the greatest fear in us. It meant he was so mad at us for waking him up and that he didn't have time to put his pants on. The only time that ever happens is when there's a fire, so we took it pretty seriously.

Of course, none of us made a peep during the exorcism as our father stood beneath the one bare bulb at the top the stairs, looming in his t-shirt and boxers, ready to take action. There were four of us up there in that attic space—my two sisters, Lisa and Christine, on one side and me, and my brother, Jim, on the other. No doors. No privacy. Six people in a house made for three, four at most.

Satisfied with the silence, our father would then turn and stomp back down the stairs. The light would go off like an exclamation point. But, in the dark, and in our memory, the underwear would linger.

When our father died two weeks shy of my oldest sister's eighth grade graduation, it was a shock to all of us. There was an outpouring from the town of food and gifts. Our mom was now alone to raise four young children on her own.

Needless to say, us kids were pretty pissed and confused that we were now forced to grow up without a dad. Our mom tried to make up the difference but she just broke down now and then at the most embarrassing times. My brother and I acted out. My two sisters acted out. My sister, Lisa, took to sneaking our mom's cigarettes, using our dad's old lighter to light them up. There was a lot of fighting among us over the stupidest of things. And, one night, it just boiled over as we were all trying to get to sleep.

This time, the light didn't come on at the top of the stairs, but we heard that familiar thump thump of footsteps stomping up the stairs.

It wasn't our mom because mom took to drinking three to four glasses of wine a night before weaving her way into the bedroom, oblivious. No, this was something else.

Our petty grievances quieted as the thumps reached the top of the stairs.

It was a moonlit night and one could just make out the outline of things. The clothes dresser. The curtains hanging in front of the rafters. And there, above the stair landing, hovering like a ghostly parlor trick, was our father's underwear.

My breath caught. I couldn't move. The underwear turned this way and that. I was sure my brother and sisters saw it too, because all I heard was my heart beating in my chest.

Mission accomplished, the underwear descended the stairs with the same thump thump until we could hear it no more.

"Jim! *Jim!*" I called to my brother with only the slightest of a whisper.

"What?" he said, annoyed.

"Did you see it?"

"See what? Go to sleep."

I realized then that my brother's eyes had, in fact, been closed. He probably thought the thump thump was one of our sisters getting up to go to the bathroom.

I got out of bed and crept over to the landing. At that same moment, my sister, Lisa, appeared on the other side. We both screamed.

"What the hell are you doing? Spying on us again?"

"Did you see it?" I said, still whispering.

"See what?"

"At the top of the stairs!" My voice must have dropped below the audible range because Lisa said, "What? I can't hear you."

"Dad's underwear!" That time I said it loud enough for everyone to hear.

Lisa stared at me for a moment. "Just shut up and go back to sleep. And stop creeping, you little perv."

She stormed off downstairs, to go to the bathroom, I assumed. She didn't seem to care that our father was still alive—even if it was just his underwear come back to haunt us.

That's when I decided to trap dad's underwear and keep him around for good.

MY BROTHER AND I once tried to catch a rabbit out in the yard using a cardboard box propped up by a stick with a long string attached. We got the idea from a cartoon. All we caught was our cat, but our cat was dumb and, besides, cats like boxes.

The second kind of trap I thought about was a camouflaged hole in the ground. We saw it all the time in jungle movies. It worked great for wild animals running through the undergrowth, but would it work on a pair of disembodied underwear? I thought not.

Then I thought of another movie trick, one specifically designed to trap supernatural entities: the force field. If I could create an electrical field, I thought, I could trap the underwear and I'd have my dad back.

Now, at that age, I didn't know much about electricity. I once tried to power a light bulb using an electrical cord that had been stripped at one end. I had wrapped the bare wire around the base of the bulb and plugged the cord into the wall. What can I say? I was a curious kid. At the time it made sense to me. Needless to say, I blew every fuse in the house and was lucky I didn't electrocute myself.

So, learning from that experience, I devised a similar plan, only combining the rabbit trap idea with the light bulb idea. Instead of a box, I pictured a series of rings dropping down from the ceiling at the top of the stairs like a big slinky. At the same time, I could throw a switch to electrify the rings. Voila! Instant force field! All I had to do was figure out how to do it.

And then it dawned on me: hula hoops. They were the perfect size. Between my two sisters we had plenty scattered around the yard and in the garage. All I needed to do was wrap wire around each one like ribbon around a Christmas wreath, space them a foot or so apart and connect them together using the same wire.

So, one Saturday, while everyone else was out playing or shopping with Mom, I spent the entire afternoon upstairs in the attic making the underwear trap. There was a half roll of chicken wire in the garage and, after a lot of cutting with Mom's shears, I had enough wire to wrap each hula hoop and tie them together. I attached the topmost hoop to the ceiling using wire and nails and accordioned the hoops together with a couple Velcro strips. I tied strings to the ends of the Velcro so I could yank them free to let the hoops fall. I then took an old extension cord, one used to run outdoor lights at Christmas time, and cut the end off and stripped the rubber down far enough to expose enough wire to connect it to the trap. I had the other end of the extension cord next to my bed, ready to plug it into the wall outlet when the time came.

It could have worked. We could have had our Dad back for as long as we wanted. I say could have because the next time our father's underwear thumped up the stairs, my sister was waiting.

It was the first snowfall of the season that day and the ground was covered in white. By the time everyone went to bed, it was late. Nobody asked what the hula hoop contraption was at the top of the stairs. I don't think anyone even bothered to look. Lisa and Christine were in their room playing music and dancing. Jim was listening to his favorite 8-track, headphones jacked into the stereo system against the wall, the cord stretched out like a clothes hanger. He usually fell asleep within the first couple tracks and stayed asleep while the 8-track cycled and cycled, clicking every eight to ten minutes, all night long. Me? I just waited. I knew eventually the noise my sisters were making would cause our father's underwear to appear. I had the velcro-release string wrapped around my fist as if I were getting ready to fly a kite. I had the extension cord ready to plug in. I even had one of those fake plastic candles people put in their windows around Christmas time, plugged into the outlet by my bed so I could see what I was doing. It was all going as planned—the noise level in my sisters' room was as annoyingly loud as usual—until the music shut off and my sisters went to bed.

I couldn't risk another night to set the trap, so I got up and went over to my brother's stereo and started flicking switches. When the 8-track cut out, my brother's eyes flew open and he popped up like an undead from an open coffin. "What the hell are you doing?" he said, still in the

thrall of the music he was listening to.

"Nothing," I said.

"Turn it on!" he said.

"I don't know how," I said.

"Turn it on, you little punk, before I get up and pound you!"

"Would you guys keep it down? We're trying to sleep!" This came from Christine.

I waited a little while longer. My brother sat up (in preparation of getting up to pound me, I assumed) when there came that familiar thump thump on the stairs. Jim's eyes widened. I flicked the switch on his stereo and he slunk back down into bed and closed his eyes, while I hurried over to my bedside where the Christmas candle light was lit and ducked down.

A few more thump thumps and, finally, there it was. Our father's underwear, glowing in the dark, just like before. Although, unlike before, I was ready.

I pulled the string and the hula hoops dropped, just as I'd planned it. Then I plugged in the extension cord. And wouldn't you know—it worked. I'd trapped our father's underwear.

The underwear tried to run but each time it bumped up against the hula hoops, it got zapped. Silver sparks flew from the boxers like from a 4th of July sparkler. I walked up to the glowing apparition as if it were some kind of rare jellyfish at the Aquarium.

"Dad?" I said. "It's me, Conner."

The underwear stopped moving for a moment. It was weird. It was as if it had recognized my voice. That's when my sister, Lisa, appeared. She had a little yellow can of lighter fluid in her hand and, without a word, she aimed the can at the underwear and squeezed. The fine stream of flammable fluid arced between the hula hoops and when it landed on the underwear, the underwear caught fire immediately. The stream also shorted out my force field and blew every fuse in the house.

With the force field down, the underwear squeezed through the hula hoops, ran across the room and crashed through the attic window. By the time my sister and I got to the window, all we saw was a pair of flaming underwear running across the yard into the woods. The snow must have put out the flames because soon there was nothing but the moonlit night and the cold air blowing in our faces. Our father was gone.

"Why did you do that?" I said.

"So you'd stop."

"Stop what?" I said.

"Stop believing that things could be different."

I started to cry then. I didn't care if my sister saw. I didn't know why but there was something final about what had just happened. And a part of me began to wonder if it ever happened at all.

My sister actually held me for a moment. She didn't cry. She almost seemed relieved it was over. "I got a piece of cardboard in my room," she said. "I'll help you tape over the window. Mom's going to want to know how it broke."

"Me and Jim were playing with the basketball," I said. "Stupid kid stuff."

"Yeah. Stupid kid stuff."

I hugged my sister back. My sister and I were always close and the secret of that night brought us even closer.

As a child, Kurt Newton was weaned on episodes of The Twilight Zone *and* The Outer Limits, *and* Chiller Theater *(which showed many of the classic sci-fi horror movies of the '50s and '60s), laying the groundwork for his fertile imagination. His stories have appeared in numerous publications over the last twenty years, including* Weird Tales, Weirdbook, Space & Time, Dark Discoveries, Vastarien, Nightscript, Black Infinity *and* Cosmic Horror Monthly. *He lives in Connecticut.*

KOLCHAK: THE NIGHT STALKER   I WALKED WITH A ZOMBIE

NIGHTMARE ABBEY

BIG PREMIER ISSUE
RAMSEY CAMPBELL
13 QUESTIONS and THREE TERROR TALES

1

STEVE DUFFY ☠ GREGORY L. NORRIS   JASON J. McCUISTON
HELEN GRANT ☠ DAVID SURFACE   ALLEN KOSZOWSKI
JOSEPH PAYNE BRENNAN   LYNDA E. RUCKER
JUSTIN HUMPHREYS   DOUGLAS SMITH
HENRY KUTTNER   ROBERT BLOCH
KURT NEWTON   A. M. BURRAGE
JAMES DORR

WHEN THRILLS BECAME CHILLS: GROWING UP WITH *THRILLER*

By Gary Gerani

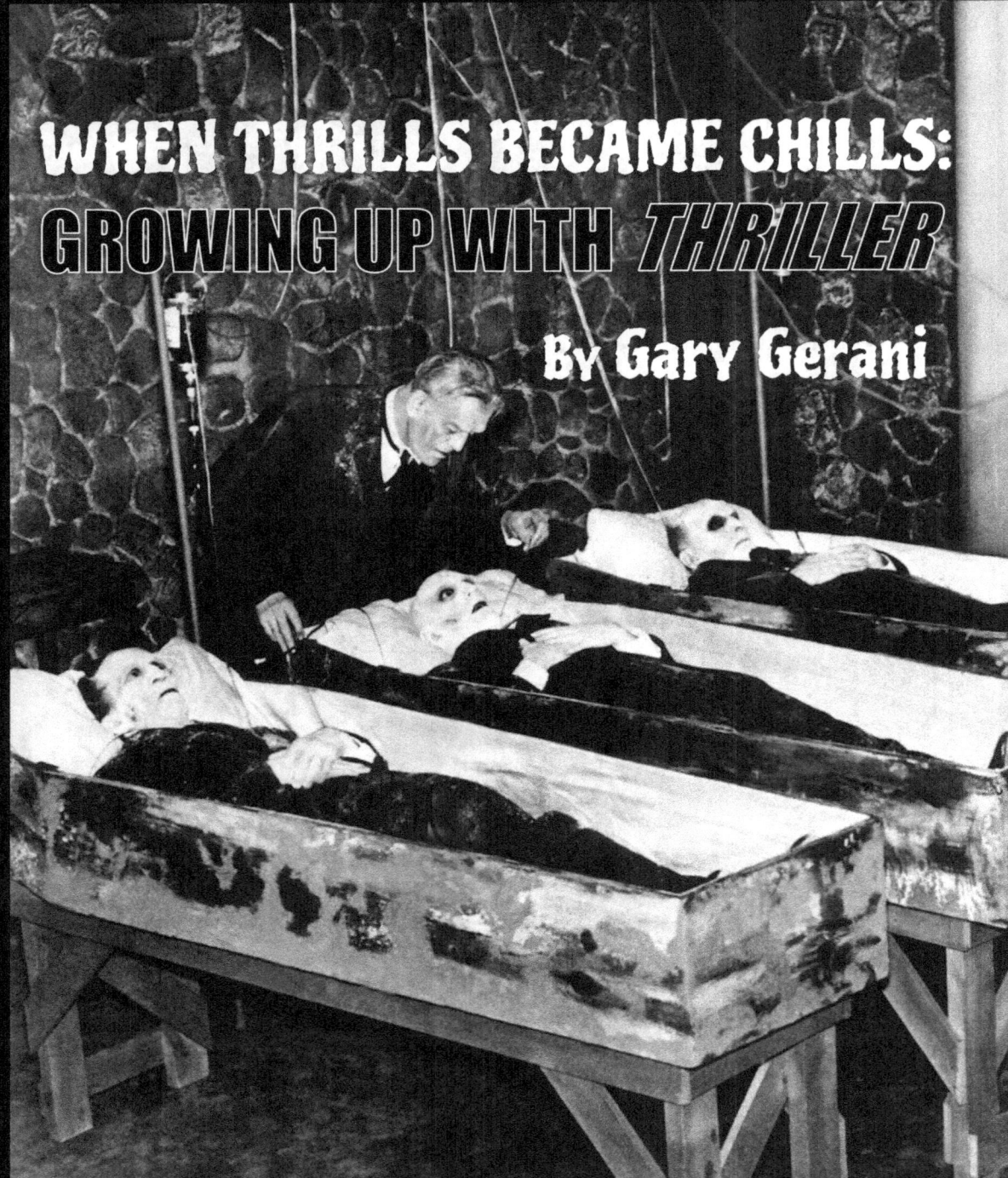

CHRONOLOGICALLY SANDWICHED BETWEEN TWO OF THE 60S' MOST CELEBRATED sci-fi/horror/fantasy anthologies, *The Twilight Zone* and *The Outer Limits*, *Thriller* (1960 – 1962) was Universal's noteworthy attempt to bring classic-style supernatural horror to the small screen. With none other than legendary icon Boris Karloff serving as host, and occasional leading man, the show spawned a number of significant episodes that remain darkly potent more than half a century later. An especially shuddery adaptation of Robert E. Howard's "Pigeons from Hell" is usually high on everyone's list of favorites, including Stephen King, who, in his genre overview *Danse Macabre*, deemed it one of the scariest hours ever presented on mainstream TV.

Sheriff Buckner (Crahan Denton) uncovers a startling secret in a decaying Southern mansion in "Pigeons from Hell." Previous page: Boris Karloff tends a trio of living-dead academics in "The Incredible Doktor Markeson." *Thriller* and all associated images copyright © NBC Television

Following page (clockwise from top left): Four scenes from "The Purple Room": the site of the titular accomodations, also used in Hitchcock's *Psycho*; Rip Torn, Richard Anderson, and Patricia Barry; Torn investigates "ghosts" with his .38 ... and encounters Anderson dressed in a Phantom of the Opera mask.

But *Thriller* gave us other creepy classics, as well: "The Cheaters," "Waxworks," "The Weird Tailor," "The Hungry Glass," "The Grim Reaper"... many of them either adapted by, or based on the short stories of, famed horror scribe Robert Bloch. His decidedly weird tales offered a special brand of occult spookiness that deftly combined ancient, often Euro-based folklore with modern American concerns, resulting in storylines that seemed vital and classical at the same time.

But that's not how things started. Created by Studio One's Hubbell Robinson, *Thriller* began life as a crime-oriented anthology, kind of a jazzier, more violent *Alfred Hitchcock Presents*. So the first batch of episodes offered no trips to the graveyard or demonic invocations, just a lot of twisted minds, criminal schemes, and reality-based murder scenarios. "It's more like Richard Widmark's *Thriller* than Boris Karloff's," quipped writer-producer Douglas Heyes, who was brought into *Thriller* during its first season when a switch from "mystery" to "horror" was initiated about a third of the way through. Heyes, veteran of some powerhouse *Twilight Zone* episodes, introduced ghosts and haunted mirrors into the universe of this curiously-evolving hour anthology, and it was newly-christened producer William Frye who found himself tasked with creating a robust spine-tingling nightmare each and every week. Pulp magazine *Weird Tales* became the torch that lit Frye's way into this dark, uncharted-for-television genre, while author Robert Bloch, famous for *Psycho*, his association with H.P. Lovecraft, and several amazing *Weird Tales* contributions, imbued the series with his own very specific brand of fantasy-terror. At the same time, traditional Hitchcock-like murder melodramas continued to be produced for the series (supervised by Maxwell Shane), far fewer in number, and these were mixed together with Frye's more exciting horror entries.

Not surprisingly, we Monster Kids eventually discovered *Thriller*, in my case purely by accident. Eight years old in 1961, I had already been experiencing Rod Serling's *Twilight Zone* for almost two years at this juncture, and, of course, couldn't get enough of this coolest of all TV series. Friday evenings actually began with *The Flintstones* on ABC and ended with *The Twilight Zone* on CBS; my parents permitted me to watch a 10 p.m. TV show because there was no school the following day. And, we should always remember, in the prehistoric 1960s, there was no such thing as DVR-ing a show for later playback. We had to be there, or wait for a rerun, if we were lucky. The compensation was, everything we experienced loomed larger and seemed far more magical, the influence and impact of these programs being strong enough to last a lifetime.

Which brings us back to *Thriller*. So there I was in '61, an eight year-old Brooklyn toddler regularly sent to bed at nine on weekdays, right after *Million Dollar Movie* (*King Kong, Godzilla, The Beast from 20,000 Fathoms, The Thing*, et al). But one Thursday

evening, from my bedroom, I could hear a lot of screaming and spooky music emanating from the television. Excited by what sounded like one heck of a spooky movie, I dared to leave my bed and venture forth, to the room with the flickering black-and-white image.

And there was a guy shooting at a misshapen monster, and my smiling mom, who raised a disapproving eyebrow, but allowed me to watch the *Thriller* episode anyway.

"Purple Room" was the Rip Torn meets the Phantom of the Opera episode, the first horror entry produced by William Frye after all those tepid crime episodes. James Cagney's *Man of a Thousand Faces* make-up was resurrected for a story that still wasn't quite supernatural (yet another murder scheme), but certainly flirted with the genre's flavors and iconography.

All well and good... but young Gary Gerani wasn't a hardcore *Thriller* fan quite yet. Besides, the show was on after my bedtime—being allowed to watch anything past nine during the week was deemed a parental favor, so I couldn't squander the privilege.

It was the one-two punch of "The Cheaters" and "The Hungry Glass" a week later that not only put *Thriller* on the Monster Kid map but inspired spirited talk among adults and my classmates at P.S. 186. "The Cheaters," of course, is one of the finest examples of Fantastic Television ever made, an uncanny adaptation of Robert Bloch's terror tale about a mysterious pair of spectacles that reveal the unholy truth about everything, and everybody. Every "body" was certainly an apt way of describing events once the specs are used to uncover murder and mayhem... and, ultimately, the nightmare that is one's very own soul.

"The Cheaters" was exciting even as the show was unfolding. My cousin from downstairs ran up to ask "Are you watching this? They're using the glasses to cheat at poker, now..." My entire household seemed captivated by the basic premise, its "know thyself" gimmick being so simple and relatable.

Significantly, *The Twilight Zone* would weigh in with a supernatural mind-reading tale of its own a few months later. That was a pre-*Bewitched* Dick York dealing with the

whimsical fantasy events of "A Penny for Your Thoughts." But the difference in type of story and tonal approach spoke volumes about how *Zone* and *Thriller* differed. Both shows could be scary, but all of us kids now realized that *Thriller* could and would go "all the way" with rotted corpse horror shock moments beyond our spookiest nightmares.

It was the climax of "The Cheaters" that set up these horror expectations. Failed writer Harry Townes, after investigating deaths caused by misusing the fantastic glasses, deduces that their truth purpose was not to read minds, but to look into one's very own soul, for profound, self-satisfied self-enlightenment. But when Townes looks into a mirror, he sees the most loathsome monster imaginable staring back at him. This weak and vain man dared to gaze into the heart of his own personal darkness, and we were all privy to the shocking results (courtesy of Jack Barron's stunning make-up, aided by Jerry Goldsmith's dread-drenched score).

Well. The entire neighborhood seemed to scream out loud at this moment of

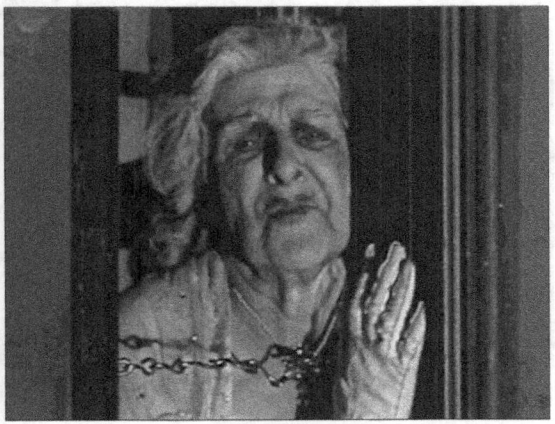

ectoplasmic manifestations making appearances throughout. Star William Shatner, in his years before *Star Trek*, was a familiar player in American horror-suspense TV anthologies, and would continue to be. (His unrestrained, blood-blanching scream, often called upon in these extreme scenarios, earned him a nickname in Hollywood casting circles as "the male Fay Wray.")

maximum horror... We could hear it from our apartment, and from downstairs, where my crazy cousin joined the frenzied chorus. Not letting up for a minute, *Thriller* followed this climax with a trailer for next week's show, "The Hungry Glass." A screaming woman being pulled into a haunted mirror (best shot in the episode, as it turned out) promised new, equally fresh and compelling fantastical pleasures. Suddenly, *Thriller* had become just as important to Yours Truly as my weekly visit with Rod Serling.

Douglas Heyes' "The Hungry Glass" was a ghost-themed episode, memorable in a low-key, moody way, with genuine

Unfortunately... and this is significant... the sometimes horror/sometimes murder-mystery juggling act of *Thriller* episodes broke the viewing pattern for us eager Monster Kids. So, as quickly as the series had come into our lives, it seemed to have vanished.

A black dog, an omen of death, visits Nesta (Audrey Dalton) in "Hay-Fork and Bill-Hook." Below: Resembling Lon Chaney's character from the lost 1927 film *London after Midnight*, Moloch (Henry Daniell) threatens Robert Penrose (Ronald Howard) in "Well of Doom." Page 101 (clockwise from left): Henry Daniell and Harry Townes in "The Cheaters"; and Ottolo Nesmith and Donna Douglas in "The Hungry Glass." Page 102: scenes from "The Hungry Glass" with (clockwise) Joanna Heyes, Elizabeth Allen, Russell Johnson, and William Shatner. All *Thriller* images copyright © NBC Television.

But not for long... Once additional horror shows started to show up, we began to notice the series again. And so, with parents keeping an eye on the family clock, and bedtime right around the corner, we kids peppered our real upcoming nightmares with a little help from William Frye, Boris Karloff, and some of the most terrifying concepts ever borrowed and adapted from *Weird Tales* magazine.

I remember hearing the evocative, richly-textured music scores of Jerry Goldsmith (years before I learned about the composer) underneath mist-shrouded episodes like "Hay-Fork and Bill-Hook" and "Well of Doom," installments I mainly experienced in audio-form, listening from my bed. But I was actually permitted to watch "The Ordeal of Dr. Cordell," which was something of a variation of 1945's Laird Cregar thriller *Hangover Square*. Pre-*Man from U.N.C.L.E.* Robert Vaughan, exposed to some weird lab concoction, becomes a batshit-crazy killer every time he hears a bell ringing. So, naturally, the protagonists agree to meet in a bell tower

at the climax of the story. Visualized through distorted lenses, Vaughan even murders a young Marlo Thomas, who was still sporting her original honker, before he's literally rung to death in the extremely loud (how could it be otherwise?) conclusion.

Next up was "Trio for Terror," and I was glad my parents let me watch this one along with them. Nothing quite matches the level

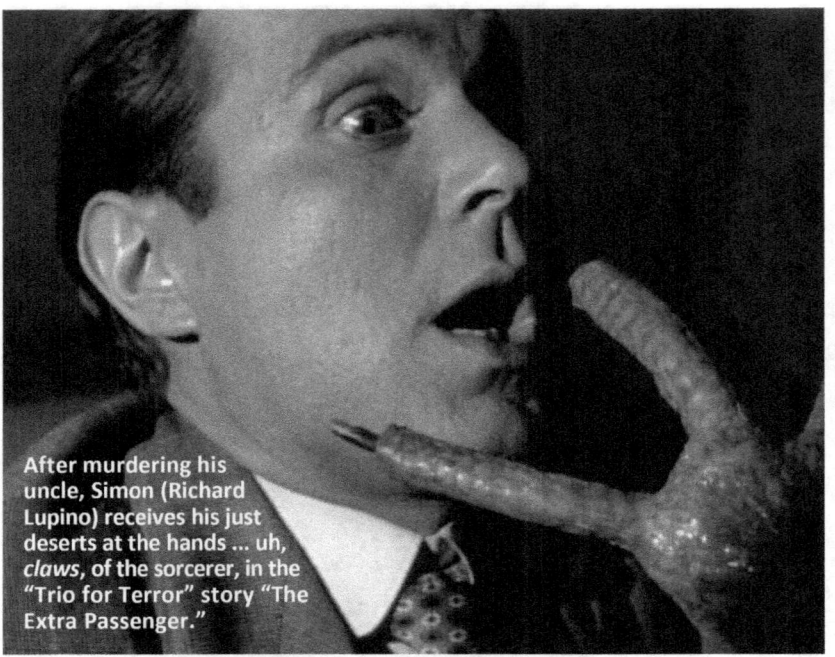

After murdering his uncle, Simon (Richard Lupino) receives his just deserts at the hands ... uh, *claws*, of the sorcerer, in the "Trio for Terror" story "The Extra Passenger."

murderous severed hands walking around were talked about endlessly in my neighborhood grade school.

Thriller's Season One drew to a horror-filled finish with two of its finest offerings ever, both golden-era television classics. No less a guru than Stephen King has christened "Pigeons from Hell," derived from a very short Robert E. Howard tale, as the second scariest network TV episode ever produced. King's Number One, for the record, was "I Kiss Your Shadow" from 1962's *Bus Stop*, also directed by "Pigeons" helmer John Newland. Incidentally, Newland's famous *One Step Beyond* series, yet another classic TV anthology from this robust era, was on at ten o'clock right after *Thriller* on Thursday nights, although on a different network (ABC).

of Lovecraftian horror achieved in the first of the three tales. After murdering a dabbler in the black arts, the killer is confronted by the dead man himself in the empty car of a night train. As the entire Gerani family watched breathlessly, a human hand became a non-human, bird-like claw, clutching at the throat of the now-mesmerized murderer. While the remaining two stories had their pleasures, it's this one moment of paralyzing terror that stuck with me, and seemed to define *Thriller* at its most uniquely disturbing.

Around the time "Mr. George" came around, I had gotten into the habit of watching the series religiously every week.... It had indeed become a second *Twilight Zone*, one with Boris Karloff-style classical horror as its main selling point. This reached another high point with "The Terror in Teakwood," an unforgettable variation of *The Beast with Five Fingers*[3] set in the world of concert pianists. Starring sophisticated Euro-types like Guy Rolfe and Hazel Court, and with the remarkable presence of ultra-weird character actor Reggie Nalder (later to shine in TV's *Salem's Lot*), "Teakwood" was another major fright fest. A few final shots of those

With a sinister but often sympathetic score by Morton Stevens, "Pigeons from Hell" plays like an extended fever-dream, ultra-gloomy and self-contained. It sets up an already unnerving situation—two tired

Guy Rolfe and Reggie Nalder in "The Terror in Teakwood."

---

[3] Director Robert Florey's 1946 film, with a screenplay by Curt (*The Wolfman*) Siodmak adapted from the short story by William Fryer Harvey. Florey also directed the *Thriller* episode "The Incredible Doktor Markesan."

young brothers spending the night in what they think is an abandoned Southern mansion—and then adds shock-horror into the proceedings, suddenly making the unreal real. What exists in the upper regions of this decaying old place is nothing less than an aged female zombie, or "zvembie," and her weapon-in-hand appearance at the end of the tale rivals Mother's at the climax of *Psycho*. This was extremely strong stuff for 1961 television audiences, darkly photographed by Oscar and Emmy Award-winning Lionel Lindon, one of the veteran masters of the painting-with-light craft at Universal. Pleased to have a project he could sink his creative teeth into, Lindon lit every shot of "Pigeons" for maximum creepiness.

Just as strong, maybe even more traumatic, was the season's final episode, "The Grim Reaper." Anticipating Rod Serling's *Night Gallery* by a decade, the show's title "character" was a grotesque painting of the infamous hooded figure of death, skull head glowering, a bloody scythe clenched in his bony hand. Once again it's male Fay Wray Bill Shatner as the episode's protagonist, chewing up the scenery as only he can. A conniving relative and willful murderer, Shatner becomes the painting's final victim in a heart-stopping climax worth recalling. First, the illustrated Reaper vanishes from its portrait, apparently taking human form somewhere in the room. Next, a brilliant "monster POV" shot is employed —the audience becomes this steadily advancing specter, zeroing in on a cringing, horror-struck Shatner, just before the Reaper's scythe sweeps across the frame. So frightening was

Above: Two brothers seek shelter in a decaying mansion that harbors dark secrets in "Pigeons from Hell."

Following a bloody encounter with one of the mansion's horrors, Johnny tries to kill his brother Tim (Brandon De Wilde).

Sheriff Buckner (Crahan Denton) learns about "zvembies" from Jacob Blount (Ken Renard) in "Pigeons from Hell."

Scared Shat-less: "The Grim Reaper," with William Shatner.

rare parody involving vampires that had *Night Gallery*'s Jack Laird written all over it.

I did manage to see a few of these 10 o'clock episodes on their original runs (mom was getting easier to break down when it came to my bedtime curfew; besides, she loved this kind of spooky stuff herself). "The Return of Andrew Bentley" and "La Strega" weren't only good horror tales, they offered genuine monsters to gawk at. The former gave us Jeanette Nolan as a creepy-looking witch —the first of many she'd play on the small screen (*Twilight Zone*'s "Jess-Belle," *Night Gallery*'s "When Aunt Ada Came to Stay"). And "Bentley" took things to the next occult level, summoning up a humanoid demon-thing known as the Familiar, a rather ambitious, one-time make-up creation at Universal. This full-fledged monster with a whale-like head was portrayed by Tom Hennesy, who had played the Creature from the Black Lagoon with admirable aggressiveness in *Revenge of the Creature*. Hennesy even wore the hand appliances created for *The Creature Walks Among Us* as part of his Familiar costume, since they were sufficiently Lovecraftian to begin with.

this conclusion that many original TV observers remain convinced that they actual saw the physically-formed Grim Reaper on screen.

SEASON TWO of *Thriller* found the series in a new, 10 p.m time slot, which meant most of us younger fans were hitting the pillow just as Karloff and company were doing their thing. "What Beckoning Ghost?" got this new slate of episodes off to a supernatural start, with "The Premature Burial," "God Grant That She Lye Still," and Robert Bloch's amazing "The Weird Tailor" soon achieving memorable moments of sanity-challenging terror. It would take reruns in syndication before I'd be able to catch up with these, and that was also true of "Masquerade," a

Of course, there was one episode of second-season *Thriller* that we kids in the neighborhood simply had to stay up for. Enthralled by lurid photos printed in *Famous Monsters* magazine, we all gathered in front of our respective TVs to experience

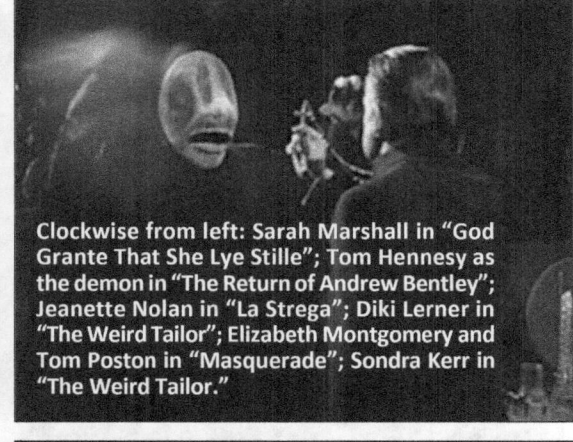

Clockwise from left: Sarah Marshall in "God Grante That She Lye Stille"; Tom Hennesy as the demon in "The Return of Andrew Bentley"; Jeanette Nolan in "La Strega"; Diki Lerner in "The Weird Tailor"; Elizabeth Montgomery and Tom Poston in "Masquerade"; Sondra Kerr in "The Weird Tailor."

"The Incredible Doktor Markesan," probably *Thriller*'s most horror-centric episode and a veritable field day for Boris Karloff in the title role. The spookiest of old houses, a misty graveyard, a hidden mad lab, and an entire roomful of shambling zombies completed this cobwebby nightmare scenario. Adapted from an August Derleth story by Donald S. Sanford, *Thriller*'s most prolific writer, it managed some welcome moments of dark poetry along with the mist-shrouded mayhem. "If I'm mad," proclaims self-resuscitated corpse Doktor Konrad Markesan, "then eternity must be madness. For I am Eternity!"

Interestingly, the next eight episodes that followed this high-watermark show were all mystery and suspense tales, not atmospheric chillers. *Thriller* never quite shook its split personality as an anthology series, still doggedly mixing conventional murder tales and blackmail suspensers with

being revamped as a supernatural-themed experience. Just as ironically, Hitchcock's episodes began to get a bit larger-than-life themselves the last couple of seasons ("The Jar," "Where the Woodbine Twineth," "The Monkey's Paw," "The Sign of Satan," etc.). The Master of Suspense even tried to launch a new horror series with continuing characters in 1964: *Black Cloak*, aka *The Uninvited*, starred Leslie Nielsen as a turn-of-the-century demon slayer. Nixed by all three networks, this well-made pilot saw life as the theatrical feature *Dark Intruder* instead.

As for *Thriller*, it went into syndication almost immediately. I caught up with many of the episodes I had missed by tuning in NY's Channel 11 during the mid-'60s. After a couple of years, however, the program was pretty much retired. Television had gone all-color by 1966, and hour black-and-white series were increasingly difficult to market (unless your show was called *Perry Mason*, of course).

It wasn't until 1973 that a serious syndication revival was suddenly underway. The show was now called *Boris Karloff Presents*

stories about ghosts, witches, and demons. The show was finally cancelled at the end of the 1961/'62 season. Many believe a jealous Alfred Hitchcock used his clout at Universal and NBC to get the series canned, with Hitch feeling *Thriller* infringed on his specific TV franchise. Ironically, it was the original "crime/suspense" conception of *Thriller* that more closely resembled the two venerable Hitchcock series (*Presents* and *Hour*). We may actually have Mr. H to thank for *Thriller*

Thriller (it was still plain old *Thriller* on screen), and a new generation of fans was poised to get the benefit of these fondly remembered TV chillers. Brand new 16mm prints were struck, with *Thriller*'s hollow-eyed, ubiquitous death's head iconography once again freaking the hell out of mass audiences ... most of whom were lining up to see *The Exorcist* at this stage of the game. But vintage black-and-white

Would you care for another bottle of plasma, my dear?

Carolyn Kearney and Boris Karloff in "The Incredible Doktor Markeson."

Previous page: Karloff and his living dead colleagues seem eager to welcome Molly (Kearney) to the party.

Copyright © NBC Television

horror still has its charms, and strengths. And there was always the invaluable presence of Boris Karloff, Mr. Horror himself, as series host and occasional star.

Today, Universal's two-season anthology stands as a television landmark, an inconsistent but often remarkable exercise in gothic horror. The show really excelled in just about all creative areas. Beyond King Karloff, wonderful actors like Henry Daniell and the aforementioned Reggie Nalder showed up time and again. As part of that first season shake-up, Pete Rugulo's perfectly okay jazzy scores were replaced by more scintillating works from composers Goldsmith and Stevens, both accomplished

pros in this particular genre. It wasn't surprising that character make-up and creative photography were always first-rate, considering that Universal was the Hollywood movie studio best known for its legendary fright flicks. Graphics for the series also struck a chord, with intrusive, animated "sticks" or lines ganging up on the frame whenever a commercial was being ushered in. *Thriller* clearly had its own distinctive identity, visually and editorially, in spite of that odd combination of both mystery and fantasy storylines.

Some of those storylines were set for

new incarnations twenty years later. A S2 episode, "Guillotine," was actually remade in color by Universal TV as an episode of ABC's *Darkroom* in 1982, hosted by James Coburn. "The Cheaters" and "Pigeons from Hell" were also being prepped for new versions… but, alas, the low-rated *Darkroom* was cancelled after only eight weeks. When my *Pumpkinhead* writing partner Mark Carducci and I were doggedly attempting to produce a new TV anthology in the 1990s based on *Weird Tales*, we learned that *Thriller*'s original producer/creator Hubbell Robinson still maintained the legal rights to the WT stories he had filmed.

Nowadays, *Thriller* can be found on cable channels, indie stations, and in Image's Rondo Award-winning DVD box set, issued close to twenty years ago. It's still available on Amazon and eBay, and I'm very proud to have co-produced the well-received special features that adorn it. They include rare "next week" trailers and a plethora of expert commentaries. Somewhere, Robert Bloch and William Frye are smiling.

Speaking of these talented gentlemen, here's a curious tidbit: both were hired by Universal to develop a follow-up TV movie and possible series based on *Fear No Evil* (1969), an excellent two-hour pilot that cast Louis Jourdan as a psychiatrist tangling with supernatural forces. Since *Fear* offered up a haunted mirror, and the overall ambience of the film was very *Thriller*-esque, Frye and Block seemed like the logical creative team to move this project forward.

Inexplicably, neither of these veteran spooky experts was able to come up with additional fantasy ideas for Evil II. I mean, c'mon, guys, how difficult could it have been? The haunted mirror concept came from *Dead of Night* to begin with, so what about a ventriloquist's dummy with demonic tendencies? The concept for *Fear*'s follow-up pilot, *Ritual of Evil*—a modern, jet-set witch using photography to snare victims—was ultimately provided by producer David Levinson. *Ritual*, by the way, won a well-deserved Emmy for its evocative cinematography, which proved that Lionel Lindon's atmospheric work could be just as effective in striking Technicolor.

So that's *Thriller*, folks. One of the Fantastic Television essentials from that golden '60s period, and a well-made anthology for any era. Looking back, I'm happy to have experienced much of it when it was first broadcast on prime-time NBC, and was quite pleased to work on the extra-filled video release from Image so many years later. Although Serling's *Night Gallery* kinda picked up the NBC/Universal horror anthology ball in the 1970s, nothing really equaled what Mr. Frye and company scared us silly with years earlier, in glorious black-and-white.

As sure as my name is Gary Gerani, *Thriller*… was a winner.

💀 💀 💀

Gary Gerani is a film/TV historian, fiction and nonfiction writer, and filmmaker. His groundbreaking 1977 book, Fantastic Television, *is considered required reading, being the first scholarly study of sci-fi, horror, and fantasy on the same screen. Other tomes include the* Top 100 Movie *series, trade paperbacks published by Gerani's own company, Fantastic Press, in association with IDW. Current/upcoming book projects include* The Art of Joe Smith *in 2020 and* The Card King Chronicles *in 2022. Gerani is also a graphic novelist (*Bram Stoker's Death Ship, Dinosaurs Attack!*), veteran product developer at Topps, award-winning art director, photo editor, designer and publisher (Abrams has published reprints of his classic card sets in hardcover book-form, with Gerani's creative involvement), screenwriter (*Pumpkinhead, Trading Paint*), producer (*Convention, special features for video releases), commentator (countless movies and TV shows), and feature-length documentarian (*Romantic Mysticism: The Music of Billy Goldenberg, *which Gerani wrote, produced and directed, was released on Blu-ray by Kino in 2022). Mr. G continues to write articles about movies and TV productions for magazines and other Internet venues.*

When guests come calling at the Abbey, we greet them with fiendish delight!
So please, let us ... er ... "entertain" you with our next big volume of ghoulish fun!

DEAD HANDS CLAPPING

by Matt Cowan

"LIVE FROM THE MAJESTIC CHRYSALIS THEATER IN LOS ANGELES, CALIFORNIA, the ICB radio network proudly brings you a fun-filled evening of live entertainment and glamour from Hollywood's biggest stars! Welcome to *The Chrysalis Variety Hour!*

"Everyone please stand and give a warm welcome to your host, everyone's favorite jabber-jaw Lionel Brunel!"

(Applause from the audience)

"Thank you, folks. Thank you so very much. I'm excited to be here once again in this incredibly beautiful theater accompanied by so many of my closest, personal friends... What's that? Who am I referring to? Well, all you lovely people seated before me, of course..."

(Laughter)

"...not to mention the millions of fans who are kind enough to join us in front of their radios every Thursday evening. Yes sir, I consider each and every one of you a close, personal friend. Just don't ask to borrow any money."

(More laughter)

"Anyway, we have a really great show tonight ... a really great show. Do you want to know who we've got?"

(A chorus of applause)

"Ha ha, I thought as much! Tonight we'll talk with famous Hollywood actor Jerry Malwyrth about his new film *The Jive Bomber*. Then talented songstress and actress Hettie Demantis will join us to chat about her new hit song "Turnabout Is Fair Play." Last but not least, the hit off-broadway acting troupe The Carcosa Mummers will make their radio debut as they perform a piece from their rendition of the world renown play Bluebeard. Jeepers! I don't know about you, but that's enough to get my knickers in a bunch! Anyway, don't touch that dial because we'll be back immediately following a few words from our sponsor, Carmichael's Liver Pills!"

"Enough to convince you it's the real deal?" asked the mustachioed man behind the counter as he clicked off the archaic looking reel-to-reel player. He'd introduced himself as Athangelos, proprietor of Athangelos Audio and Visual Archive. Barriston was surprised the man bothered with a brick-and-mortar store, the oil-smelling cluttered hovel that it was. Surely he could reap the same income from online sales without all the overhead.

Barriston rubbed his chin, as he processed what he'd heard. After so much time searching and so many disappointments, had he finally found it? "Could be," he said, "but if it's genuine, how'd you come by it?"

Athangelos' long, weathered face stretched into a wide grin. "It's what I do. Some people track down criminals, some scour libraries in search of lost books. I rescue audio rarities from the forgotten tides of time."

Barriston frowned. "Look, I know a thing or two about these 'rarities' as you call them, and a recording of the final episode of *The Chrysalis Variety Hour* recorded the very night of the tragedy … well, that's rarer than hens' teeth. I need to know how you, here in Indianapolis of all places, happen to have one before we start talking price."

Taking a moment to smooth his thick, black mustache, Athangelos cleared his throat. "The guy who sold it to me said it had been recovered from the premises of the late Dexter Glimp."

"Glimp? Wasn't his body discovered in his apartment three days ago? Murdered, as I heard it. Was he even cold yet when your source "recovered" the tape?"

Sweat beaded on Athangelos' brow. "Didn't ask. None of my business. None of yours either. You want to buy it or not? Makes no difference to me. I've more than enough other interested parties to sell it to if it would spare you your conscience."

* * *

GUSTING WIND SPATTERED against Barriston's face, causing him to pull his hood tighter as he darted across the busy downtown street across from Athangelos' shop. The negotiations hadn't taken long before a mutually beneficial price had been agreed upon. He must have done an adequate job disguising how desperately he wanted the recording. Athangelos, on the other hand, had been less

successful hiding his nervousness regarding the possibility of questions being raised over its attainment. Still, it hadn't come cheap and would likely take a solid year of belt-tightening before his bank account recovered from the purchase, but he hadn't hesitated when presented the opportunity. Barriston upped the volume of his SUV's radio to blaring, letting the thumping chords of Great White's "Desert Moon" thrum its way through his body as he negotiated the winding, rain-soaked interstate toward home.

* * *

"So I understand you had an unsettling situation during filming. Care to fill us in, Jerry?"

"Certainly, Lionel. It all came about when I spotted the upper story of this rundown old Victorian peeking out above a mass of overgrown hedges on my ride to the set everyday. I was really intrigued by it, for whatever reason. So one day when there was a break from shooting, I decided to check it out. I hired a cab to take me and told the driver to stop back by in an hour to pick me up. His English wasn't too good, but I was able to make out he was trying to talk me out of it … until I offered him enough money to allay his concerns, that is."

(Audience Laughter)

"Anyway, I was forced to hack my way through the thickest underbrush you can imagine to reach the place. Luckily, I'd had the foresight to bring along a machete or I'd never have made it."

"I have to tell you, Jerry, I'm half-expecting to hear Boris Karloff met you at the front door!"

(More Laughs)

"No, the place was in such a terrible state of repair there was no question it had been abandoned long ago. The front door had swelled into its frame so badly I couldn't force it no matter how hard I tried. I ended up having to fight my way through thistle weeds and chest-high grass to find another entrance around back. That one I was able to get open."

"Did you ever consider maybe it might not be worth the effort, Jerry?"

(Laughter from the audience)

"You know, that very thought hit me immediately upon stepping through the back door, Lionel!"

(Nervous laughter)

"Well, don't keep us in suspense! What'd you find?"

"It opened into this long dining hall covered in broken glass and pottery shards. The air smelled stale and laden with mildew, with a thick layer of dust covering everything, which wasn't unexpected, of course. A couple things certainly did unsettle me, though—the chairs, for instance."

"I'm sorry to be the one to break this to you, but it's not that uncommon to find chairs in a dining room. Why, I even have some in my own, as a matter of fact!"

(More laughter)

"Yes, but every single one of these, about twenty or so, had been pulled out from around the table and set facing directly at the back door I'd just walked through. I've performed on stages before thousands of people before, but never in my life have I felt more observed than right then in that empty, old house. It sent a chill down my spine, I have to tell you."

(Murmuring from the audience)

"Alright, that's kind of creepy. What was the other thing that set your nerves a jitter?"

"That would be the footprints in the dust headed toward the big bannistered stairs leading up to the higher floors. Keep in mind, I'd just spent ten minutes cutting my way through years of overgrowth just to get inside. These footprints looked fresh, like they'd been made days, hours, maybe even minutes before I arrived."

"I take it you hightailed it out of there at that point, right?"

"No, call me foolish if you like, but I was curious. I felt I had to find out about those prints or the mystery of the whole thing would drive me mad."

"Honestly, the fact you worked so hard to get into that place already marked you as mad, so you had nothing to lose."

(Murmured laughter)

"Either way, I climbed up a set of rickety old stairs which twisted past two lower landings to a narrow hallway with several closed doors at the topmost level of the house. I decided to try the one at the end where the footprints led. I know it sounds crazy, but I knocked on the door and ... well, I heard something on the other side that sounded as if someone, or something, had darted swiftly across the room. Then it sounded like someone cried out briefly before going silent again."

"And that's when you fled the house, never to return?"

"Ha ha, no, but I did consider it for a moment before opening the door and entering."

"Jerry, it's an absolute wonder you've lived this long with that sort of decision making!"

(Laughter)

"Alright, tell us what you found inside the room of this death house?"

"I opened the door to see a man wearing a bizarre-looking hat standing directly before me with this shocked look on his face."

(A collective gasp from audience)

"This guy was exceptionally handsome. He actually reminded me a lot of myself ... because that's exactly who it was—myself, reflected in a dingy vanity mirror. What I'd initially taken for a hat was actually just a large black raven that had perched atop the mirror on the opposite wall."

(Heavy laughter)

"So there was no one else there?"

"Not a soul, but that bird was plenty, let me tell you. It took to the air, so I decided to ignore it and look around the rest of the room. I found an old book lying on this little end table, and when I reached to pick it up, that raven landed atop a nearby bookcase and let out the loudest screech imaginable. I nearly leapt out of my skin. Then it flew out the door. Anyway, I didn't find anything else in the house, so I left and had my cab take me back."

"What about the footprints? Did you figure out who made those?"

"No, that one remains a mystery, I fear."

"Did you end up taking anything back with you from the house?"

"Two things, the book on the bed, which turned out to be an 1807 publication of *Macbeth*, and an unwanted pet."

"An unwanted pet? How's that exactly?"

"Every day since then, I've seen that big raven. It's like he's attached himself to me. How he followed me all the way across the country I have no idea, but boil me in oil if I didn't see him perched over the entrance to this very theater when I walked in tonight, squawking at me the whole while."

* * *

BARRISTON STOPPED THE recording after the segment ended. It had shifted to discussions of Jerry Malwyrth's new film and his family life for another ten minutes before commercial breaks for Brylcreem and spark plugs took over. As excited as he was to listen to it in its entirety, work had patched through an emergency call out to repair a broken water pipe under a nearby house. He didn't want to go, but the overtime would help recoup some of the cash he'd just dropped on the recording. Listening to the rest would have to wait.

* * *

THE JOB HAD BEEN a tough one, keeping him out late into the evening. By the time he got home he headed straight to bed. Thoughts of Malwyrth's discoveries inside the creepy house tussled with his body's intense desire for sleep. Knowing the fate that awaited the actor along with everyone else inside the Chrysalis Theater on that evening lended the story added meaning. There had been warning signs. If anyone could have recognized them, perhaps things would have turned out differently for them and ultimately for himself.

* * *

BARRISTON HAD SPENT the majority of his life believing the couple who raised him were his birth parents, but upon reaching his late fifties he learned otherwise. He was at his adoptive father's funeral, having already lost his foster mother to cancer four years previous. At the reception following the service, a man he called his Uncle George approached him, the perpetually kind look in his eyes tinged with sympathy and something else, revelation. He placed a hand on Barriston's shoulder to pull him in close.

"There's something I need to tell you—something your father never wanted you to know while he was alive, but it's something you need to know."

What followed was the untold story of his life. His birth father's name was Grady Hollister, an on-the-rise actor at the time of his death inside the Chrysalis Theater disaster of 1955. Boasting a broad six-foot-six frame with a thick, lantern jaw and a head full of curly red hair, he was poised to become the next big star. He had appeared in three films before his death, each role larger than the previous one. There was far less information available regarding his mother. He knew her name was Caroline, and he'd managed to unearth a grainy orange-tinted picture of her sitting beside Grady in the front row of The Chrysalis Theater, both of them smiling and clapping their hands. Uncle George was prevented from expanding with further details due to his own death from a heart attack two days later. Barriston spent the next eight years since the revelation searching for everything he could find about them, but other than repeatedly watching all his father's existing movies and listening to a handful of radio interviews he'd done, he hadn't learned much. He wasn't sure what he hoped to learn from the recording of the show where his parents had died in attendance, but even the realization that the applause issuing forth from it included those produced by their hands made him feel some connection to them he'd never had before.

* * *

"So Hettie, what's this I hear about you having a twin sister?"

"Ha! Well, I don't have a twin sister, per se, but I did recently discover I have an identical twin of sorts."

"So, you have an identical twin to which you aren't related in any way. How does that work?"

(Laughter)

"Well Lionel, I don't know that I can really explain the how of it, so I'll just relate what happened and let you be the judge. I made this rather startling discovery while recording for "Turnabout Is Fair Play"—my new hit album which you should all rush out and buy tomorrow morning."

(Laughter)

"I tell you Lionel, it's the strangest thing I've ever encountered in my life. It all came about when my flight from California to the recording studio in New York was delayed a day due to inclement weather. When I finally did show up for the recording session, my producer Wallace greeted me with the biggest—very unexpected hug—and let me tell you, Wallace has never been a hugger. Then he said to me, 'You look worlds better! We were ever so worried about you after last night's session.'"

"But, you hadn't even boarded the plane at that point!" Lionel interjected.

"Right, and that's exactly what I told him. I should say repeatedly told him, but he didn't believe me no matter how many times I tried!"

"Why on Earth didn't he believe you?"

"Because, no less than three people there swore they saw and talked with me during that time—those being the building's doorman, an audio technician, and Wallace. Each of them said I came in around 6:30 that evening, which was later than we usually start a session, but they claim I insisted on recording a tract right then and there."

"Wait, you're saying this other 'you' made a recording?"

"That's exactly what I'm saying. I've even heard it."

"And, to think just moments ago I thought Jerry's story was the craziest thing I'd ever heard! So, this 'double' looked and sounded exactly like you?"

"Well, not exactly like me. They all said she looked like me only she was much thinner and paler than me, and she had very deep, dark circles around her eyes as though she had been sick for some while. As to her voice, I brought along a copy of it which I gave to your producers to play if you'd like to hear for yourself."

"That sounds fantastic! What do you say audience, do you want hear this song Hettie's long lost, previously unknown twin recorded in her stead!?!"

(Heavy applause)

"All right, Producer Clifford, play that recording!"

(A hum and crackling followed by somber piano and violin music)

(A husky-voiced woman begins to sing)

A fair warning Delilah chose not to heed

From the Temple of Dagon she refused to leave

Safe amidst the crowd, or so greatly she believed

She soon felt full impact of blind Sampson's final heave.

* * *

BARRISTON STOPPED THE TAPE. The singer's voice did sound remarkably similar to Hettie's, only deeper and sharper. The amalgamation of menace and amusement this "double" conveyed gave the song such an unnerving quality. He was surprised the studio of the day had agreed to air it. Barriston had heard Hettie sing during his quest to track down his father's appearances. She had been the female lead in a musical cowboy film where his father was cast as the villain's henchman, a role he'd managed to make memorable despite having no lines of dialogue.

During the remainder of the segment, Lionel put voice to Barriston's decades-later assessment that although it sounded like Hettie's voice, it had too unnatural a quality to have actually been her. They soon moved to talking about her new album, from which she sang the title song as they went into a commercial break about Colgate Shampoo.

Only one unheard segment of the program remained before the show would be brought to its premature, tragic finale. He paused the recording again. He didn't know how much of the incident and its aftermath would have been picked up, but he knew he was about to be listening to the last few moments of his parents' lives. He took a moment to steel himself, then reached forth to press play again.

* * *

"And we're back, folks! You've made it to the end of this great, if decidedly odd, show tonight. I want to thank Jerry Malwyrth and Hettie Demantis for joining us and offering up such wonderfully bizarre stories to keep us all entertained. I just hope we're able to sleep tonight after hearing them."

(Laughter)

"As for myself, I think they've managed to convince me to never set foot outside this theater again!"

(Heavy Laughter)

"What do you say folks, are you ready for our final performance of the night?"

(Applause)

"Courtesy of the off-broadway acting troupe—way off broadway in this case—I present to you The Carcosa Mummers performing "In the Pale Moonlight" from the play *Bluebeard*. Isn't that the one about the guy who murders his wives? *Ay Caramba*, are we certain this isn't a Halloween episode?"

(Laughter before music begins to play)

(A loud snap)

(A quick snippet—the beginnings of an explosion—then static)

* * *

IT WAS OVER. Barriston hadn't realized how tensed he'd been during that entire last section until it ended. He was drained, both physically and emotionally. Grabbing a bottle of sangria, he collapsed into his recliner and flicked on the television. He needed the background noise to keep him from feeling so alone. It was well after 1 a.m. and he didn't feel like scouring his streaming services for something worthwhile, so he settled on a random network that replayed old television programs. In a haze, he watched a couple episodes of the '50s-era *Adventures of Superman* show staring George Reeves. After awhile, with his consciousness ebbing away, the bottle dropped empty from his hand. The screen wavered before him, playing disjointed images of hamburger-toting clowns and mischievous elfin creatures harassing pizza delivery men.

* * *

Barriston found himself hovering in a void of darkness. Reaching out a hand and taking a step forward, he felt nothing. The "Hello," he called out echoed back to him, awakening a ruckus of murmurs and shuffling. Finally, the blackness eased enough he could make out his surroundings.

He was on the stage of the Chrysalis Theater standing beside Lionel Brunel before a sea of well-dressed men and women populating the audience. Everything, including himself, was devoid of color, painted only in shades of black and white.

"So tell us what brings you from so far in the future to be here with us today?" Lionel asked, his deeply set eyes hidden amidst pools of shadow.

Barriston surveyed the audience until he spied the happily smiling couple in the front row, his birth parents both alive.

Pulling his eyes away from them, Barriston struggled to clear his clouded mind. "I don't understand why I'm here?" he mumbled absently.

Lionel's smile stretched even wider, the studio lights further deepening the darkness clouding his eyes. "Well, to tell us about the future, of course. What sort of exciting lives do we have in store for us? Will Jerry become the next Jimmy Stewart? Hettie the next Grace Kelly? Will I star alongside the likes of Bing Crosby or Audrey Hepburn?"

Barriston averted his gaze from Lionel's intense, eyeless stare without answering.

"Don't keep us suspense. You can at least tell us what sort of bright future your loving parents have ahead of them! Does your dad become the next big Western film star?"

Looking at the couple in the front row smiling up at him, the couple he'd never actually known but for whom he felt such a strong connection so many years after their deaths, he couldn't bring himself to tell them the truth. "Yes," he mumbled instead. "You all go on to great success."

There was no applause this time, just complete silence. Looking back at Lionel, he saw his unnatural smile had vanished, replaced by an angry sneer. "Liar," he sputtered, then rose from his seat to tower over Barriston.

(Chants of "Liar" reverberate
throughout the theater)

As the chanting continued Barriston looked out at his parents. They sat expressionless, no longer smiling as they joined in repeating the chorus of the audience. Unable to take it anymore, Barriston stood up, pushed his chair aside and raced toward the back of the stage, seeking an exit.

"Don't worry, Barriston! You'll be joining us soon enough!" Lionel yelled after him as the sounds from the audience reached a crescendo.

(Deafening Applause)
* * *

THE SCREAM OF HIS cell phone snatched Barriston from the nightmare. It took a few moments to orient his thoughts enough to dispel the hellish pseudo-reality of his dream. Apparently, he'd successfully made his way into bed last night but hadn't removed his work clothes. A glance at his phone proved an unexpected surprise when it displayed Athangelos Audio Visual Archive on the screen. After attempting to clear his groggy throat, he answered the call.
* * *

THIRTY MINUTES LATER, Barriston was adjusting his van's visor against the blinding morning sun rising from the horizon. The conversation had been brief. Athangelos said he'd acquired an ultra-rare reel of an unfinished film called Dynamite Canyon, a low budget western which was to have been Grady Hollister's first leading role before his death in the Chrysalis Theater explosion led to its cancellation. Athangelos suspected how desperately Barriston would want it and would price it accordingly, but he would find a way to pay no matter how deep a financial hole it dropped him into. Thinking about what awaited caused Barriston to further depress the van's accelerator. Reflected in his rearview mirror, a large, black bird kept pace with him as he drove.
* * *

THERE WAS ONLY ONE other vehicle in the store's parking lot when Barriston pulled up. Immediately upon exiting the van, a huge black shape launched itself at his head, screeching full into Barriston's face before sweeping up to perch atop an arch overhanging the shop's entrance. A hulking raven tilted its head sideways to fix one bulbous eye upon him. After taking a moment to recover, Barriston entered through the front door.

A drone of static crackled from the shop's overhead speaker system. The spot behind the cluttered front counter, normally occupied by Athangelos, sat empty.

"Hello?" Barriston called out toward the rows of metal shelving.

Silence, then the garbled fragment of a transmission broke through static which was emanating from the speakers overhead.

(...around back...)

Despite the heavy interference, the voice sounded familiar—Jerry Malwyrth.

Moving slowly forward, Barriston concentrated on listening for any hint of movement but could make out nothing over the ever-present, incoherent murmurings from the comm system. As he passed between the tightly packed shelving units of film and audio canisters, a voice from the speakers again became momentarily audible.

(...The air smelled...)

It was still Malwyrth, and seemed to be from the very episode he'd been so invested in of late. Athangelos must have made a copy of the recording. He couldn't blame him considering its rarity. That particular fragment of the recording did cause something to register with him however—a foreign smell piggybacking upon the shop's normally stale air, like rotten eggs, or... Barriston halted his advance—a gas leak! He instantly turned to flee the shop and alert the authorities. An ignited gas leak had been ruled the cause of the Chrysalis Theater explosion so many years ago, and as much as Barriston longed to explore every aspect of his parent's lives, he had no interest in sharing their fate.

(...heard something...)

Something shifted from the back of the building followed by a groan. Someone else was inside the shop.

"Athangelos?" Barriston called.

The groan repeated, causing Barriston to turn back around and run toward it.

(...it's an absolute wonder you've lived this long with that sort of decision making...)

Ignoring Lionel Brunel's decades old quip from above, Barriston made his way through the opened back-office door. Inside, stacks of metal canisters dominated much of the floor space leaving just a narrow path to a grimy desk under a wall of monitors surveilling every aisle of the store. Athangelos lay slumped over a toppled mass of reels on the floor.

Barriston knelt down to pull him up, trying to rouse him all the while.

Athangelos gazed at Barriston through glassy eyes.

"We have to get you out of here!" Barriston yelled as he struggled to lift Athangelos, who was not light, from the floor. It wasn't easy, but adrenaline allowed him to get the man semi-upright and propped under one shoulder for support.

Attempting to leverage Athangelos out of the building proved a slow and exhausting process forcing him to further inhale the poisonous air with each step of their excruciating journey.

(...Did you ever consider maybe it might not be worth the effort...)

As Lionel Brunel's weirdly prescient interlude played from the staticky recording, Barriston pulled out his phone with his free hand and dialed 911, blurted out the address, and warned them of the leak.

* * *

"THANK YOU FOR helping me," Athangelos murmured as Barriston helped him from the building and across the street to prop him up on a bench. "When this is over, you can have that film you wanted, no charge."

"The film!" The sudden recollection of why he'd gone there in the first place hit him like a ton of bricks. "Where is it?"

Athangelos, his consciousness wavering, didn't answer. Barriston shook him by the lapels. "Where's the film!?!"

"My office ... where you found me..." Athangelos muttered, then slumped over into unconsciousness.

With sirens blaring through the early morning air, Barriston took off across the street, back into the store.

Making his way to the back office, he began rummaging through the scattered film canisters. Casting aside reel upon reel, Barriston could feel his head begin to swim.

At last he spied the one he sought, *Dynamite Canyon*. Snatching it up with a cry of triumph, Barriston turned to leave when the speaker chirped to life again, blaring Lionel Brunel's voice much louder and clearer this time.

(...Are you ready for our final performance of the night?!...)

The sudden, unexpected burst of volume startled Barriston to a momentary halt, slowing him enough to notice the figure wavering on one of the surveillance monitors. Standing at the forefront of the store, Barriston saw himself—a dark-eyed, sickly-looking copy of himself smiling crookedly at the camera—at him. Unable to pull his gaze away, he watched his double raise his hands up and begin to clap, slowly at first, then faster with each successive one. Every time the doppelgänger's hands met, its smile grew wider, impossibly so, until its mouth stretched to absurd proportions.

All around him Barriston heard a sudden roar of applause arise to join in unison with his malformed twin on the monitor. The sound of thousands of furiously clapping hands reverberated off the shop's walls to form a deafening cacophony. Barriston dropped to his knees, holding his hands over his ears. Suddenly, it came to an abrupt halt. The resulting silence lessened by an incessant ringing in his ears. Looking up, Barriston saw his black-eyed double still standing at the forefront of the store on the flickering monitor, its contorted, face-splitting smile displayed a mouth overfilled with gleaming white teeth. Struggling to his feet, the overhead speakers crackled to life again. No words this time. All he heard was...

(A loud snap)

(A quick snippet—the beginnings of an explosion...)

Matt Cowan's love for the horror genre stretches back beyond his earliest childhood memories. At a young age he stopped having nightmares once he began enjoying them too much. Since their departure, he's been forced to craft nightmares of his own devising on the printed page. He's had short stories published in various horror, science fiction, and crime anthologies over the years, including regular entries in the Deathlehem *series of Christmas-themed horror stories. A few of his stories have been featured on podcasts, including* Pod of Horror *and* Tales To Terrify. *In addition to his fiction, Matt penned numerous installments of his popular movie review column* Matt Cowan's Threat Watch *for* Black Infinity Magazine.

Being a voracious fan of short horror fiction, Matt frequently writes about classic and modern tales of terror—and their authors—for Nightmare Abbey *in his regular column* Horror Delve, *as well as for his eponymous blog (which served as the inspiration for his magazine column)* HorrorDelve.com

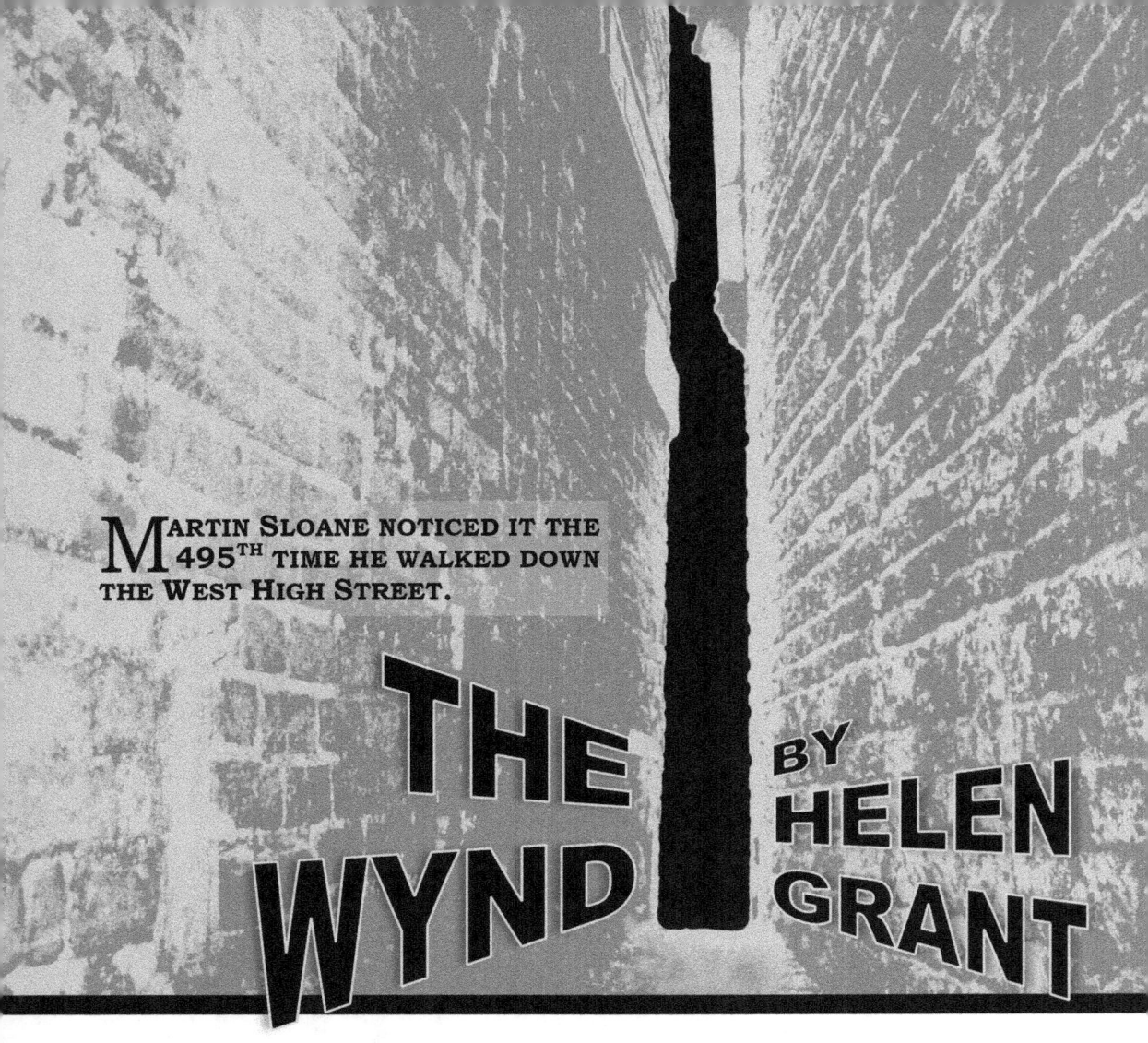

MARTIN SLOANE NOTICED IT THE 495TH TIME HE WALKED DOWN THE WEST HIGH STREET.

THE WYND
BY HELEN GRANT

He was dressed inconspicuously, a lit cigarette in his hand, and the lingering taste of bad coffee and indignation in his mouth.

You win some, you lose some, he said to himself without conviction. In spite of his intention to forget the whole thing, to write it off as a bad lot, fragments of the previous day's debacle would keep coming back to him. Mainly he remembered Hetty's father, a solid, patrician-looking man upholstered in a dark pinstripe, saying *Your name isn't even Martin Sloane; I've checked. You must be mad if you thought I wouldn't, considering what Hetty is worth.* And Hetty not looking at him. She'd sat there in the peach silk dress that had cost a ridiculous amount of money and suited her so badly, her hands twisting nervously in her lap. She had looked at her father, out of the window, down at

the table—anywhere but at Martin. That was when he had known it was all up. He had made a half-hearted attempt to say that Hetty's wealth was an irrelevance, that he adored her for herself, but that had been mostly face-saving. Shortly afterwards, he had risen from the table making a great display of dudgeon, and stalked out of the restaurant, being sure to leave Hetty's father with the bill.

It was very hard not to feel aggrieved. He had invested a considerable amount of time in the whole affair, not to mention the cost of flowers and chocolate—and the ring, which was set with cubic zirconia rather than diamonds as he had claimed, but which had still required a decent outlay. And after all, Hetty—who was pale and somehow rather watery—would have had Martin's good looks and charm in return, at least for a while, and some useful life experience to boot. But now here he was, walking down the West High Street with a bitter little pucker at the corner of his mouth and twenty pounds to his name.

It was perhaps the need to find a new project to fill the gap precipitously left by Hetty that made him more receptive than usual to his surroundings. He had walked down this street a great many times before, after all, but generally he had been preoccupied with this and that; today he was scanning the scene as if literally looking for the main chance.

What snagged his gaze first was a glowing seam between two very tall buildings, one a nondescript grey apartment building, the other a grimy set of disused offices, also grey—the sort of places the eye normally slid past from lack of interest. The strip of light was so bright that for a moment his brain interpreted it as neon, and Martin felt a brief spark of surprise at the incongruity of it. Then it faded and he realized that what he had seen was a narrow gap between the buildings, brilliantly illuminated by a serendipitous shaft of sunshine. Without it, the gap was barely noticeable.

Martin shot a swift glance over his shoulder—the habitual action of those who wish to avoid observation—and then he wandered nonchalantly over to take a closer look. It was a curious sort of gap: not wide enough to be considered a thoroughfare, but not so narrow that you couldn't go down it at all, though you might have to turn sideways. It was unclear why the builders had bothered to leave a gap at all, since it was so awkward to traverse, and an inviting repository for rubbish.

He'd have lost interest then, except he glanced up and saw that there was a street name sign high up on the left-hand wall, very much faded and worn, so that the words were barely legible. The first one he couldn't make out at all, although the final letter might have been a K. The second one was WYND.

In addition to a lately-acquired name, Martin had a plummy southern English accent which was very different from the

one he had grown up with. As a child he had often run through city alleys marked *wynd* or *vennel*, not infrequently clutching someone else's property in his grubby hands. He didn't recall ever seeing such passages described as wynds since he moved south.

Well; none of this was going to restore his failing fortunes. He thought he'd better get on—go to the barber, perhaps, and refresh his style a little; after that he might haunt an upmarket coffee shop or wine bar for a while and scope the place out for a replacement for Hetty. He stepped forward, and then all of a sudden he had a view right down the wynd, to the end.

It was light down there—clearly the wynd opened out into a courtyard or perhaps another street—and he could see a vertical strip of building. That it was a church was obvious from the pointed window arches and the profusion of carved detailing on the façade; no house or office block ever looked like that. The sun came out again and suddenly it blazed gold in a myriad of places where the carving was adorned with gold leaf.

Martin froze, looking. He did not consciously say to himself: *there are valuables here, ripe for the picking.* It was a very long time since he had pilfered lead from a church roof, or portable items from inside; he had grander ambitions these days. But he felt the siren song of ill-guarded opulence, and given that he had nothing else in particular to do, the decision to *just go and have a look* was swiftly made.

When he tried to enter the wynd he discovered that it really did require him to turn sideways on. The span of his shoulders would not fit into its width. If he had been any stouter he might not have managed it that way either; as it was, his chest was almost touching the grimy stone wall.

Good thing I'm not claustrophobic, he said to himself as he inched his way down the wynd, persuading himself as much as anything, to keep the tiny prickles of alarm at bay. The air was faintly damp in here, and mineral smelling, and sound was magnified, so that the shuffling of his shoes on the ground and even his own breathing were loud in his ears.

Halfway down it occurred to him that there must be another way to the church; it couldn't possibly *only* be accessed through this unnervingly narrow space. But he was committed now. He went on, feeling as though he should be extruded from the end like toothpaste from the tube.

At last he approached the end of the wynd, and the magnificence of the church's façade opened out in front of him, the gilding gleaming in the shafts of sunlight. It was very tall, its Gothic pinnacles at least as high as the tops of the surrounding buildings, and very highly ornate, textured all over with finely chiseled figures and motifs. Martin was not an expert in church architecture, his interest in such places being entirely commercial, but even to his untrained eye it looked very old.

He looked about him, and found that he was in a very small court with stone flags underfoot. The church took up one side of it, and the other three sides, with the exception of the slit through which he had passed, were made up of high blank walls. There were no windows, no doors, no fire escapes or ladders—simply dark grey stone walls, as though all the surrounding buildings had turned their backs. All the sides were so high that if the sun had not been directly overhead, the entire court would have been sunk in shadow. Most probably that was why he had never noticed the wynd before; he had never passed at exactly the right time.

The church had a heavy oak door with black iron strap hinges, and that was curious because it implied that people would go in and out the way Martin had, through the wynd, which seemed very inconvenient. Presumably access had been freer when the church was constructed, and it had been built around later. He supposed there was another door, one leading out into the street on the other side.

Martin looked back down the wynd. At the far end, beyond the close-set walls, he could see the street he had left: light, modern, reassuringly dull. Nobody was passing. He turned his back and went over to the church door, putting out his hand for the handle.

To his surprise, it wasn't locked; it opened easily. Martin stepped inside, feeling a subtle change in the air temperature; out in the court it was cool, even a little damp, but inside the church it was dry and rather warm. He was assailed by a lot of different impressions: not only the warmth, but the sound of his feet on the stone floor, and the aromas of furniture polish, dust and incense. Light tinted many different colors dappled the flagstones and the heavy oak pews. There were, he saw, stained glass windows set into each of the walls, which was unexpected; he'd thought the sides directly adjoined other buildings, but no, the church must be surrounded by open space. He didn't recall seeing a church on the scale of this one in this area. Even if you weren't interested in ecclesiastical buildings, you could hardly miss one this size, but seemingly he had.

Disappointingly, there was nothing that was moveable. There were plenty of exquisite little carvings of fruit and flowers, animals and figures, but all of them were integral to the heavy oak pews, the pulpit and the lectern. There were brasses on the floor, mere shapes of people, so worn that he could not make out any recognizable feature, but they were flush to the flagstones, and he soon abandoned his half-hearted attempts to prise one of them up. Then he looked around for chalices, crucifixes and candlesticks, but there were none, save a large cross suspended over the altar, which was too big to be of interest, and out of reach anyway.

He had now, rather unwillingly, examined almost everything in the church. The entire enterprise was depressing. There was nothing he could surreptitiously remove, and it simply reminded him of what might have been: himself and Hetty, standing before the altar, she simpering as he pledged undying fealty to her and more importantly, her money. He thought about that money with something akin to lust, but he knew that it was useless. Hetty's father had seen to that.

Martin decided to leave. He was wasting time here. There might be some plump widow with a huge annuity nursing a mojito all on her own in the chic little bar around the corner. *Onwards and upwards*, he thought. He cast a last eye around, and it was then that he noticed the stained glass windows. He'd been aware of them before, of course, but he hadn't really *looked* at them, because they did not offer any kind of opportunity to such a one as himself; they couldn't be carried away and sold.

All but one of the windows—he thought there were about twelve—were of the most higgledy-piggledy appearance. Martin seemed to recall that glass from windows which had been smashed, for historical reasons quite obscure to him, was sometimes reinserted in fragmentary fashion. Why anyone would do this was equally obscure; the effect was chaotic. Here he saw a hand pointing, there a fold of drapery, and below that a section of pattern he couldn't identify at all. It was impossible to guess what that window— or any of the others—had originally repre- sented. It had people—or a person—in it, that was pretty clear, but you couldn't tell what they had been doing, or even if it was a man or a woman. The light positively *glowed* through the glass, warm and peachy, and he supposed the glazing must have some kind of tint to it. It made a glittering mosaic, an incomprehensible beauty, of all the tiny fragments.

All the windows were like that—but one. Naturally Martin's eye was drawn to it, and to the figure which dominated it. It was a curious image for a religious setting: not a crucifixion or ascension, nor a nativity, but a man seemingly climbing out of a window, bent under the weight of a sack he carried on his shoulders.

A thief, thought Martin.

It was wonderfully well done. The archi- tectural detailing of the window and the wall that framed it suggested affluence: there were little crenellations running across the top, and fluted pilasters to either side. The figure wore a flowing green tunic and yellow hose, and there was an evil-looking short sword attached at his waist. His hands sup- ported the bulging bag on his shoulders, and his face was turned to the viewer.

Martin felt an unpleasant thrill of recog- nition. The face was remarkably like his own. He'd been meaning to go, but now he couldn't help himself; he went over to take a closer look. The resemblance was striking, although the painted face in the glass was somehow tainted with dishonesty; it was handsome, framed with thick fair hair, but it was a false, gloating face, the eyes sharp and furtive. He prided himself on the fact that whatever faults he had, they were walled up within a pleasing exterior, and he did not like to see them displayed like this. The likeness must have been coincidental, but Martin felt an irrational flash of anger, as though the artist had purposely carica- tured him. The more he stared at it, the more the features seemed to leer down at him.

He stepped back, still staring angrily at the window, and then he saw there were words underneath the figure—a motto or quotation of some kind, written in spiky Gothic script. With a little effort he read: *Ye shall not steal, neither deal falsely, neither lie one to another*; and after it, *Leviticus 19:11*.

So the figure was indeed a thief, and now Martin saw that he was also a deceiver; behind him, framed in the corner of the window, was a woman in a scarlet kirtle, her long hair loose and her face turned aside in shame.

Martin thought of Hetty, quite involun- tarily—generally he felt no guilt at all, since the world was a hard place and a man had to live. Now he felt obscurely that he was being attacked, and that made him first angry again and then defensive. Women weren't *ruined* any more these days; Hetty had had her fun too, he'd seen to that, and it wasn't as though he'd ruined her prospects, or anything so Victorian. The window was a piece of outdated and quite frankly offensive morality. If he'd thrown a brick through it he'd have done the world a favor.

He turned his back at last and went over to the heavy oak door, thinking of the street outside and the chic little bar around the corner, once he had negotiated the gloomy length of the wynd. So concentrated was he on this pleasing idea, that it took him a moment to react to the fact that the door wouldn't open. He pushed the iron handle down, and nothing happened. Then he leant a brawny shoulder against the oak and shoved. The door didn't move—there was not so much as a tremor. Martin leant on the handle, hard, pressing it down, thinking that perhaps he simply hadn't depressed it far enough. Then he pulled back and *thumped* it with his shoulder. It still didn't give.

Was it possible that someone had come and locked it from the outside without his hearing them? It seemed unlikely. Martin stooped and examined the door but he couldn't actually see a lock at all. There was just the ineffectual handle. After giving the door a couple of stout kicks he gave up and went to look for the other door out.

There wasn't one.

He made a complete tour of the church, following the walls, going into every corner and feeling with his hands where the shadows were too deep to see properly. After five minutes of fruitless searching he concluded that there *was* no second door. There was the one which led out to the wynd, and no other.

Martin stood in the middle of the nave and put a hand to his head, considering. It seemed incredible that the only entrance and exit to such a grandiose building should be through that narrow wynd. There *must* be a second door. He must simply have missed it; it might be somehow superficially concealed. He went around the church again, and this time he never let his fingertips leave the wall, thinking to find a rim or crack or a change in texture. Still nothing. There was solid stone all the way round, except for the oak door he had come in by. He gave a small incredulous laugh. Then he tried the door again. It was immoveable.

Martin sat down on an oak pew with a grinning horned face carved into the end, and took out his phone. Whom could he call? The list of saved contacts was lamentably short.

Hetty? he wondered, and immediately dismissed the idea. He might have prevailed on her alone to come and rescue him, whatever his sins, but he was pretty sure her father wouldn't countenance it. If he heard that Martin was trapped inside a church with nothing to amuse himself with except a stained glass window representing dishonesty, he'd probably think it served him right. It would have to be the police, then. No doubt they'd be annoyed, but he'd blame it on whoever owned the church.

He entered the number. Nothing. No signal.

Martin thought about the toweringly high walls surrounding the entrance to the church. Was it possible there was no reception because of those? It seemed unlikely.

I'm in the middle of a bloody city, he said to himself. The stirrings of anger that he had felt at the image of the thief were slowly inching him to the limits of his control. It was warm in here, warm and dry. If he was stuck here for any length of time, his tongue would soon be hanging out. He remembered the restaurant, and Hetty's father in his expensive suit glaring at him. The carafe of mineral water on the table, crystal clear, glittering in the sunshine. In his memory, everything seemed plump and moist, bursting with water: the little pats of butter in a dish, the fat blossoms on the table.

"God damn it," said Martin aloud.

He got up again and paced about. He loosened his collar. It was too warm. Hot, even. He couldn't get out. The thief in the stained glass window smirked down at him with his own features. His face. It was an insult. Martin ground his teeth. He couldn't get out. He couldn't—

At last the anger boiled over. There was nothing moveable in the church, that was true, but he had his phone in his hand. With a howl of fury he flung it at the stained glass window as hard as he could, thinking to punch a hole in the middle of it.

With a crash like a wave breaking, the entire window erupted, bursting into thousands of tiny, bright, razor-sharp shards that arced through the air with deadly force, like a swarm of shrieking insects. Glittering fragments blasted into Martin, *through* Martin, with the force of a hurricane. He didn't even have time to scream before he was engulfed in a perfect blizzard of flying glass. Mere seconds later, the last pieces pattered down onto the flagstones around him, with a series of tiny pops and cracks. Then there was a very long silence.

THE DAY SLID PAST, the shadows lengthened and deepened. Inside the church, nothing moved. Nobody came to investigate the sounds, the signs of damage. The oak door stood closed. Outside, the little courtyard became a black pit that smelled vaguely of damp stone. The wynd itself, entirely unlit, became imperceptible. Its walls were so close that they seemed to press together; a person might have walked past it a hundred times and never noticed it.

Hetty *did* walk past it, the next day. She was tear-stained, clutching a balled-up handkerchief in her left hand, but resolute. If she could find Martin, whom she imagined in a bar, gazing miserably into a large Scotch, she meant to defy her father and give him another chance. She said to herself that she was over thirty; it was up to her what she did with herself and her money. The wynd did not even penetrate her consciousness; she walked past it as if it weren't there at all.

Beyond the wynd, the church stood silent and self-contained in the slender shaft of sunlight that descended to the little court. The oak door was still closed. Within, if there had been anyone to smell it, there was a faint aroma of furniture polish, incense and dust. In front of the rows of heavy pews with their ornate carvings the stone flagstones lay cool and clear and clean. A warm gentle light gleamed through the twelve stained glass windows.

They were curious, those stained glass windows. Not a single one of them depicted anything you might have recognized. All of them seemed to be composed of the broken pieces of some now untraceable scene, re-inserted into the window frames in random fashion.

One of them had lately depicted a thief climbing out of a window, a sack slung over his shoulders, although nothing of that design was now discernible. An observer could only have guessed at the original content of the picture from details that could be made out on the fragments. Here, for example, was a triangular shard of yellow hair, rippling realistically. Here was a single eye, rolling as in terror, with the white showing all around the iris. Here, fingers closed around what might have looked to an untrained eye remarkably like a modern mobile phone. And here, weirdly disembodied amongst a cluster of unidentifiable shapes and textures, an open mouth, screaming desperately, silently, and forever.

Helen Grant writes Gothic novels and short supernatural fiction. Her latest novel Too Near the Dead *(Fledgling Press, 2021) was listed among the Guardian's best recent fantasy, horror and science fiction in August 2021.*

Helen's short stories have appeared in Weird Tales, Supernatural Tales, All Hallows and anthologies including Egaeus Press's acclaimed Crooked Houses, *Swan River Press's* Uncertainties 2 *and Black Shuck Books'* Ars Gratia Sanguis *(Great British Horror 6). Joyce Carol Oates has described her as "a brilliant chronicler of the uncanny as only those who dwell in places of dripping, graylit beauty can be." A lifelong fan of M.R. James, she has spoken at two M.R. James conferences.*

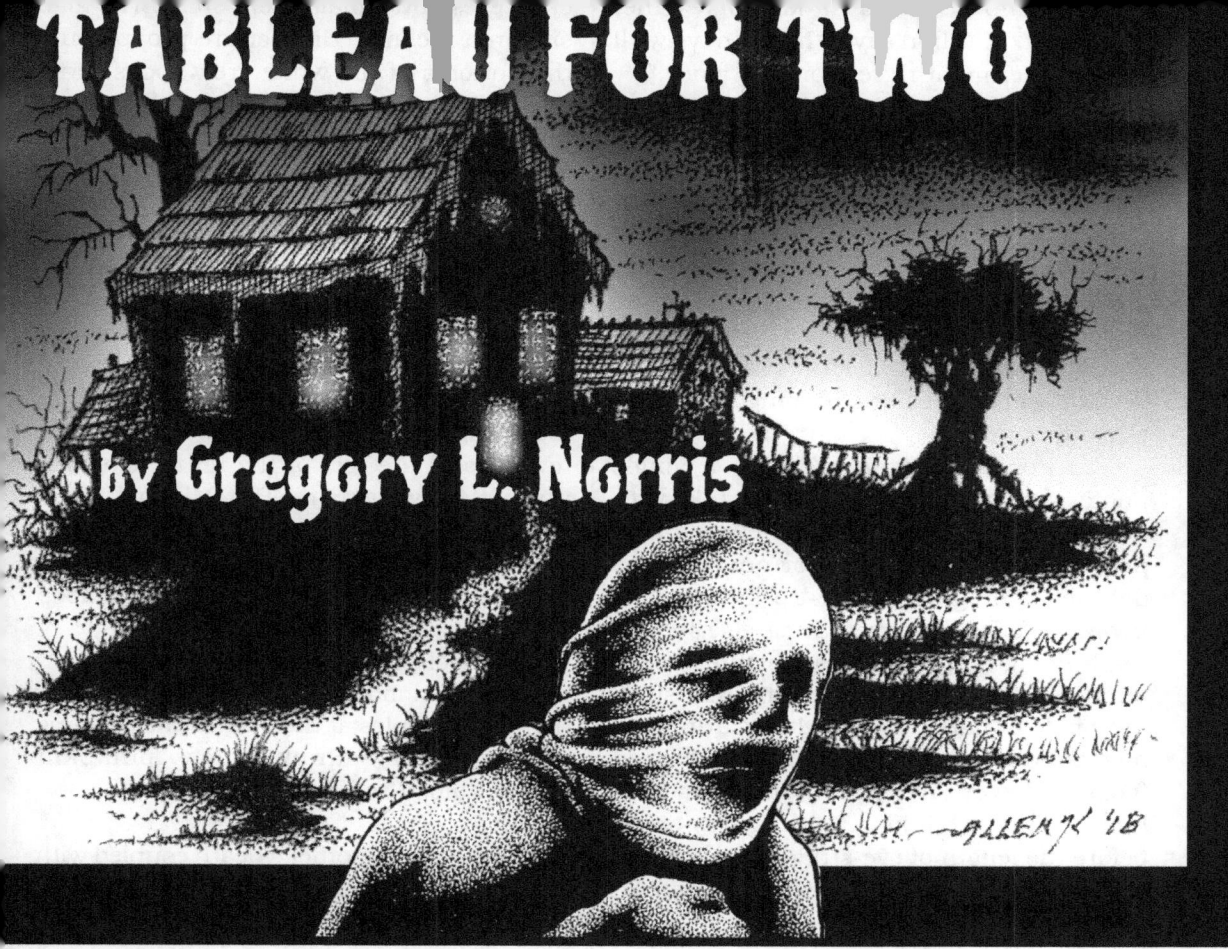

TABLEAU FOR TWO

by Gregory L. Norris

IT IS A HAUNTED DAY FILLED WITH GHOSTS. OUTSIDE, A STIFF OCTOBER WIND HOWLS AROUND THE APARTMENT HOUSE, moaning in a disembodied voice and clanking chains made of colored leaves. Inside 2-08, the two brothers labor to clean out their late mother's one-bedroom unit. In the closet, under a stack of shoeboxes filled with shoes, Michael discovers the old photograph album. It is gray, its cover showing a pastoral meadow scene with a snowy mountain rising in the background. Inside the album, the plastic sleeves have yellowed with age, the pages filled with old photographs, the subjects missing names, the events dates.

Carlton, the older brother, works in the kitchen, dumping plastic ware and plates into a box for donation to the local church junkshop. That's the destination for most of the late Elaine Dearden's relics. A growing stack of garbage bags in the living room where the phantom of her perfume lingers tells of the rest.

There is no music here, no cable TV. They could plug in phones, activate data, and listen to tunes, but this is a somber, unwanted obligation, and so the brothers have opted to perform it in silence. Carlton realizes no sound comes from the bedroom. Only the wind speaks. He dumps another handful of food containers into a cardboard box from the local packy, sets it on the cluttered countertop, and peeks around the corner. Michael stands inert, the old photo album opened in his hands. From the angle, Carlton sees his brother's eyes narrowed on the page.

"Hey, no trips down Memory Lane, remember?" Carlton says. "In two days we'll owe another month's rent on this place."

Michael blinks. "Huh?"

"Hustle. Move your ass."

Michael doesn't. Carlton turns back to the chore of their late mother's kitchen, but a chill embraces him. They've switched off the heat. This cold goes deeper than the brisk October grayness hanging over the day like a shroud.

"Mikey?" Carlton asks.

Michael comes out of the fugue. "I don't remember this."

Carlton approaches. *This* is a single photograph, the kind you used to take with a camera and film before cell phones, printed up in a drugstore or one of those defunct photograph drive-up kiosks. The image is faded like everything else in this tomb being emptied of its worthless contents. Knotty pine paneling, the real stuff, not made of particles and glue. Carlton remembers how the knots sometimes formed faces and eyes that stared at him in that house without blinking. Two figures stand before the length of eye-studded wall. Boys, he assumes, because they're dressed up in Halloween costumes.

One of the little ghouls is a ghost wearing a shiny white toga and a white plastic mask decorated in arching black eyebrows and matching sockets. The other is some generic green-faced goblin, his toga black. Goblin stands a few hairs taller than Ghost. Cheap, store-bought Halloween costumes, on his next shallow sip of air Carlton can almost smell the plastic. Maybe it's a lingering trace of what he's been boxing up in the kitchen. Or a memory window inching open —one more apparition released to haunt the day.

"You don't remember?" Michael asks, his voice barely louder than a whisper.

For another second, Carlton doesn't. Then the memory window is thrust open, and he's back in that house, on that night. Their mother's record player trills with spooky music. Carlton blinks. Across from the snapshot of the two Halloween specters is another that terrifies him more. It shows a man with dark hair, handsome but with cruel eyes and a malevolent smile. The man sits on a recliner. His feet are propped up, the bottoms of his white crew socks dirty. The knotty pine walls are visible behind him. There's a boy seated on his lap. It's Michael.

Breathing becomes difficult. Carlton expels the stale air in his lungs and gasps himself out of the growing trance. "Pitch it."

"What?" Michael protests.

"The junk pile. No one needs to keep any of that."

Carlton reaches for the photo album, intending for it to join magazines, old dishtowels, and the rest of the refuse stacking up in the living room. But Michael turns away and holds on.

"No," he says.

"Why? Why would you want to keep *that*?"

Michael doesn't answer.

The wind moans, stirring leaves shed by the row of maples at the back of the building past windows—sunny yellow, pumpkin orange, blood red.

MAYBE IT'S THEIR mother's death coupled with the burden of cleaning out her little place in a town he rarely visits. Or it could be the time of year with its short, dark days and commercialized fright. All of it. None of it. Something *other*.

Carlton goes through motions aware of a chill that pursues him like an unwanted, second shadow. A kind of solar eclipse stains the days even when the sun is out. And at night, he returns to that Halloween in a past that can't be completely forgotten, no matter how deeply he buried it.

In the shadows of the bedroom where he sleeps alone, embalmed by his memories, Carlton travels back through time, to another October night. It's Halloween. They're living in that house, the small bungalow near the lake, the one with the knotty pine walls. The walls have faces and eyes and always seem to stare at him. He and Mikey share the bedroom at the back of the little house.

Halloween means candy even in this remote prison at the end of the world. The nearest neighbors live halfway around the lake on Bella Vista Road. Carlton will look out for Mikey—he'll take the big flashlight, the one that belongs to their father. They'll—

"No, I've got something better planned," she says.

With the old man on the road driving for Faulk & White Trucking, she's become both Mother and Father, and the eldest son rarely questions her. But it's Trick-or-flipping-Treat. Candy bars galore!

A shadow crosses her face, the one he knows to never underestimate. "I want you home, both of you."

And there's Mikey in his stupid ghost costume from the store, haunting the house's narrow strip of hallway, in front of the bathroom that doesn't have a tub, only a standup shower wedged in one corner beside the water heater. He doesn't speak.

"No need to worry about razorblades in apples, little bro," Carlton says, real cool. Inwardly, though, he winces at the mere suggestion. The concept of disguising apples with razorblades unleashes a chilling mental picture whenever the season rolls around, one of unsuspecting mouths biting down on crisp, sweet fruit, an explosion of pain as massacred gums and cheeks sever, and then the blood. So much of it.

She's doing that thing again, cheerleading in the face of suffering, an unconvincing smile on her face. "Like I said, something even better!"

So Carlton dresses up, too—in the cheap green mask and shiny costume that reeks of plastic and newness, while she presents the better alternative to Trick-or-Treating. As dusk descends and the October wind spirits around the little house, scattering dead leaves, she completes preparations for a Halloween party. There are only three guests, but she continues to dart her gaze at the clock above the stove and at the front door as though anticipating a fourth.

She puts a record on the player—the soundtrack to an old soap opera she watched as a teen called *Dark Shadows*. The spooky gothic music grates on Carlton. So does the insanity of what follows. There are donuts strung from the ceiling on thumbtacks. Two. Plain. He and Mikey are expected to eat them off the string without using their hands. First to do so wins a prize. And she's hauled in their little plastic swimming pool from the previous summer, filled it with water and apples from the tree in the backyard. She wants them to bob using only teeth, again no hands.

Carlton took a bite from one of those sour, misshapen apples a week earlier. The concept nauseates him almost as much as the mental snapshot of the mouths savaged and bloodied by razorblades.

"Isn't this fun?" she cheers, lifting up the camera from the counter to record their misery. "Carlton, put on your mask."

He does. She snaps a photo and several more over the course of the next long hour as the party wears on, and her mask drops.

HIS TEARS HAVE DRIED, leaving his face sticky, but hers continue, audible through the gaps in the knotty pine walls. Carlton tries to not hate her. Part of him forced to grow up in advance of his years pities her. The effort to make a memorable Halloween for him and Mikey should matter. And she has, though not in the way intended. Oh yes, this rotten, dark night will always be with him.

He'll bury it deep under mental strata until his kid brother finds the old photo album, exhumes the sole surviving picture from that night, an artifact that should have been thrown out long ago and erased from history.

The memory is loose again though not complete. There's more. Something Carlton should recall but can't, not until the bed begins to quiver around him, the walls to shake, the entire house to tremble. He's at the epicenter of an earthquake, the present and past linked by vibrations so powerful he feels them in his molars, his marrow; deeper, his soul.

Carlton jolts awake. The world continues to rumble around him, keeping him paralyzed under a glaze of invisible ice. He stares without blinking into the darkness. Drool seeps from one corner of his mouth. He utters a loud, throaty moan and is sure he'll wet the bed for the first time since—

The ice thaws. He makes it to the bathroom and vomits up the little in his gut.

CARLTON STARES INTO the mirror. Between blinks, the reflection of his tired, unshaved face reverts from a man past forty to a boy in a green plastic Halloween mask. He rinses his mouth again and brushes his teeth for the third time. The apartment has ceased shaking.

He recalls that missing detail. The little house with the eyes in the walls—after his tears dried but his mother's didn't, it shook. How it shook!

Because, at long last, the party's fourth guest arrives well after the dry donuts are choked down and the wormy apples dumped outside the back door along with the water inside the kiddie pool. Pulled up to the house in the woods in his big rig.

Their father's returned home on Halloween night.

APPROACHING THE DOOR, Carlton shudders. Those vibrations from a night long ago are inside him, echoes of the past. His bones trapped them and now they've been released through memories.

He recalls something else—what he heard through the wall after his mother's screams replace the brief sound of her joy at the old man's arrival.

"I know he isn't mine," their father shouts.

She tries to convince him that, yes, both of the brothers are his sons, but he won't hear her. For the first time, Carlton questions why Mikey's hair is dirty blond while his—and their father's—is dark.

"Carlton?" Mikey calls from the darkness.

Carlton hastens through the shadows to the other bed. Mikey trembles against him. He hugs the boy, sharing his terror. Disappointment over the night's earlier events no longer matters. Footsteps cut across the short length of hallway, heavy and ominous, making his young heart gallop. Carlton forgets how to breathe. The door opens. Their father stands at the threshold, a wall of obsidian backlit by the glow from the other bedroom.

"*No*," their mother shrieks.

And the memory ends, cut in two like an old film coming apart in a projector.

Carlton wakes in the present, outside the door to the small house his brother rents. A cold October twilight is falling early thanks to the clouds. As he readies to knock on a door festooned with fake cobwebs and an enormous plastic tarantula with furry legs and red eyes, a thousand little orange lights activate, filling the front hedges with a Halloween effulgence. Three pumpkins guard the brick steps, one apiece for mother and two sons, Carlton thinks.

He knocks. The spider eyes him through eight malevolent lenses. The door opens. Michael stands there, a towel wrapped around his waist, another around his head. The air smells sweet, like donuts, caramel apples, and candy.

"Hey," Carlton says.

Michael gives him a tip of his chin, nothing more, and recedes from the door. Carlton enters the small house.

"You got a minute?" Carlton asks.

Michael turns to the bedroom at the back of the house. "Not really. It's Trick-or-Treat time soon."

Carlton notes the big pumpkin made from neon orange glass, its insides filled with candy bars. It's Halloween night. The chill around and inside him deepens.

"I'll be quick," he says.

Michael pads off to the bedroom. "You got me as long as it takes to change into my costume."

There's a tone Carlton doesn't like. Even more worrisome is what he glimpses after Michael enters the bedroom, shaking the towel from his head. That brief flash reveals black hair, there one instant, gone the next as Michael moves out of view.

"The other day at Ma's old place," Carlton stammers. "The photo album. That picture."

"What about it?" Michael asks.

"There was more. After the Halloween party. After, in the night, when our father came home. That was the last time, remember? He was gone after that."

Michael doesn't comment.

"I remembered something. What came after."

Silence. Only the wind speaks, its slither through the leaves around his brother's rented house adding to the growing sense of wrongness.

"What he said—"

"What he said about me not being his real son?" Michael asks.

Then he's in the doorway, his body a mass of shadow. As he steps forward, his footfalls ominous, familiar, Carlton sees that Michael has dyed his hair, cut it to resemble their late father's. Even the clothes he wears evoke memories from that other time and place.

"What do you think?" Michael asks, a slippery grin curling on one corner of his mouth.

A shiver teases the nape of Carlton's neck. He resists, fails. The shudder tumbles, sending the world around him out of focus. When it stabilizes, he is staring at the image of his father, recreated in the son that wasn't really his.

"What are you doing, Mikey?" Carlton asks.

"Me? Honoring my late father."

"He wasn't—"

"Mine?" Michael interjects. "Oh, I remember what he said through the wall and him standing at the bedroom door. I thought I'd forgotten all of it, but then I saw that photograph, and it all came back to me. It was all there, just hidden away like a picture in an old album."

Michael snorts a dismissive laugh through his nostrils. His eyes narrow.

"You're still my kid brother. Always have been, always will be."

Michael hovers, keeping his distance. "You don't get it, do you? After all these years."

"Get it?" Carlton parrots.

"When he found out about Ma's infidelity, him gone for all those weeks, sometimes months at a time."

"Michael?" Carlton whimpers.

"I was his real son. *You* weren't, Carlton. He told me the truth."

Carlton chokes down a dry swallow. "He told you? But he's dead. He's been dead for a long time."

Then Michael smiles, and Carlton gazes into his kid brother's eyes, and the cold inside him worsens, for it is like staring into the face of a ghost frozen in time; like staring at an old photograph.

Raised on a healthy diet of creature double features and classic SF TV, Gregory L. Norris writes regularly for numerous short story anthologies, national magazines, novels, and the occasional episode for TV or film. Gregory novelized the NBC Made-for-TV classic by Gerry Anderson, The Day After Tomorrow: Into Infinity *(as well as a sequel and a forthcoming third entry into the franchise for Anderson Entertainment in the U.K.), a movie he watched as an eleven-year-old sitting cross-legged on the living room floor of the enchanted cottage where he grew up. Gregory won HM in the 2016 Roswell Awards in Short SF Writing. He once worked as a screenwriter on two episodes of Paramount's* Star Trek: Voyager. *Kate Mulgrew,* Voyager's *"Captain Janeway," blurbed his book of short stories and novellas,* The Fierce and Unforgiving Muse, *stating, "In my seven years on* Voyager, *I don't think I've met a writer more capable of writing such a book— and writing it so beautifully."*

In late 2019, Gregory sold an option on his modern Noir feature film screenplay, Amandine, *to the new Hollywood production company Snark-hunter LLC, owned by actor Dan Lench, a devotee of Gregory's writing. In late 2020,* Snarkhunter *optioned Gregory's tetralogy Horror film based upon four of his short stories,* Ride Along. *That same month, his short story "Water Whispers" (originally appearing in the anthology* 20,000 Leagues Remembered*), was nominated for the Pushcart Prize.*

Gregory lives and writes at Xanadu, a century-old house perched on a hill in New Hampshire's North Country with spectacular mountain views, with his rescue cat and emerald-eyed muse.

Follow his further literary adventures at: www.gregorylnorris.blogspot.com

LA NIÑA ATARDECER

BY STEVE DUFFY

IT WAS DUSK WHEN HE SAW HER, UNDER THE CLEAN NEON LIGHTS OF A LONELY GAS STATION ON THE OUTSKIRTS OF GUADALAJARA. He'd fueled up for the night's drive and was waiting for a thunderous convoy of trucks to pass before rejoining Federal Highway 15, and there she was, standing by the exit ramp with the setting sun behind her. She was slim, with long dark hair and a short summer dress, and his first thought was that she was a *fichera* working the trucker trade. His second thought was that this was no place for a girl who wasn't a *fichera* to find herself when night fell; his third was that either way, he should probably do something about it. And so he rolled his borrowed muscle car over to where she was standing, leaned out of the driver-side window and asked, in his approximate Spanish, "*Disculpe,* um*, necesita,* ah*, necesita lleve*?"

The girl smiled. "I do," she said, to his relief. "Would that be OK?"

"Fantastic." Fantastic, not least, that he'd made himself understood. She scrambled into the passenger seat, unencumbered, he noticed, by baggage or possessions. "Travelling light," he said, pulling out on to the highway, "that's cool. So, where you headed?"

"Mazatlán?" she said apologetically. "It's a long way."

"Unbelievable, me too." The prospect of company on the six-hour drive was agreeable. And now that he could get a better look at her, the prospect of her company in particular seemed more than agreeable. "So what's your name?"

"Bianca," she said, rolling down the window so that the highway breeze flared through her long hair.

"Pleasure to meet you, Bianca. I'm Wayne. So what's in Mazatlán?"

"Oh, I have an appointment," she said. "Will we be there before dawn?"

"That's the plan," he said. "Driving by night, it's cooler, less traffic. We'll be there in time for breakfast." He glanced to see if she'd picked up on this oblique invitation, but the whole of her attention seemed to be on the road ahead.

They drove on past the last straggling suburbs of Guadalajara, through the first of the tolls and out into the scrubland where no lights shone. In the west the red remnants of the sunset smoldered over the low hills. The light of the dash shone palely on the girl's face as she gazed in wonder and contentment at the ribbon of the road. "We can push it up to sixty now," Wayne said, and grunted with satisfaction as the Valiant Super Bee picked up speed. "Hey, do you want a drink? There's beers in that cooler in back."

She shook her head. "No thanks."

"Mind if I smoke?"

Another shake of her head, and a flash of that captivating smile. He couldn't decide whether she was Mexican or American; her voice had a subtle inflection, but it seemed almost more musical than regional. Her dark complexion and black hair might have placed her origins south of the border, as might her white linen dress embroidered at the breast, but then again, what did it matter, really? The night was balmy, the road was straight and empty and seemed to lead to endless possibilities. He took a pack of Marlboros from the dash, tapped it so that a cigarette protruded. "You want one?" he asked.

She glanced round, saw what he was doing and reached over in alarm for the wheel. "No worries," he said, taking the cigarette between his lips and lighting it single-handed. "I've been doing this for a while now. Did you want a cigarette?"

"You should be careful," she said, shaking her head no. "There are accidents on this road. Look," and she pointed to the roadside where a rough wooden crucifix and a wreath of dead flowers marked the site of a past fatality.

"Oh, I'm an excellent driver," he said.

"That's good to know," she said seriously.

He drew on the cigarette, exhaled happily. A fragment of song ran through his head, and he tapped out the rhythm on the wheel. Beneath his breath he sang, "On a dark desert highway, cool wind in my hair, warm smell of colitas..."

"That's a pretty song," she said. "Did you make that up?"

He laughed, then stopped when he saw she wasn't joking. "You never heard that song? Really?"

She shook her head. "It's nice, is all. I like the melody."

"Yeah, it's nice." So, maybe not American. Surely everybody had heard of the Eagles.

"Warm smell of colitas," she sang, approximating the tune, and he picked it up with her, "...rising up through the air. Hey, you smoke? I don't mean like these," indicating his cigarette, "I mean, you know, the *yerba*?"

Another shake of the head. "You need to keep your head clear when you're driving."

"Oh, I'm not holding," he assured her, and left it at that. No need for her to know the reason for his trip to Mazatlán, which was to broker a deal behind the backs of the Sinaloan cartel for a new smuggling route *el otro lado*, across the border to the States. Think of this as more of a first date, he told himself. You don't talk about work. Keep it conversational.

Which, for the next hour or so, he tried to do, with limited success. Before they'd gone too many miles, it became apparent that Bianca wasn't a talkative passenger. Though she'd always respond with a smile or a nod, still she'd manage to swerve any direct questions about herself, her past, present or future. Eventually he gave up, not wanting the whole scene to come across like an interrogation. After all, he told himself, there was plenty of highway still to ride. Instead, he filled his head with thoughts of how it would be to live life in the fast lane, when the deal was cut and the greenback dollars started coming in. He could imagine a babe like Bianca on a lounger by the poolside, white bikini and mirror shades; one day, he told himself. All in good time.

In the high hill country around El Platanar the twists and turns of the gradients made the going more arduous, and kinks began to knot up Wayne's neck and shoulders. With relief he spotted the lights of a roadside *venta* up ahead. "Hey, I'm gonna stop here a minute, get some more smokes, maybe a coffee. You want anything?"

"Uh, I'm good. Do you really need to stop?" There was something fretful in the way she declined the offer. Not for the first time, he wondered if she might be running from something, or somebody.

"No worries, we're making good time," he assured her, pulling up in the parking lot. "Can't run out of cigarettes in the middle of the desert, you know? *Desastre*. I'll get coffees to go, I'll be five minutes, less."

She stayed in the car, drumming her fingers on the dash. Wayne stretched luxuriously in the cooling night, feeling the breeze where the sweat had plastered his shirt to his back, and slipped through the beaded curtain at the door. There were few customers in the *venta*, all of them locals he guessed, and he was served at the counter by a grumpy man in a sweat-stained singlet who apparently had no Marlboros or Pall Malls to sell him, only Delicados, which would at least keep him awake.

When he returned to the Valiant with two coffees *sin leche*, Bianca was hanging across the open passenger door, pushing off the gravel on her tiptoes so it swung restlessly back and forwards, glancing up and down the road. Before he could offer her one of the waxed paper cups, she'd bounced back inside the automobile.

"Got you this," he said, settling alongside her. She took the coffee, but didn't drink from it, only cradled it between her hands. In a few gulps he'd finished his, and she handed over her own, untouched. "Thanks," he said, and she smiled at him. Now they were moving again she seemed a little less on edge.

Around the borderline between Jalisco and Nayarit the highway snaked through a series of gaps blasted in the bedrock. As Wayne was approaching a slow right-hander through one of these defiles, Bianca spoke: "Careful, there are roadworks up ahead, better go slow."

"I don't see any signs," he started to say, but halfway round the bend he saw bollards along the median strip, a single lane in operation. He braked quickly and skirted the works. A wilting spray of flowers had been threaded through the steel mesh fence between the lanes, just ahead of a mangled section where the concrete abutment had been gouged out in a collision. On the shoulder of the road a shredded truck tire had unraveled itself; the skid marks on the road showed the accident had been recent. "How'd you know about that?" he asked her, glancing at her with curiosity.

"I saw the sign back there," she said. "You must have missed it." He was pretty sure there hadn't been any sign back there to miss.

"I think you got the sixth sense," he said, making it into a joke. But she didn't smile back. Clear of the obstruction, he leaned on the gas, and the V8 engine rasped as the torque kicked in. That smoothed out her frown momentarily, and they drove on in the hydrocarbon mesquite dark.

Bianca acted nervous all through the next stretch, he thought. She spoke very little, only in response to direct questions, and then it was in monosyllables. In between times she just seemed lost in the road's ghostly unwinding, shifting in her seat, one foot tapping an agitated rhythm, and Wayne noticed that she was gripping the arm rest hard. He wondered if she was one of those people who are unduly spooked by accidents, or the prospect thereof. He'd never given the matter any thought, which in his line of work was just as well. The sheer number of things that can go wrong in even the simplest dope deal would leave a nervous person gibbering behind a locked and bolted door, but he had an innate belief that confidence and right thinking left no room for that stuff, which in his view was what gave you cancer.

Speaking of business, he was aware that at some point during the trip he was supposed to check in with the Mazatlán end of the operation. They were driving now across the old lava fields on the shoulder of Ceboruco, sour scrub clinging tenaciously to the harsh black volcanic pumice, and he resolved to stop at the next roadside *cantina* and phone the number he'd been given. Maybe Bianca would take a drink, he thought; a drink might take the edge off a little. He really didn't want her nervousness

to become contagious. Whether she was too far away from her destination, or not far enough from her starting point, she needed to come down a notch or two.

Miles of chaparral, empty highway streaked with the skid marks of past emergencies, road signs to places Wayne would never visit and didn't want to, until finally he found what he was looking for, colored bulbs strung across the porch of a shack by the roadside and a sign that said *Descanso de los Viajeros*. "Gonna stop here," he said, turning off the blacktop on to the rough track, "need to call someone, get a drink maybe. Join me? Little tequila, little beer? I'm buying."

"You can't stop again!" She seemed almost angry, which Wayne didn't like at all. Who was in charge here? He was beginning to tire of her insistence on uninterrupted forward motion. Enough already. "We're losing time, all the time..."

"Look." He parked up alongside a big old Peterbilt narrow-nose truck, tapped the clock on the dash. "We are totally on schedule, Bianca, making real good time, road's empty, easy riding, plus, I really have to make this call, okay? There's ... people I need to speak with, plans to make, and what's the harm in one little glass of beer? You need to trust me here, everything's copacetic. Whatever it is, the boy is on top of it, don't you worry."

The electric bulbs outside the *cantina* painted midnight rainbows across her anxious face. "I really think you should keep going," she said. "You know the phone doesn't even work in that place."

"Huh?" She was doing that thing again. "Why would it not be working? I mean, how can you tell? You been this way before or something?"

"Whatever," she said. "Believe me, the best thing is keep on going."

"Look," patiently, trying not to show his irritation, "I absolutely have to make this call. I'll be ten minutes tops. Just chill, okay? No need to get hung up." He put a hand on her shoulder, and found to his surprise that her skin was clammy cold. "Chill," he said again, aware of the irony. Strange that it felt so uncomfortable touching her, when he'd thought of little else for the last couple of hours. Something about that cold skin gave him the creeps, and for a second the thought crossed his mind, *Ditch her? Here?* That wasn't a gallant thing to be thinking, and he forced himself to pat her shoulder one more time. "You should come in, stretch your legs at least."

She didn't answer, just stared at him mutinously. "No?" She shook her head. "Well, okay, I won't be long—"

Now she reached out for him, and he was so unprepared that he actually pulled away in surprise. "Stay," she said, and though she was trying to make it sound inviting, it came out just a little crazy. "I don't want you to go in there, stay here, please..."

There ensued a brief struggle between the various parts of Wayne's brain, in which the lizard instinct of the basal ganglia urged him one way—*back in the car, man, she's down to party*—and the higher processes of the neocortex said *huh-uh, really bad idea, no way José.* The mammalian side won out, just, and Wayne disengaged himself from her clutches. Perhaps if her hands had been a little warmer, her nails a little shorter, who knows? Even as he stepped backwards from the Valiant, he was only half sure he was doing the right thing. *But maybe,* the thought came unbidden into his head like the toss of a bad penny, *maybe the time for doing the right thing was back in Guadalajara.* Shrugging, he entered the *cantina*.

At first it seemed that déjà vu had kicked in, some after-hours hallucination of the road. The place was a ringer for the El Platanar establishment he'd stopped at a while back. It had its own morose *jefe* in a singlet, its own ceiling fan with flies weaving lopsided spirals between the blades, and it even had its own bum, a scroungy Willie Nelson-looking *viejo* slumped at a corner table. Wayne could live with all of that, though, because next to where the bum was seated was a payphone in a recess.

"*Oiga señor,*" Wayne greeted the impassive *jefe*, "*¿Tienes una cerveza fría?*" Not that he didn't have his own cooler of beer in the backseat, but he felt it was good manners to put down some rent for his use of the phone, plus he needed the change. He took the bottle over to the phone booth and fed in a handful of centavos. Dead air. He tapped the cradle impatiently. Nothing. *Holy shit,* he thought, *but she knew. How did she know?*

"Out of order, kid." It was Willie Nelson at the next table; a fellow American, or so it seemed. "Been that way for a week, apparently."

"It has?" Wayne was finding it hard to process this latest development.

"Sit down," the bum said expansively, and pushed a seat towards him. "Our host here's sick of the sight of me, and that guy over there, he's kinda the silent type, you know?" Indicating the only other customer, the Peterbilt driver, Wayne guessed, who was scratching an itch between his shoulder-blades with the spoon he'd been using to eat his bowl of chili. "But you got a minute, ain't you?"

"I'm in kind of a hurry, you know," Wayne said, but he sat down nevertheless. Make Bianca wait, teach her a lesson. Wayne operates on his own time, baby.

"Say, that a Tecate you're drinking?" He nodded, and the bum eyed it appreciatively. "Good beer, man." He was watching that beer go down the way Wayne had watched Bianca by the roadside.

What the hell. Wayne signalled with the bottle, first towards the *jefe* and then at his new drinking buddy. "*Otra cerveza* for, um, what's your name, man?"

"Lanny," the bum said, with his eyes on the beer as the *jefe* clanked it down on the tin tabletop. Before Wayne could clink bottles with him, Lanny had downed half of it in one steady pull. "Oh god, that's good. Ohhh, man. Beer for my men. Tell you what, man, make my night and let me hitch a ride to Nogales, 'fore I wake up and find I'm dreaming."

"I'm not going to Nogales, man," Wayne told him hastily. Talk about giving an inch and taking a mile.

"Sonora? Anywhere?"

"Mazatlán is all, man, sorry. And you know, I already got a passenger, so..." He made a sad face.

Lanny shrugged. "Eh, them's the breaks. Beer's good, though." He drained the rest of the bottle and nodded in agreement with himself. "That Tecate, it really hits the spot."

"How come you need a ride, anyway?" Wayne said it to make conversation, but really he was thinking about Bianca, how she could possibly have known about that phone. And then what was with the roadworks back there, she'd known about those as well.

"Crashed my car," Lanny was explaining, "three days ago. Totaled the damn thing. Waiting for my woman to come fetch me, I guess that's not gonna happen now. Soooo, Nogales. And from Nogales, back across the ol' borderino." He saluted, and hummed the first bars of the Star-Spangled Banner. "For better or worse. *Salud*, Bianca."

That got Wayne's attention. "Say what?"

Lanny snorted. "The ladies, god bless 'em." He hoisted his empty bottle, turned it upside down and let the drips fall on the linoleum floor. "Wish I'd asked Ángel about it," pointing towards the *jefe*, "back when I stopped here. Tell you this, I wouldn't be here now, that's for sure."

Ángel interpreted this gesture as another order, and brought a fresh one to the table. Lanny looked guiltily at Wayne, but he waved it away. "Told you what, man?"

Lanny made a start on the new Tecate, wiped his mouth with the back of his hand. "Yeah, see, Ángel hipped me to the whole backstory, man, once I got stranded here. It's a crazy goddamn story, but I dunno. I mean, I heard crazier things, you know?"

Wayne didn't doubt that. There were Lannies by the dozen in Mexico, battle-scarred casualties of the war on drugs, seekers after enlightenment turned panhandlers for pesos, each with his hard-luck story of the deal that didn't come off, the sure thing that blew up in his face, the holy peyote quest that left him stranded in some one-horse town with just the Jesus sandals on his feet, was all. Every one of them had a yarn to tell, and all of those yarns were fool's gold and monkeyshines, the flyblown detritus of dreams, tall tales of Spanish castles in the air. But Lanny here: he'd dropped that certain name, and Wayne wanted to hear some more about that.

"You said Bianca, is that right?"

Lanny nodded. "Name she went by, that time at least. I mean, seems like she got other names, you know? Ángel, he told me a few. But it was Bianca back in Guadalajara, man, when I seen her by the roadside with her thumb up."

"No freakin' way." Wayne was staring at him now, in a way that probably nobody had stared at Lanny since the draft board marked him 4-F. "Guadalajara?"

"Next leg of the journey, man, Guadalajara to Mazatlán. Easy stages, drive by night, all the way to Nogales to hook up with my woman. That's the plan. And me, *estúpido*," slapping his high sunburned forehead, "I gotta blow it all, give the lil' *niña* a ride."

"And?" Wayne's teeth were practically grinding, he felt so wired.

"Says she wants to go to Mazatlán, and that's where I'm headed, right? So there we are, we're tooling along, making good time, you know, everything fine, and this chick, she don't talk too much, but that's okay, she don't have to talk, you know? In that little white dress and all, hair blowing free, mm-mmm, that's what papa like."

Across the room the trucker's chair squeaked as he pushed back from the table, gave his spoon a final lick, and dropped some bills on the counter. Ángel nodded in acknowledgement, but he stayed alongside Lanny's table; maybe he couldn't believe this stuff either, thought Wayne. The bead curtain rustled as the trucker strode out into the night.

"So," Lanny was saying, "like I said, we're making good time, only it ain't fast enough for her. Go faster, go faster, that's all she says, we ain't gonna make it by sunup. And I say to her, baby, this ol' junker here, it's about as old as I am, and we both of us going about as fast as we *can* go, if I push it any harder the whole damn engine's gonna blow, and anyways, ain't we got the whole night? I got it all worked out, *no hay problema*, dig?"

"Damn," muttered Wayne. This was unreal.

"Right? But she ain't buying it, hell no. Then I stop here, get a cold one from Ángel, take it back to the car and she's about ready to blow, why did you stop, get moving, we're gonna be late, and I'm like, okay, okay.

"And she don't stop, not ever. Faster-faster-faster, yadda yadda, till in the end I'm pouring it on just to make her shut up, you know? Like, she got to me, somehow, got inside my head. And then we come upon a truck, this is just back down the road a way, and he's kinda dawdling along, you know, and Bianca grabs a hold of my arm, 'pass it, pass it,' like it ain't a suggestion, you know, like it's life and death? And here's the thing —she grabs me, and her hands are *cold*, man. Colder than this beer," holding up his bottle, "like ice cold? Like … I dunno, man. Like creepy cold."

Creepy cold. Wayne nodded, feeling the throb of recognition. "I hear ya."

"And she's hauling on my arm, and whoa, we're out in the fast lane, and I just jam on the gas, like, get past this damn truck and then kick her crazy ass out the car, right? And I'm almost there, and then *bam*, the goddamn front tire blows. Kaboom. Can't steer, I'm hauling on the wheel, and then we're bouncing off the center rails, spin off the side of the highway, *bang*, there's a tree, *bang*, there's a big ass rock, and before ya know it I'm upside down, I'm covered in broken glass, I've got like ten seconds to get out before the goddamn gas tank blows, and I just barely get my ass clear when *whoomp*, up she goes."

"And the girl?" Again Wayne felt that unwelcome sensation of a cold hand placed on his sweating skin.

"'And how are *you*, Lannie?'" He seemed a little put out that Wayne hadn't asked. "Why just fine, thank you, pardner, seeing as I narrowly avoided being turned into a goddamn roadkill fricassee? Once I picked all the goddamn glass out of my head while I watched the whole of my earthly goods go up in smoke?" His crossness subsided, as if the mystery was greater than his indignation. "I don't know how the girl was, man. She was gone, like split, like outta there, brother." He made a flying-saucer whirr, spiraled a finger up into nothingness. "Nowhere in sight."

"But how could she—"

"Hell if I know. Like, I'm upside down in the wreckage, but I'm by myself? So she was thrown clear, maybe? Maybe. But when I get out, when I look around, I don't see her. There's the car on fire, there's the truck stopped to see if I scratched his goddamn paint job, and there's me, and that's all. Wasn't any sign of her. Gone. Vanished. *Desapare*-frickin-*cida*, baby." He brought his hands together in the contemplation mudra, then spread them wide hangdog style, how'd ya like them apples?

"Unbelievable," Wayne breathed. "Sorry, no, man, like I do believe you. It's crazy, but I believe you. I don't want to, but I got to. This Bianca?"

"*La niña atardecer*," Lanny said, his wild eyes faraway someplace. "That's what Ángel calls her, man. The sunset girl. But Bianca, yeah. What about her?"

"I got her outside in my car, man," Wayne said.

Total silence in the *cantina*. Then Lanny spoke, throatily, as if the beer had left him desert dry. "You got her what?"

Wayne repeated it. "In my car, right out there."

"Same chick?" Lanny's eyes were darting back and forth between Wayne, the proprietor, and the door of the cantina, where the bead curtains were swaying as if from the passage of ghosts.

"Come take a look," Wayne said. "Same chick, man, I am one hundred percent certain."

"Journeys end in lovers' meetings," Lanny said, but he didn't move.

And still nobody moved, until Ángel broke the tableau. He'd been sitting at the next table, frowning at Lanny while he told his tale, at Wayne when he dropped his bombshell, and now he got up and made for the door. As if the spell was broken, Lanny and Wayne followed him outside.

Where the girl had disappeared.

The passenger seat of the Valiant was empty, which to Wayne was almost as disconcerting as Bianca still being there would have been. "She was right there," he said, and then it struck him that apart from his own car, the parking lot was empty. "The truck, man!" he exclaimed. "She must've gone with that guy in the Peterbilt!"

Lanny, one of nature's slow reactors, was taking a while to process this series of disclosures. It was Ángel who spoke, for the first time, his voice like bitter chocolate. "It was her," he said, "and yes, she went with the trucker."

It was as if the night air had muttered a secret in their ears. Bombshell dropped, Ángel turned and went back into the cantina, and Wayne and Lanny trailed along after him like obedient children. "What did you tell him?" Wayne wanted to know. "You saw this girl as well?"

"Not this time," Ángel said. "But yeah, I seen her. She's known on this road."

"Holy shit," Wayne said, "you mean she pulls this trick all the time?" Struck by suspicion, he slapped at his pockets. Wallet and passport were both still there.

"On this road, people know her," changing the order of the words but still seeming to be evading the real answer, the answer that lay deeper, that wouldn't necessarily be apparent to the passing traveler, here only to go.

"Did you see her with him?" Meaning Lanny.

Ángel shook his head. "He come in alone," he said, and Lanny finally found a point at which he could re-enter the conversation.

"Yeah," he said, sounding croaky still, "yeah, I came in to get a drink like I said, she stayed in the car like she did with you. Got my beer, I split, we drove on, she was acting loco, and then like I told you," his hand smacked into his palm, "the crash. And then I had to haul my ass back here on foot, took me an hour, man, and then like I say, Ángel tells me the story."

"What, that she's a lunatic? A grifter?"

"That she's a *fantasma*, man," Lanny said, "*un espectro. Hada del camino.*"

"What?"

Lanny couldn't look in his face and say it, but he stood by it nonetheless. "Believe it, man. I know it's crazy, but this man here, he's seen some stuff, he don't deal in fairytales. It's the road, man, strange days on the highway, strange days and crazy nights."

Wayne was about to scoff, but he glanced at Ángel and thought better of it.

The big man was eyeing him levelly, just daring him to disagree, and there wasn't a trace of whimsy about him. "This what you told him?" he managed to ask.

"It was," said Ángel, in a way that left little room for negotiation. So there it was.

Were they serious? Were they putting him on, was it all some highway hazing thing? Whatever. Wayne was about done with the whole scene. "Hey Lanny," he said, coming to an instant decision, "you still want a ride as far as Mazatlán?" He slapped the tin table. "'Cause I am rolling, brother, as of now."

"A ride—oh, do I ever, man?" Lanny's fervor was touching. "Hey, I gotta tell you, Ángel, this has been a special few days and I owe you big time, but I am outta your hair as of now, amigo. Swear to God, once I get to Nogales, I'll send you cash money, whatever, and I'll be glad to do it, man, whatever's right, you deserve it just for putting up with me, just, hoo Jesus, don't let this sinner pass this way again. No hard feelings, you know?"

Ángel took their parting stoically. All he said as he accepted Wayne's fistful of pesos was, "Don't chase her, man. Don't get too close." But as Wayne strode out to the Super Bee, he was thinking exactly the opposite. He'd shaken off the bat whispers of fear, and in their place was anger, anger at being played, at having been made a fool of by some chick in a white dress who dumped him for a trucker, of all people.

"Get in, Lanny," he said, and settled behind the wheel. Ángel watched them drive off, watched their red taillights recede down the empty highway until they were swallowed up in the country blackness. For a long while he stayed there in the doorway, and his eyes, had anyone been there to look into them save the fugitive ghosts of the road, were unreadable.

Wayne was driving fast, and the sensitive suspension of the Valiant bucked at every imperfection on the blacktop. Lanny seemed to be caught between relief at finally getting a ride, and apprehension of Wayne's driving, or possibly of the object of his high-speed pursuit. "Going a little fast there, man," he observed, and Wayne just nodded.

"Pays to be careful on these roads," Lanny said.

"Mm-hmm."

"Can't trust the highways after dark, man."

No response.

"You chasing her, right?" Lanny said, going there at last. "Chasing that truck, see if Bianca got a ride with that guy?"

Wayne nodded, not taking his eyes off the road ahead. "That's not cool, man," Lanny said uneasily. "You heard Ángel back there, man, he's got dark wisdom for this stuff, you know? He knows this road, man, he knows about *la niña*."

"Yeah, I know about *la niña* too, okay?" Wayne was being stubborn, not least because he could see just far enough ahead to glimpse the edge on which Lanny was teetering, and he wasn't going to let that scroungy sonofabitch drag him back over it if he could help it. To think that way would be too weird, too massive, too disruptive of his whole philosophy of being; and maybe too close to the gut sensation he'd felt back when the girl had gripped his arm with those cold, cold hands. So he stuck to his guns, "Here's what I know, I know she was right there in that same seat you're in, and she wasn't no ghost. She grabbed my arm, man, same as you said she grabbed yours. That ain't a ghost."

"There's all sorts of ghosts, man," Lanny was talking fast, urgently, like a preacher in a down-home revival tent. "You think there's a line you cross, like this here's life and that's death, black and white and no shade? It ain't no line. What it is, it's like the way day turns into night, see, like there ain't no time when you can say that was day, now it's night, no, it's a process. There's a blur, man, and the name we give the blur, we call it dusk, and that's where our girl's at. *La niña atardecer*, remember? Sunset girl. That's where she's at, that's where she does her thing. That's when we seen her, man, sunset, remember? She comes with the sunset.

"And Ángel, okay, he says you don't ever see her leave. It's only afterwards you find she's gone, that's all, only after the hammer falls, and that's 'cause she ain't ever gonna get to where she's going, see? She ain't ever gonna get to no Mazatlán. The road, her fate, her curse, whatever, it don't let her. You seen all the crosses and stuff by the roadside here, man? Crashes, rollovers, accidents, whatever. Old burnt-out wrecks in the desert, flowers and calvaries? That's how long she's been trying to get to Mazatlán."

He was practically yelling by now, testifying to his wild and secret truth, with Wayne a mutinous member of the congregation. Out of the dark, Wayne saw a flash of movement, a big buck *conejo* darting out of the brush. Too late to brake, too late to swerve, and thump went old jackrabbit under his wheels. "Now see what you made me do," he snapped at Lanny.

"Bad mojo," Lanny said, which only fed Wayne's irritation.

"Don't you ever switch off, man? Everything's bad mojo and Twilight Zone with you!" He'd half made up his mind to jettison his passenger in the next town, whenever they came to the end of this long desert stretch. "Can you not just kick back for once?"

But Lanny's attention had been caught by something up ahead.

Out in front of the Valiant, the highway plunged blade-straight into the pit of the night. At the bottom of that pit, out beyond the edge of the darkness, shone two red eyes, pinpoints unblinking, the taillights of a truck. *The* truck, Wayne decided, for no reason other than instinct, and he accelerated again. "Don't ever see her leave, huh?" he shouted at Lanny over the growling engine. "Well, we're gonna see her now, me and you, man, I promise you that."

There was no other traffic coming or going on the freeway, and the Valiant soon bit into the Peterbilt's head start. Wayne wasn't thinking clearly about this wild pursuit, or even about what he'd do when he caught up with the truck. Maybe he saw it as chasing after the laws of reality, the chance to reassert all the things he'd thought he believed, to say to Lanny *see, no mystery here, no such thing as ghosts, just a chick who likes to game you*. Or maybe he really just wanted to see Bianca again, to assure himself that she was flesh and blood and not some indefinite condition of the sunset.

The truck began to take shape in the headlights. It was pounding along at a speed well over the limit, laying an acrid trail of smoke from its exhaust stack, and now he'd caught up with it Wayne thought twice about overtaking. One mistake, he told himself, and they would all be toast. Accordingly he dawdled in the slipstream, and Lanny took the opportunity to restate his case.

"Look, man, we can just let that truck go, carry on to Mazatlán nice and easy, forget about this whole damn thing."

"You gonna forget all this?" Wayne thumped the steering wheel. "Was round about here you went off the road, that right? Damn near got your ass incinerated? You gonna forget a thing like that? Don't you wanna ask her what the hell happened?"

"Way I see it, forgetfulness is a skill, man, and you need to pick it up." Lanny was almost beseeching him. "You know, I got lucky, walked away from it, but we—you and me, right here, right now—we might not. Not this time."

Wayne was exasperated. "Hell, you got me into this!"

"I got you? *I* got you? You got you into this, you damn fool! You did the exact same as I did, saw a pretty girl with her thumb out, gave her a ride, and it all played out the way it always does, 'cause that's the fix, the fix is in, and it always ends the same. You don't mess with that stuff if you can avoid it, and that's exactly what you're doing right now, getting the both of us into something we can't just walk away from, 'cause you're too damn stubborn!"

"You and your goddamn *fantasmas*!" They were yelling at each other above the combined racket of the two engines, the Vanguard and the Peterbilt. "You goddamn hippie burnouts, you're all the same, you make this stupid junk up 'cos you can't deal with the real world!"

"Oh yeah?" Lanny was choking with indignation. "Well, try this on, man, what if it's the other way round? What if straights like you just *made up* this *real world*," complete with scornful air quotes, "so-called real world, 'cause *you* can't deal with the dark side, man, can't deal with the freaky-deak? How about that?"

Wayne took his eyes off the truck for a long moment to glare at Lanny. He wanted to say so many things, but he didn't know how; didn't trust himself to keep it on the straight and narrow, or even to keep the car on the road while he did it. And so he just said, "That doesn't even make sense. You know what? Look out the window, man. See what you can see."

With that he stamped on the gas and swerved on to the hard shoulder, and made to overtake the Peterbilt on the blind side.

There was dust and debris on the edge of the blacktop, and the car was jouncing and kicking up dust as Wayne tried his best to keep a straight line. Steering by instinct, he leaned out of the open driver-side window and squinted up at the cab of the truck.

There was a face in the cab, passenger side, lit by the dash, he assumed. Afterwards, he wondered about that. A thin face, surrounded by blackness.

A horribly thin face.

In the instant that he saw it clearly he took his foot off the gas, perhaps in shock, perhaps because at last his self-preservation had kicked in, and they fell back behind the Peterbilt. Not a moment too soon: the driver must have seen him making his move, and swung across his path, missing the nose of the Valiant by inches. Desperate to avoid a smash, Wayne hauled the wheel and made for the fast lane. Encountering no obstruction, the truck ran all the way off the road, and tilted at a crazy angle on the raised berm by the side of the highway. Almost in slow motion, it began to lurch over on its side. Wayne hit the gas again, praying to whatever gods protect dumbass drug dealers and superannuated freaks that he could outpace the toppling truck.

He made it, just about. With a grinding crash, the Peterbilt hit the highway on its side, and went screeching along the blacktop like a banshee in the Valiant's wake. In his rearview Wayne could see it close, so close, too close, and then the friction, or the gods, whichever, slowed it down and he was clear. Once he was sure it had stopped he slammed on the brakes, adding his own squealing to the tortured metal of the truck. They fishtailed to a halt about fifty yards along the road.

"Jesus," was all Lanny could say for a little while, perhaps still in his crazy preacher persona. Wayne was getting his own breathing back under control, still gripping the wheel so tightly his knuckles showed bone white beneath his tanned skin. "Jesus," Lanny said again, shakily. "Did you see that?"

"Did *you* see it?" Wayne was almost whispering.

"Did I see it? I was right here, man! I wasn't anyplace else!"

"Did you see her face?"

"Her face?" Lanny was thrown for a moment. "I couldn't see jack from my side, man, you were in the way, the cab was too far up. You see her face?"

Wayne thought about it for a long moment. Perhaps if he'd given himself a while longer, he might have lied about it, tried to keep on the right side of reality, avoid a one-way trip to Lannyville. As it was, he stated nothing but the truth, or at least the truth as he'd seen it: "Her face, yeah, I saw it, man. Looked like a skull."

Lanny stared at him dumbfounded. For the first time in their brief acquaintance he seemed lost for words.

"Looked like," Wayne said, already trying to walk it back some. "I mean, I dunno, I only saw it for a second."

At that moment, fire sprang up in the rearview.

Wayne threw open the door of the Valiant and started running back down the highway. He was peripherally aware of Lanny coming after him, heard the flap-flap of his sandals on the blacktop as they neared the toppled truck.

There were flames lapping in back of the cab, where Wayne guessed the fuel line was broken. He tried to remember where the tank sat in a Peterbilt, how many gallons it could hold. At the same time he was trying to squint through the starred and shattered windshield, to find out if what he saw now would be what he'd seen for a moment back then.

With a tinkling smash, the truck windshield blew out. Was punched out, rather, because there was the trucker, hard up against the steering wheel, struggling to get clear, it seemed. There was blood on his fists and trickling down his face, and if he'd seemed taciturn back at the *cantina* he was desperate now. He looked to be tangled up in something, something that dragged him back, impeded his escape, and at first Wayne thought it was his seatbelt. Then he realized it was something white, something that flapped and wound itself around him.

A white dress? *White bones in a white dress*, whispered his subconscious? Wayne stopped in his tracks. Which was just as well, because at that moment the tank blew, and the blast of the fireball knocked him off his feet.

When he could see again through his scorched eyeballs, Lanny was helping him sit upright. The truck was well ablaze, beyond any possibility of intervention, even if they'd dared get near enough. Inside the cab was all flame, and from out the center of it one terrible dying scream, a sound which would stay with both of them for the rest of their misbegotten lives, reappearing out of nowhere to splinter the bright midnight, scatter sleep to the desert winds, sweat them and chill them simultaneously. In its aftermath, nothing but the roar of the fire and the pounding of their hearts.

"What did you see, man?" Lanny was asking him. "What are we gonna tell people? What do we tell the cops?"

That did it for Wayne. He got to his feet, leaning on Lanny at first but slowly regaining his balance, or his physical equilibrium at least.

"We don't tell 'em nothing, man," he said. Lanny was about to speak, but he took a look at Wayne and decided, wisely for once, to keep it to himself. "No cops, nobody. You see anybody here?" He waved a hand at the highway, at the scrubland that surrounded it, lit in fitful firelight. "We got a chance to split, and no one any the wiser. So what we do, is we get in the car and we hightail it all the way to Mazatlán."

"Man..." Lanny seemed torn.

"Or what, do you want to hitchhike? Get

a ride with *la juda*, maybe? Maybe land both our asses in a Mexican prison cell?"

He'd spoken the magic words so far as Lanny was concerned. One mention of the police was all it took. He stumbled abjectly after Wayne back to the Valiant, took his place in the passenger seat, kept his own counsel as they sped away from the scene, a spark in the mirror, one staring hellfire eye that winked out into nothing.

Once or twice in the hours that passed, Lanny would start to say something, as for instance, "Said you saw a skull?", or "Was she in that cab at the end, man?", or something as simple as "What do you think...?" An upraised hand from Wayne silenced him each time. As dawn touched the edges of the country dark and they approached the outskirts of Mazatlán, he said simply, "Here's good, man." Wayne pulled up, watched him get out, and while he was still stretching his stringy old frame sped away before Lanny could say so much as *vaya con dios*.

WHAT HAPPENED IN Mazatlán, so far as the rest of Wayne's story goes, stayed in Mazatlán. He was in no real state to rep himself and his scheme with the badass *hombres* at the meeting, and after an uncomfortable denouement found himself thrown out on his ear with an admonition to live a better life, put less euphemistically and with more threats of violence. He treated himself to a lost weekend in the local bars and bunny ranches, spending most of his waking hours blasted and insensate, until he acknowledged the need to get back to Guadalajara and break the news to his co-conspirator.

Understandably, he drove by day. He kept a steady pace, fast and controlled, slowing only when he passed by the site of the accident, across the highway divide. There was a scorched place on the blacktop, a heap of wreckage by the roadside, and a solitary bunch of gas station flowers wedged into the fencing.

Back in Guadalajara he endured an uncomfortable rapprochement with his bud, the upshot of which was that they both decided to revisit Mazatlán for one last shot at resuscitating the deal. They set out in the Valiant, Wayne relinquishing the wheel to its rightful owner, and with one thing and another the sun was almost down by the time they hit the road.

The road, naturally; back on Federal 15, a journey Wayne could have lived several lifetimes without feeling the need to retrace. He kept his eyes in the footwell as they cleared the suburbs, houses giving way to vacant lots and tumbleweed, funeral parlors, whorehouses, truck stops, the ragged edge of the metropolis, of civilization, the beginnings of an older dispensation.

He looked, though, in the end. He had to look. Raised his head at the exact moment they sped past the gas station, past the clean neon lights, past the pretty girl in the white summer dress, standing at the roadside with her black hair blowing in the scented dusk, waiting for a ride, for the same old ride, waiting to keep her appointment.

💀 💀 💀

Steve Duffy lives and works in North Wales. His most recent collection of weird stories, Finding Yourself in the Dark, *was published by Sarob Press in 2021; he's currently in the process of putting together his next. Steve was the winner of the International Horror Guild's award for Best Short Story 2000, and in 2015 he received the Shirley Jackson Award for Best Novelette.*

WE HOPE YOU WILL RETURN TO
NIGHTMARE ABBEY.

WE PROMISE WE'LL DIG UP SOMETHING SPECIAL FOR YOUR NEXT VISIT.